Rehearsal for Love

Also by Faith Baldwin
in Large Print:

Innocent Bystander
The Office-Wife
Make-Believe
District Nurse
That Man is Mine
The Heart Has Wings
Enchanted Oasis
Rich Girl, Poor Girl
For Richer, For Poorer
Face Toward the Spring
Evening Star
And New Stars Burn
Arizona Star
District Nurse

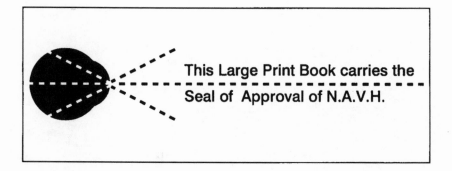

This Large Print Book carries the
Seal of Approval of N.A.V.H.

Rehearsal for Love

Faith Baldwin

Thorndike Press • Thorndike, Maine

L
F
BAL

Published in 1997 by arrangement with
Harold Ober Associates Incorporated.

Thorndike Large Print ® Candlelight Series.

The tree indicium is a trademark of Thorndike Press.

The text of this Large Print edition is unabridged.
Other aspects of the book may vary from the original edition.

Set in 16 pt. Plantin by Juanita Macdonald.

Printed in the United States on permanent paper.

Library of Congress Cataloging in Publication Data

Baldwin, Faith, 1893–
    Rehearsal for love / by Faith Baldwin.
      p. cm.
    ISBN 0-7862-1239-X (lg. print : hc : alk. paper)
    1. Large type books. I. Title.
  [PS3505.U97R44   1997]
  813′.52—dc21   97-36279

To Doctor John B. Wheeler with the hope that it will amuse him for an hour and with the affection of its perpetrator.

Chapter I

The night that Eloise, Inc., dress shop extraordinary, threw its annual party before the autumn showing, Kathleen Roberts, sitting on a divan beside Mitzi Lambert, the newest rave in musical comedy stars, wished she had not come.

She had come with, and because of, Hannah Arnold, who designed sports clothes for Eloise and was Kathleen's closest friend. She had seen little of Hannah since their arrival and now, after talking to a dozen people whom she knew well or slightly, she was feeling bored.

She listened to Mitzi, ticking off the frailties of everyone who passed with a deadly and feline accuracy, and wished herself at home and in bed. The rooms in which the guests were gathered were spectacularly like anyone's rooms, provided that anyone had a good decorator and a better bank balance. Dove gray, with strange introductions of ivory and black, a splash of purest coral and three magnificent flower paintings, the particular room in which Kathleen sat was a background for any woman's beauty.

The room was crowded as well as decorated. The fashion show had taken place and all were huddled in small or large groups discussing it, and each other, avidly. The air smelled of expensive perfume, good wine, excellent accompaniments, cigarette smoke, roses, and face powder. Kathleen wished heartily that someone would open a window. She wished, further, that Hannah would appear or that she would have the energy to rise, press through the throng, find her, make her excuses, and go on home. And at that moment of indecision she saw Hannah coming toward her with Paul McClure.

She recognized McClure at once; his pictures popped up, now and then in the press and for a long time one more personal, and in a silver frame, had adorned Hannah's dresser. Paul McClure, the playwright. Paul McClure, New York, Groton, Harvard, whose first play had been an astonishing success. He had a reputation as a heartbreaker, and a wit, an income from his deceased parents, and currently, no ties. He was called the handsomest man in town, which didn't mean much. Kathleen admitted, regarding him with curiosity, that he was very good-looking, not too tall, broad-shouldered, fair, with a thin expressive face and blazing blue eyes. People said he was more sophisticated than a Noel Coward character and Hannah, two years ago, had been desperately in love with him. But that had been over for some time.

Hannah was a designer. She had been with Eloise, Inc. since its inception. She was twenty-seven, four years older than Kathleen, and she was a small redhead, with narrow brown eyes and a magnificent figure.

Totally dissimilar, she and Kathleen had known each other for years but Kathleen had gone to college while Hannah was studying at a school of design, and afterwards in Paris. Now she was very successful, designing the simple, costly sports things for which Eloise was famous, daring in color contrasts and flawless in cut.

"Darling," she cried, above the orchestra, "this is Paul at long last and he's perishing to meet you."

Mitzi had risen a moment since and drifted away, wondering if she dared return and order "Tonight is Ours" — a divine Grecian affair in white and silver . . . Would the show run that long? Would her present — patron stand for it?

So Kathleen was alone on the divan.

Paul said, "A masterpiece of understatement," and sat down beside her. Hannah, very busy, for this was no evening in which she could take off her mental shoes and be purely social, darted off again. She waved her hand and screamed, "Be nice to him, Kate, but not too nice. He broke my heart a century or two ago — don't let him have any truck with yours."

"A splendid recommendation," commented Kathleen, smiling.

McClure offered her a cigarette. She refused it, shaking her head. "I've smoked two and my mouth tastes like a cardboard box," she said.

"May I get you some wine?"

"I rarely use it," she told him.

He looked at her with frank approval but not because of her abstemiousness, and his pulses quickened in familiar warning. He told himself, "Steady on, old boy, remember that you've been fancy free for a long time now and you like the sensation — or lack of it —" But he went on looking.

Kathleen was not pretty, as Hannah was pretty, nor smart and veneered, as Hannah was. She had something that is very rare in this age of chic and standardized women. And that was authentic beauty . . . in the spacing of her gray eyes, the clear clean modeling of her face, the shape of her head, the way her chestnut-brown hair grew.

When she smiled at him he saw that she had an absurd dimple at the corner of her mouth. The line of her cheek was still heart-breakingly young and her fine-textured skin owed little to the cosmetician.

He said, "I suppose you're a devotee of Eloise, Inc."

Kathleen laughed. She laughed as a child laughs, heartily, spontaneously, and Mc-Clure liked that in her. Too many women shrilled or giggled or just made silly noises . . . while their eyes remained untouched by humor.

"On the contrary," she said frankly, "I can't run to it. I don't know that I'd want to, if I could. . . . I'm Hannah's despair. I won't, and can't, make a fetish of clothes."

Her frock was simple, gray, the color of her eyes. It had a bright twist of orange velvet at the slim waist. Hannah could have told him . . . thirty-nine fifty, and named the shop. Mitzi Lambert, now standing across the room talking to a motion-picture producer who was here to persuade the genius of Eloise, Inc. to come to the coast, was wearing an Eloise . . . at three hundred and fifty.

He asked, "If you don't like clothes, what are you doing here?"

"Hannah," she explained. "We've always been great friends. I'm awfully proud of her success."

11

"I haven't seen Hannah for a couple of years," he said carelessly. "I've been here and there, a trip around the world, a try at Hollywood. Now I'm back again."

She said, "I liked your first play so much."

"And my second?"

"Not as well."

"Neither did I." He made a rueful face. "The critics and the box office gave me the big head. I patterned the second on the first. It didn't come off. I have had two flops since, not to mention Hollywood. But I'm on my way back."

He was sure of himself, she thought, far too sure. He had, she had noticed, at once, fine nervous hands. His lean face was continually dissolving into conflicting expressions and the slant of his crooked eyebrows, darker than his hair, above the queer, blazing blue eyes, lent him a mildly satanic expression.

"Tell me about yourself," he demanded, leaning closer to her.

She thought, Hannah's right, he's attractive, he has an approach . . . It was, she judged, second nature with him. He looked at you and you could believe you were the only woman in the world, the one person on earth with whom he wanted to be. But if you realized this about him, she thought com-

12

fortably, it couldn't disturb or impress you at all.

"There isn't much," she began obediently. "My father's a lawyer, a very good one. My mother . . ." She hesitated and stopped. She couldn't talk about her parents rationally and she certainly wasn't going to turn irrational in this setting. She could imagine just what Paul McClure would think about the close relationship between her and her parents. He'd give it some long dour psychologist's name, he'd tell her she wasn't adult . . . or he wouldn't believe it at all. She went on, presently, "I was born in New York, some twenty-three years ago. School, private. College, Smith. I graduated at twenty-one. I've had a business course and I've been working in my father's office."

"You," he said, amazed, "in your father's office!"

She asked, somewhat irritated:

"Why not? And don't tell me that I'm taking the bread out of some poor girl's mouth. My father wanted me to be a lawyer. I couldn't see it. So I chose the business training instead . . . and may heaven bless Mr. Gregg, who gives the girl without specialized talent her priceless opportunity. I needed experience and so my father let me have a typist job. Recently, however, he's

13

been rather ill and as he's had to be at home I've acted as his secretary there, when his office secretary has been busy or has had more important things on her mind than his personal letters and telephone calls and the cataloguing of his library. He's a collector in a modest way," she added.

He said, "You don't seriously intend to go on working?"

She didn't like the way he said, "working."

"Why not?" she asked again, rather defensively.

He shrugged. "Of course," he said, "it's the fashion. But there are a lot of girls, you know, who have to support themselves."

Their glances crossed, sharply, like rapiers. She said, "I suppose you'd approve if I went in for modeling?"

"You've the figure for it," he murmured, "or mustn't I say so?"

"Or the stage or night club singing or dress designing or autobiographical novels," she went on rapidly, ignoring his comment. "No one seems to mind that. But business! They shudder and grow socially conscious, quite suddenly. Well, look here, Mr. McClure, my father brought me up to be independent. He said if he had a million dollars he wouldn't want a daughter who couldn't take care of herself. Things happen

14

to a million dollars, you know, and then where on earth are you?"

"Generally at the Ritz bar," McClure replied and she could have slapped him.

She said, hotly:

"Don't be absurd. I have a small income from my grandmother's estate. I came into it when I was eighteen. I've dressed on it and used it for my personal needs ever since, and therefore learned something of the value of money. If I live at home it's because I like to be with my people. But someday I'll be entirely on my own. I want to be, and my father approves."

He said, laughing, "My dear girl, a job in your father's office or doing his personal telephoning for him at home isn't being on your own."

"Are you being deliberately disagreeable?" she demanded.

"No," he said gently, "merely interested. I won't ask you to forgive me when I tell you that you are very young . . . and quite beautiful. You'll hate being called young, though I've yet to meet the woman who threw things when a man told her, sincerely, that she was lovely. In a year or less you'll be married and living in a nice little apartment on the East Side. So that's that."

"Unfortunately," said Kathleen, "I prefer

my freedom. I haven't, as yet, met the man for whom I'd give it up."

"And when you do?" he inquired.

She laughed, in spite of herself.

"You're hopeless," she said, "personal and rude and . . . well, you don't deserve an answer. But here it is. When I do, I'll marry him so fast that his head will swim, whether it means a walk-up in Brooklyn or that hypothetical apartment on the East Side."

"Incredible!" said McClure, sighing. "I can't believe it. But I must. Is it possible that you have ideals?"

Kathleen flushed. She asked gravely, "You believe they're outmoded?"

"Among this crew at all events," he answered. His face settled into adult lines of disillusionment. Mitzi called to him, something unintelligible, and waved a hand which looked as if it had been tipped in blood, and an older actress smiled as generously as was compatible with her most recent face lift. Young playwrights are popular with actresses, old and young, especially if they have had success.

Kathleen said energetically:

"It isn't like you to talk like that."

"Like me? But you don't know me!"

"I am beginning to think I don't," she said, frankly disappointed, "but I used to fancy

16

that I could know the man who wrote *Nothing Is Lost*."

He was silent, looking at her. He said presently:

"How many men have told you that you are better than beautiful?"

"Only one," she said.

"And he?"

"My father," Kathleen told him, "but you must allow for a certain understandable bias."

"I'd like your father," he said instantly. "Look, tell me something about the people who run this show."

"Eloise, Inc.? But surely Hannah must have told you? She's been with the firm ever since it started three years ago."

"Hannah," he said, "talks best about herself."

"That's rather catty," Kathleen told him, offended.

"I didn't mean to be. She is an engrossing subject, Hannah," he said, smiling. "But I'd like to know about the brains of this business. It interests me. A good house, a good neighborhood. Even the window dressing is exciting because it's so expensively simple. A needlepoint chair, a chinchilla wrap."

"Bolero," corrected Kathleen.

"Bolero then, and a pair of gold slippers.

17

And then this party — Hannah assures me that this is the most spectacular, lavishly patronized custom dress shop in town . . . that its two previous parties have made Elsa Maxwellian history, the talk of columnists."

"Did you see the invitations?"

"Hannah just dragged me here, I'm a gate crasher," he admitted.

"They were printed on pattern paper," she said, "scissored into fantastic shapes . . . and I trust you notice the press, flocking, certain of vintage champagne, pâté de fois gras, sliced pheasant breasts. . . . Society too," added Kathleen, smiling, "wondering how good its credit is, Broadway looking for laughs, and Literature looking for material."

He said, "I wouldn't think you could be cynical. You look like a romanticist — your eyes, for instance."

"Perhaps I am," she said; "Hannah says so. But you can't be romantic about this sort of thing, can you? Yet in a way you can be, about what's back of it . . . that is to say, Rosa and Sammy Davenport."

"I met them," he said, "a couple of years ago." He was silent and she wondered if he was thinking of the time before he and Hannah had their quarrel. "I liked them both," he added.

"A legend," said Kathleen, "a two-headed

calf. One dynamic young man, one dark woman in her forties."

"Davenport's not their name, is it?" he asked idly.

"No," she answered. "He changed their name by law. Which made his mother Mrs. Davenport . . . whether or not she liked it. Hannah says it was because Sammy's late, unlamented father was born in Sofia!"

They laughed together comfortably. Paul McClure, offering Kathleen his cigarette case, was aware that he had never met a girl with whom he so earnestly wished to talk and laugh the hours through. She shook her head at the case and said:

"I am beginning to think I should leave."

"Stay," he begged her. He thought, Any excuse, it doesn't matter. "Tell me more about the Davenports."

"You should ask Hannah, my information is merely secondhand and lacks all the color of her embellishments."

"I like statistics," he said gravely.

"Rosa," said Kathleen, "left her husband when Sammy was three, and supported the child and herself by dressmaking. She must always have had a great gift, I think. Later, when Sammy was in school, she went to a Fifth Avenue shop in the custom-made department as a fitter. After that to Paris, taking Sammy with her. She had saved some money, Hannah says, and her husband had drunk himself into a peaceful grave and had to her, and probably his own posthumous, astonishment kept up his insurance. To do him justice," Kathleen added, "he probably loved her and the boy and hoped they would return to him."

"And Sammy," asked McClure curiously, "was he always like that?"

He indicated Sammy fleetingly passing them, making too many gestures, talking in a high-pitched, excitable voice. A slim dark young man, sharp featured, very like his mother, and with definite personality.

"Hannah," Kathleen said, "tells me that he was not appreciated here, in school — they made rude noises when he went by. But in Paris — well, he learned to chatter French — he still does, and Rosa worked hard. They stayed there until Sammy was almost grown. He had for some time shown a talent quite equal to her own, and real executive genius."

"He's an interesting human being," said McClure thoughtfully. "When I first met him I didn't like him. The next time I discovered that he was extremely intelligent."

"He's a superb artist," said Kathleen. "And he told me once, having had too much to drink, that he liked very little but loved a

20

few things passionately."

"What, for instance?" asked McClure.

"I would say offhand," she answered, "himself and his mother, the sound of scissors ripping through satin, the feel of furs, and velvet, and his drawing board."

"Did she send him to college?" McClure asked.

Kathleen looked at him tolerantly.

"Is that your yardstick?" she inquired. "Not all boys, even the brilliant ones, are university material. Sammy didn't need college, he did a good job on himself. Art school he had, of course . . . and practical experience."

"I imagine," said McClure, "that the atmosphere of dressmakers' workrooms must be something stupendous. Exciting, petulant, and frenzied. I have seen that atmosphere around Hannah on occasion."

Kathleen laughed. "Hannah adores her work . . . and she's very fond of Eloise, Inc. There isn't much more to it than the Davenports. I believe there's an honest bookkeeper and, of course, a number of young American designers like Hannah. They'll all strike out for themselves one day but there will be others."

Sammy came back with Mitzi in tow. He was smiling. He passed Kathleen and

McClure and waved at them. He didn't especially like McClure but he respected him for his undoubted talent. Sammy was fond of Hannah in his way and he resented the fact that McClure had at one time made her excessively unhappy. He regretted, recalling that she had been vocal about it in the modern manner. Today's girls not only carry torches but they keep them burning by a species of emotional petrol. Sammy, the most articulate of men, liked reticent women. He liked Kathleen Roberts, whom he did not know well. She was not especially reticent but she had repose, charm, grace. He wished he might dress her. She was a beautiful young woman but he could make her spectacular.

He loved this party. He thought with affection of the banker who had financed the shop venture. He had agreed with Sammy during their first interview that women dress mostly for women and would do so at enormous expense whether or not their husbands were jumping off roofs or blowing out their financial brains. He agreed, further, that those who had always been rich were poor pay but good advertisement and that those who were more recently affluent — and there were some — were prompt with the checkbook and that, while stage folk were notoriously backward when asked to please remit, you could afford to dress the most popular or the prettiest and they would bring in customers.

Hence, Eloise, Inc.; and the banker had no reason to regret his investment, which paid him pretty dividends, and as Eloise also dressed his wife, a plain woman, with such éclat that he fell in love with her again, he was more than satisfied. For falling in love with his wife was much less expensive than certain other of his pursuits, undertaken in boredom and because of advancing age, during the long period when he was not at all in love with her.

Tonight's party, thought Sammy, surpassed its predecessors. He wove his way through the crowd and charming women greeted him with shrieks. As a rule Sammy was visible only by appointment, and his mother rarely appeared except at the parties, as she spent her time in the workrooms and in conference. The saleswomen were handsome and expert. Two bore titles, the English girl had married hers, discarded the incumbent but kept the title. The Russian girl was born that way.

"A swell shindig," commented a famous columnist, giving Sammy the genial elbow. The columnist was a little drunk and had not one but two blondes hanging on his portly arms. Sammy smiled and was properly gratified. He didn't like columnists but they had their place in his scheme of things. He knew how to treat them, without servility and yet without indifference. He looked from the columnist to the archway between the two rooms, bulging with people listed in Bradstreet, Debrett, the Almanach de Gotha, the Social Register, and Who's Who. There were so many pretty, or apparently pretty, women that they surfeited the eye. There were tail-coated men — husbands, sons, and lovers of these elegant ladies. Stage and Screen, Colony, and 21.

Park and Fifth, Westchester, Long Island, and Connecticut, they had all come to drink the wine, listen to the newest swing band, applaud the latest singing wit, who alone at the piano and without much voice could slay his tens of thousands like an earlier classic example . . . and they were here also to watch the absurdly beautiful models wearing the fall collection. One actor, the portly columnist, a polo player, and Sammy had acted as masters of ceremony to announce the unlikely names of the frocks.

Sammy went in search of his mother, satisfied and smiling. He stopped when he saw Hannah, in animated discussion with a client. He said because, although he was fond of her, he was also malicious:

"You'd better look out for your boy friend, Hannah . . . he's completely engrossed in Kathleen Roberts."

Hannah raised an eyebrow. She said, "He has always had good taste, Sammy," and went on talking. But a little later she went to see for herself. But Kathleen and McClure had gone.

Kathleen had said:

"I've talked enough, I've told you all I know. Hannah is the fountainhead — which reminds me that, although I came with her, I should go even if I must go without her. I've a date, tomorrow early."

"Man hunting?"

"Job hunting," she said indignantly.

"Really? If I see you safely to your door, will you promise to tell me about it?"

"You'd laugh," she said.

"I promise not to."

"But you came here to meet Hannah, didn't you?"

"Yes, and we met. We've buried the poor little hatchet," he assured her, "and are having dinner together tomorrow night. She can spare me now — this is business with her and not pleasure."

A little later as they were taxiing uptown

McClure reminded her, "Now, about the job . . ."

She said, leaning back against the upholstery:

"It's this way. My father has been ordered a long vacation. And lest you get notions about us, we aren't financial tycoons, whatever that is, it's always sounded like a tropical storm to me. At any event, an insurance policy is coming due and he and mother are shutting up the apartment and going for a long cruise, after which they plan to stay in England for a time. My father's sister is married to an Englishman."

"Roberts," he said reflectively. "Oh, of course, your father is Lawson Roberts . . ."

He looked at her with increased interest. Lawson Roberts was quite a figure in his profession. Owing to his passion for the underdog, he did not make a great deal of money. His honor was unimpeached, his love for the law and for justice — a different matter — a byword in legal circles. McClure had once attended the trial of a criminal case in which Roberts was the defense lawyer. It had been rather unusual as the young man accused of the murder of his wife possessed no glamour for the newspaper reader, had no money and no political friends. He had been acquitted and there hadn't been a cent in it for Roberts. McClure had gone to court because at the time he was writing a play which dealt with a murder trial. He recalled Roberts, tall and stooped, with a superb speaking voice and delivery, and much of the actor about him, but not the sensational actor. He was too honest a man for tricks.

At the time it had been mentioned in the papers that Lawson Roberts's sister was the Duchess of Ainslee.

"I heard your father in court," said McClure; "it was a magnificent thing to hear and witness."

Kathleen smiled at him.

"Thank you," she said. "I like to hear that better than almost anything else you could have said."

"I believe you're telling the truth!" He went on, after a moment, "Now, about the job?"

"Oh, Father knows some people," she said carelessly, "and I'm to see them. And Hannah told me yesterday that if I don't want to live alone I can share her apartment with her. Her cousin married last month, you know, and she has a long lease and an extra bedroom."

McClure whistled. He said:

"I can't quite see you and Hannah —"

"Why?" she asked sharply.

"You're so different!"

"We're friends," said Kathleen.

He digested that for a moment. Then he said, "Well, brace yourself, Miss Roberts. They'll probably call you Bobbie in the office."

"Over my dead body!" she said indignantly.

"Hannah calls you Kate," he said reflectively.

"My father does," said Kathleen; "she picked that up from him."

"It suits me," he agreed. "Quote, 'For you are called plain Kate, and bonny Kate, and sometimes Kate the curst,' unquote!"

She asked, "You think me a shrew?"

"You forget," he told her, "that it goes on 'But Kate, the prettiest Kate in Christendom!' Yes, I like your little name. As to the shrew, I'll tell you after we know each other better."

She was amused and exasperated. The cab slid to a stop before her door, and McClure got out. When he followed she asked carelessly, "What makes you think you're going to know me better?"

"The working girl," he answered, "is the prey of all horrible young men about town. Besides, I've made up with Hannah and something tells me that I'm going to see a

28

lot of Hannah — or at least her apartment — in the near future."

"I'll warn her," said Kathleen solemnly.

"Do so, by all means. That will only put her on her mettle. Good luck," he added, "with the job. I hope the boss is old, fat, very, very bald, and is afraid of his wife." His eyes laughed but his mouth remained grave. "Good night, sweet Kate."

Chapter II

The Roberts apartment did not possess a fashionable address. It was on the top floor of an old, well-kept house, and all the rooms were big, with many windows and much sun and air. They were comfortable, they had a muted, unobtrusive elegance and charm, due entirely to Marion Roberts's excellent taste and love of homemaking. She was a pretty woman, with dark hair going gray, shorter than her daughter, and a little on the plump side. She had Kathleen's gray eyes, wide and merry, and, so her husband and daughter believed, the sweetest face in the world.

They had had their servants, a couple, for a great many years, and one of Lawson Roberts's chief objections to his doctor's orders was that he couldn't throw Mary and John out into a cold world. After eighteen years, he said, of the Roberts menage they'd never fit into another household. But John, practical and firm, took a high hand with his master. It was all right, he said, he and Mary had long wished to return to England and see their friends and relatives. They would do so, if Mr. Roberts was closing the apartment. They had saved, their small investments had prospered, thanks to their employers' generosity and wisdom. They would take a long vacation and would return to the States with the Robertses.

Mr. Roberts was discoursing on John's intelligence when, after the butler had left the dining room, he was alone with his wife and daughter. "I must say," he remarked, "his decision took a weight off my mind."

"You worry more about him and Mary than you do about me," said Kathleen without rancor.

Her father smiled at her affectionately. "I can't afford to worry about you. I'd stay home in that case," he said.

Marion Roberts shook her head. "Kathleen has common sense, and we've brought her up to think for herself, and if . . . well, she knows enough to go to Dr. Hamilton." But she paled a little as she said it.

"Darling," said her daughter, "don't look like that. Nothing's going to happen. I'm as strong as a horse, a percheron. I've had all the childish diseases and the last time I went to old Ham he said that if his other patients were as healthy as I am he'd shut up shop and go in for wood carving. You are *not* to fret."

"I won't," promised her mother meekly.

31

She looked at her husband with concealed anxiety. Surely his color was better this morning? He must be her first concern, she must take him away, hoard his strength, watch over his diet, see that he had relaxation and entertainment and sleep. He'd slept so badly these last months.

Kathleen said:

"If you worry about me I'll run away with the grocer boy or go to Hollywood as an extra just to give you something definite to stew about. You did your best, you offered to take me along. But I was stubborn and ungrateful. I preferred to stay at home and work."

She thought, My dears, how much I'll miss you, I don't know how I'll stand it . . . But she couldn't let them know it, a long trip, leisurely, unhampered, together. She thought, I'd wreck it, I've too much vitality and curiosity, they'd want to keep up with me, and they couldn't; besides, it would bore me eventually and they'd know it.

Her father laid down the morning paper and made a gloomy comment on the headlines. He said, looking from his wife to his daughter, "Kate can take care of herself. She's proved it before, in minor ways. Now's her chance."

"I wonder," said Kathleen. "Tell me about

Patrick Bell — You haven't said a word except that you ran into him at some club or other and that he said I was to come see him and maybe he could give me a job."

"I don't know him well," admitted her father, "although I've seen him around for some years, and run into him now and then. We got talking over a drink at the bar —"

"Lawson!" said his wife, appalled. One of the new dietary rules was no alcohol.

"Mine was ginger ale," he said hastily, "cross my heart, Marion. Well, to go on, he's young . . . in his early thirties and the head of a big firm of general contractors. City work, I believe, I don't know much about it . . . but they do subways and bridges and city buildings and all that sort of thing. The outfit was started by his father, who died last year. Young Pat told me he wouldn't go to college although his father was anxious to send him. He went right into the business from high school. I asked him if it wouldn't have been easier for him had he been an engineer and he said calmly that he employed a lot of high-priced engineers . . . His name isn't Bell, by the way."

"What in the world is it?" asked Kathleen, interested.

"I've forgotten. A long Italian name. His father changed it, when he started the firm

. . . someone told me once that the old man was a holy terror. He said he had too many relatives, in Italy as well as here, and once they got wind of his success they'd all want to be foremen or office workers. So he cut it short to Bell."

"Where does the Patrick come in?"

"An Irish mother, I imagine," said her father. "He's an interesting young man, Kate. All the drive in the world, a little too fast for my blood, he left me gasping. Something of the steam roller about him. You'll find him a very rough diamond, indeed."

"It will be a relief," she said, "after all the polished ones I've encountered of late. I met one last night not only polished but in a platinum setting."

"Who was it?" asked Marion. "And you haven't told us about the party. Did you get in late?"

"Not very; before one, I think. Oh, the party was the last word . . . hot music and cold champagne, entertainers and the *most* beautiful models in the maddest clothes. It gave me the shivers to think of the fat elderly women who'll turn up at Eloise, Inc. today and buy the little numbers they saw displayed last night, believing they'll look marvelous in them, the very twin, say, of the tall blonde who showed 'em. But at that I suppose the shop adapts them or persuades the customers to something else . . . they couldn't afford such bad publicity! Hannah was in her element. Her sports things are really something; everyone raved about them. I might save my dividends once I'm on a salary and buy myself one. The colors would make your mouth water, the combinations are amazing . . . turquoise and maize, cerise and purple . . ."

"You're way over my head," said her father, "throw me a life line. Who was your polished diamond?"

"By name Paul McClure . . . by profession a playwright, New Yorker born and a great friend of Hannah's. At least he used to be. She wrote me about him all through my last year at Smith . . . I thought it would be wedding invitations and a trip to Honolulu. But something went wrong. He's been away a lot since, is just back now. She was careful not to let me meet him when we got together on my vacations," explained Kathleen, laughing, "but now she doesn't care. She has that Georgian prince, or whatever he is, in tow now."

"I'm not sure that I approve of your plan to live with Hannah," said her mother, "she knows the oddest people!"

"They've no affinity for me nor I for them,"

said Kathleen, "so don't worry. I sit on the side lines and watch. Spectator sport stuff. It's fun; besides, Hannah does know nice people really. You've never got over the shock of having her bring Sammy — that is to say Eloise, Inc. — up to your table one evening."

"She didn't receive half the shock I did," said her father grimly. "Did you say Paul McClure?"

"Yes, why?"

"I heard him speak some years ago," said her father. "Clever youngster . . . I seem to remember a play . . . can't think of the name . . ."

"*Nothing Is Lost*," said Kathleen, "it was a marvelous play . . . it had great acclaim. But he's not done very much since."

Marion's pretty brows were creased in an effort to capture an elusive memory. She said finally:

"Oh, now I know. I knew his mother, years ago. You did too, Lawson, we used to play bridge with her at the Harpers'. A pretty woman, wasn't her name Paula? She was a widow then. It seems to me that I heard afterwards that she died of the flu. . . . A very attractive woman, a Southerner, with the prettiest accent."

"Oh, of course," said Lawson, "I remember."

36

"You should," said Marion reproachfully, "you were quite crazy about her!"

"Nonsense." But he laughed sheepishly, and his wife and Kathleen laughed with him. "Perhaps you've forgotten the Coldstream Guardsman, that friend of Butch's, Marion," he countered.

Butch.

His Grace the Duke of Ainslee was Butch to his wife, friends, and in-laws.

"That will do!" ordered Kathleen. "I've no time to discuss your loose life." She jumped up, bestowed a kiss upon her mother's cheek, her father's temple. "I must dress," she said, "and hustle to my appointment with Mr. Bell. Hold your thumbs and pray for me."

She was gone. The sunlight fell on old silver and clear thin crystal, on the bright orange marmalade. Mrs. Roberts said despondently, "It scares me!"

"Me too," admitted her husband, "but it's for the best, believe me. I sometimes think we've been too happy, too close, we three. When she was a little bald-headed baby in a bassinet we agreed that the finest thing we could give her was her independence. And we have done so, I think. Now she'll have a chance to prove our theory right or wrong. Right, I think. She's had you as an example,

Marion. We've told her all the rules of the road and the traffic lights, we aren't turning her out into the highway without knowledge of the way in which the law operates."

"This man Bell," began his wife.

"Clever, young, pushing, completely business," said her husband, "and not Kathleen's type at all. Don't worry. McClure sounds more up her alley, and if he's at all like his mother —" He smiled teasingly at Marion and she made a little face at him and rang the bell for John to clear the table.

At eleven that morning Kathleen sat waiting in the offices of the Bell Construction Company. They occupied a floor of a building which was, so the legend read, the Bell Building. The rooms were big and light but the reception room was utilitarian in the extreme. No soft carpets, lush draperies, or divans. There was moderate comfort, a lot of telephones, and ash trays, and at the desk an elderly woman with a sharp, hard face.

Kathleen was aware of her appraising eyes, which expressed neither approval nor disapproval. She opened her compact and stole a look at herself. She didn't know what she expected to see, she saw merely the face with which she had lived for twenty-three years, although she'd reached fourteen before she became aware of it. It was a nice face, she knew that; she wasn't in the least vain but she had eyes in her head, nice eyes, a nice head. And McClure had said —

Oh, why think of McClure . . . even if she had been doing so off and on all morning. He was a disappointment to her, she told herself firmly. A man with all the promise and gift of that first play! She had expected someone quite different . . . brilliant but responsible, grave and utterly honest. Instead he had proved to be a good-looking, wisecracking lightweight, with an eye for every woman he met and not a serious thought in his mind. He was amusing, she liked, rather than disliked him, it would be entertaining to meet him again and quarrel a little with him. But she had built up a picture of him in her mind ever since seeing the play, ever since Hannah had talked about him. And he had fallen far short of that picture. He was young, he couldn't be much older than Hannah, if any older . . . It was too bad, she thought further, that he had money of his own. Perhaps, if he had to work he would. And do something worth while. Hannah had told her, during their luncheon together the other day, of the fabulous amount he had made in Hollywood, adapting two of his plays for the screen — *Nothing Is Lost* wasn't screen material at all — and adapting other people's plays as well. But when they were ready to take up his option he hadn't seen it their way. He'd thrown it in their startled faces and headed east.

She looked up and through half-glass doors into an office filled with girls at typewriters. The clatter came to her faintly. In the distance a door opened and a man came out as if catapulted. He recovered himself and walked unsteadily down between the rows of desks. Kathleen watched him with interest. Was he ill? she thought with a pang of pity, or, with less pity, drunk? The girls typing didn't seem curious, they hardly glanced up. Perhaps they were used to disheveled men staggering through, arranging their ties and brushing at their coats with futile hands.

He came into the reception room and slammed the door after him. He looked over at Kathleen and she saw that his right eye was swollen. He had the making, she saw and tried not to smile, of a superb shiner. He went over to the desk and spoke to the woman behind it. Kathleen heard what he said. He said, "P. S. He didn't get the job!"

The woman said something sharp and low, and he nodded and went to the elevators and kept his thumb on the button. Presently the doors slid back and he disappeared from view. Kathleen thought nervously, "Well, if Mr. Bell treats all applicants like that!"

A telephone rang on the receptionist's desk. The woman spoke into it, and then looked over at Kathleen.

"Mr. Bell will see you now," she said. "Go through that office and turn left . . . first door."

Kathleen thanked her and rose. She made her way between the rows of desks and was conscious that here and there a machine ceased, momentarily, its metallic chatter and that a good many eyes, brown and blue and gray and hazel, followed her. She heard a buzz of voices which, stopped instantly as a woman in a tailored frock came through the aisles and stood aside to let Kathleen pass. Office Mrs. Legree, thought Kathleen, more alarmed than ever.

She was aware that her Oxford-gray suit was simple but well cut, that her hat was new and a little on the dashing side. She thought, Perhaps I should have left the sables at home! But they were modest, only two skins, if soft and dark, and they had been a Christmas present from her father.

She reached the end of the big square room and turned left. A door was open and a man was shouting into a telephone . . .

"O. K., Murphy," he was saying, "I've

41

sent him back to you and he can stay there. Next time you'll know better . . . I won't be blackmailed into giving jobs to your misfit relatives. You can take it and like it. And you're out the price of a good juicy steak. No, you fool, not for his stomach! For his eye!"

He was laughing as he hung up, swung around and saw her standing there.

"Oh," he said, and grinned at her, "sorry. Come in, Miss Roberts, and you might shut the door after you."

She did so, coming forward and sitting on the chair he indicated. The room was big and rather bare. A great untidy desk, a steel safe, and files across one wall. A picture of a man hung back of the desk . . . a fat, dark man with heavy eyebrows. On the other walls unframed blueprints.

He said, "I thought you were older!"

Kathleen leaned forward.

"I'm twenty-three," she told him, "and that isn't, I hope, too young," she tried to smile. "At times, it seems almost elderly."

He said, still staring at her, "You must forgive the confusion of this room. I just had a little argument."

Now for the first time she noticed the overturned chair, the metal scrap basket spilling wastepaper, the small table tipped drunkenly, the books it had held sprawled open on the floor. She said impulsively, "I saw the result!"

"No man," said Pat Bell, scowling, "can blackmail me!" He shook his head and smiled at her. "I like your father," he told her abruptly, "he's a swell guy. I knew I'd like his daughter. Tell me about yourself."

She said, "The usual schooling, and graduation from Smith. Business school after that and almost a year in my father's office. I was just a typist there but sometimes I filled in when the secretaries were busy or ill or on vacation. I can take dictation, Mr. Bell, I have good speed. I type clearly. I'm perfectly capable of writing letters on my own. . . . That is —" she hesitated, trying to explain — "when I'd fill in for Mr. Howard's secretary — Mr. Howard is my father's partner — he'd say, 'Tell him to go to the devil, I wouldn't speak at that dinner for a million dollars, I hate the man like poison,' and I'd write the letter and explain how honored Mr. Howard was, and how much he regretted, etc., etc. You understand."

"Perfectly," said Patrick Bell, laughing. "Go on."

"That's all. Except that since my father has been at home I've taken care of his personal mail. Of course, during my time at the office

I became familiar with legal terms . . ."

"Good," said Bell. "Look here, I've a man secretary for the business end of things, he's trained in our particular kind of language. What I need is a personal secretary. One who will keep the wrong people out, and let the right people in; look after my personal bills, remind me when to send my mother flowers, and argue with the school about kid sister's bills. You know, all that sort of thing. There will be business letters too, but that's not the main idea. Jim can't handle this sort of stuff and it's getting a little beyond me. I'm moving across the hall into other offices, with an anteroom . . . that would be yours, if you want it."

She cried, "Of course, I want it. I hope you'll give me a trial."

"Can you come Monday?" he asked her.

So she was not to be catapulted out of the office with whatever equivalent of the summer she might expect to suffer at his hands. She looked at him, and away again. When she had first come in she had met his eyes steadily but now she couldn't for long. It was as if they laid a burden on her. But she knew what he looked like.

Big. Big shoulders, big frame, big large-knuckled hands. His eyes were blue and his heavy voice had a curious lilt in it . . . that was the Irish mother. He was almost too meticulously dressed, his tie matched the handkerchief in his pocket a little too well, his socks matched too. His shoes were highly polished, his short square nails manicured. He had the whitest teeth she had ever seen and the most belligerent square chin. He had the vitality of ten men, it emanated from him, it made itself felt across a room. He didn't have to move or speak to have it reach you and take you by the throat and make you a little breathless.

He said, "We haven't talked money."

She looked at him now, directly. She said:

"It's up to you, Mr. Bell. I've been frank with you, you know just what experience I've had. It isn't much, yet I believe that it is something on which I can build. I am careful and accurate, I can take orders, and I can learn. My father paid me a purely nominal salary. I didn't think it fair to accept more . . . so I took a little less."

He said, "Good. I like an honest woman, they're rare as hen's teeth. I'll pay you thirty-five to start. If you're any good to me you'll get fifty by the end of the year. How's that?"

"It's more than generous," she said, startled.

He rose; obviously the interview was over. Kathleen rose too, a little bewildered. He said, "I'll take you to the elevators . . . I'm going that way."

He made it clear that if he hadn't been going that way she could have found her own way out. All right, she liked that in him. She liked him. She was faintly afraid of him but she liked him. He was as refreshing as a strong wind blowing from the sea. He could be, she already had proof of it, a hurricane, a tornado. Someone had shown him the fashion magazines for men. His suit was conservatively dark but the cut was not conservative. His hair, she saw now, was unruly and curly. There were cigarette stains on the fingers of his right hand.

They walked down the aisle together between the rows of desks. Here and there he spoke to a girl in passing, put a hand on her shoulder, said, "Well, Betty, how goes it?" to one; to another, "How's the kid brother?" and to a third, "If I get a minute this week I'll run into the hospital to see your mother, Joan."

There was adoration in the eyes they raised to his and Kathleen felt her throat tighten.

He stood with her by the elevators. He said, "You may be taking more on your plate than you know. But we'll talk about that Monday."

The elevator came up, he smiled at her, the doors closed, and she dropped into space. But the elevators had never affected her heart before, not even the magic ones which run to the top of the Empire State Building. Still, her heart was pounding. She wanted to run and sing.

She thought, forcing her steps to be sedate, as she turned toward the subway, "Well, I've got the job!"

She couldn't wait to reach home. She turned into the nearest cigar store, to stand in a close-smelling little booth and dial her number. She wanted her father and her mother to know the news at once.

"I'm hired," she said triumphantly when her mother answered.

"Come home at once," said Marion, "and tell us all about it."

In the subway she planned what she would tell them.

Nice man. She liked him. He looked stubborn as a mule, but as honest as daylight. She was sure she would like the job.

That sounded a little pale, a little cool. She didn't feel pale or cool. She felt flushed with excitement and warm with anticipation. She'd never seen a man like Pat Bell. And every other man she had known seemed pallid and tepid by comparison with this one brief glimpse of him.

Beginning Monday she would see him every day for, she assumed, five and a half days.

Chapter III

The Roberts apartment was being disman-
tled, silver and rugs sent to storage, valuables
put away. It was in one of the first co-opera-
tive houses, and Lawson Roberts owned it.
In accordance with his character, as soon as
it had been settled that Kathleen would not
live in it during her parents' absence — "I'd
rattle around," she said, "like beans in a
gourd . . . jumping beans for choice" — he
had refused to consider renting it but decided instead to lend it to one of his clients
who, having lost all he had some years since,
was making a slow, modest comeback. As
the client had three obstreperous children,
Marion tempered her husband's generosity
with precaution and left the new tenants her
less precious china, her plated flatware, and
removed her orientals and certain personal
belongings which she prized.

Mr. Roberts's small, but fine, collection
of books was housed in a room sacred to
himself, and opening off the library proper.
This room, which would be of no use to
the Hitchens family, was locked and the key
delivered to Kathleen, who promised to

come in at stated intervals to air, dust and, otherwise see that the books remained in order. The Hitchenses, nice, married people, were delighted to be relieved of the responsibility.

Preparations went on, Kathleen went to and from the office. Because of the new interest and excitement of her work she found the signs of departure less harrowing than if she had been left behind to twiddle her thumbs. She was taking some of her own things to Hannah's apartment and between work, helping her mother, moving her clothes and belongings, little by little, her time was very full.

The Robertses sailed on a cold, sunny autumn Saturday and John and Mary, remaining in the apartment to settle the new tenants, would leave for England the following week. Kathleen, sitting with her mother and father in their comfortable stateroom, swallowed a large lump in her throat and talked fast and furiously about everything and nothing.

The stateroom was filled with flowers, books, bottles, the inevitable baskets of fruit. Kathleen, rising to walk restlessly around, read the card attached to one ornate container of flowers. "Pat Bell!" she exclaimed, startled. "Why, how nice of him!"

"Very," said her father, "be sure you thank him properly."

Bands were playing, people calling to one another, the public rooms, corridors, and lifts were crowded. Stewards bustled past with luggage, followed by a chattering stream of people. Nice people, for the most part, Kathleen thought, observing them. She hoped her mother and father would find good company aboard for the four months' cruise . . . four months was a long time; a year much longer!

Callers knocked at the door, Lawson Roberts's partner and his wife: "The office will go on," he promised, "and we'll keep an eye on this infant for you"; the junior partner and his recent bride, clerks, Roberts's secretary, Miss Jervis . . . friends, acquaintances . . . the stateroom was much too small, everyone talked and laughed and smoked, the bottles were opened . . .

Kathleen waited until the very last moment. The others had left, thank heaven. She could take her mother in her strong young arms and hug her hard. She could put her arms around her father's thin shoulders.

"Don't cry, mother," she said. "What a way to begin a second honeymoon!"

Marion sniffed. "I started my first in tears," she declared with a catch in her voice, "my shoes hurt me dreadfully and my corsets were too tight!"

"All ashore that's going ashore . . . all ashore . . ." the warning cry reached them and they started and looked at one another. Kathleen said fiercely, "I won't bawl!" But the tears streamed down her face. She cried, "Oh, have a marvelous time, you two. Send me silly postals with 'wish you were here' and 'X marks the spot.' And *don't* worry!"

Her mother said, choked, "Don't stand on the pier. It's always so silly — waiting for a boat to sail . . . people hanging over the rail and shouting . . . no one hears, and the people who are going wish they could leave the deck and go below and the people who aren't going —"

They were propelling her along the corridors, they had reached the gangplank. She let herself be swept down by a crowd of shoregoers, and once on the pier fought her way forward, and looked up to see if they were still on deck. They were, hanging over the rail just like the others whom her mother had deplored. They were waving . . .

So she waited, scarcely seeing, until she couldn't endure it another minute, until the frantic gestures of her father told her as plainly as words, "Move on, my girl, get going."

And she moved on.

She taxied back to the apartment to cry a little with Mary's good arms around her and John timidly patting her shoulder. There were a few last things to be taken to Hannah's, over on the East Side. She thought, with a perking of her spirit, "Well, Paul McClure was right, a little East Side flat! My destiny."

When she was ready to leave the telephone rang and it was McClure. She said, astonished, "I was just thinking of you."

"Very flattering. Good thoughts?"

"So-so. I was considering your flair for prophecy as I am moving to that little East Side flat. Only the catch is, I knew it the night of the Eloise party and you did too. Hannah's flat."

He said, "Hannah didn't say when . . ."

"Now, in a minute, I was just about to call for a taxi."

"It's a grand day," said McClure, "how about my coming over to help you move?"

"Thanks, no," Kathleen said, "I'm in no condition to receive a gentleman."

"What, not decent!"

"Decent, but depressed. I've just seen my family off, they sailed a little while ago."

"How about having dinner with me tonight? By the way, I assume you got the job."

"I did," she said and could not keep her

elation from her voice. "And I will."

"You sound as if you liked your work," he said curiously.

"I do," she answered.

"And that sounds like the marriage ceremony. I'll stop for you at seven at Hannah's."

He rang off and her spirits went on perking, like a coffeepot. Any port in a storm, even Paul McClure, she thought; these first few days would be so difficult, adjusting herself to Hannah's haphazard ways, and to being alone.

She had finished rearranging her pleasant bedroom with its view of the oily, lively river when Hannah blew in, her hat on one side and her welcoming smile lipsticked in Chinese scarlet.

"Lamb," she cried, "it's marvelous!"

"What?" asked Kathleen. She had on an old skirt, an older sweater, and her sleeves were rolled up. She had unpacked her clothes and books and put out her photographs and hung three pictures she loved on Hannah's peach-tinted walls. She liked the room, it had charm and an odd, engaging shape. There was a funny narrow ell-shaped end to it, containing a chaise longue on which Kathleen had put her own pillows and a lopsided sinister giraffe made of gingham which her father had once won in a shooting gallery and which had spent four years with her in Northampton.

"Your being here. I'll be more popular than ever, and that's saying something," Hannah explained modestly.

"I won't get in your hair," Kathleen promised. "Tell me when to stay away — it will all be fifty-fifty . . ."

"My precious, I didn't mean that at all. I meant . . . Oh, hell, figure it out for yourself." Hannah collapsed on a divan and shouted, "Amelia!"

Amelia appeared. She was fat and black. She was a magnificent cook, a superbartender. She had a way with headaches. She understood white nights and mornings after. She swept into the corners and under radiators but Hannah, who had had her for three years, forgave her and had a cleaning woman in once a week.

"Martini," said Hannah, "and you'd better join me, Kate, as a sort of celebration."

"Too early in the day."

"Darling, you aren't going to be too pure, are you?" asked Hannah anxiously.

"No," said Kathleen, smiling, "just pure enough."

"Well!" Hannah drew a deep breath. "Family get off?"

"Yes. They've a nice stateroom and the passengers looked interesting . . . it's a lovely ship too. Mother was crying and Father kept swearing and blowing his nose. I bawled like a two-year-old. But I'm so happy for them. If only they won't worry about me."

"They will," said Hannah calmly, "and seems to me that they have something to worry about now."

"What?" inquired Kathleen with interest. "Don't tell me I've been in a scandal already and my poor parents not eight hours out at sea!"

"Scoff on," warned Hannah, "but meantime I have had a glimpse of your boss."

"Pat Bell." Kathleen's dimple appeared briefly. "Where," she demanded, "and how?"

"Oh, even designers get around. I had lunch at India House yesterday, with a very nice but rather wacky man. I encouraged him, as I think he will steer his wife to Eloise, Inc. — that is, if I can make him feel sufficiently ashamed of himself for daring to make passes at an innocent wide-eyed little undesigning designer. Yes, he'll send her to Eloise and tell her to go the limit and it will be the *amende* expensive. Where was I?"

"In India House."

Amelia waddled in with a tray, two bread sticks, a cracker spread with caviar, a tiny shaker, and one glass. She set it down, looked with love at Hannah and approval at Kathleen, and waddled off again.

"Oh, yes," said Hannah, pouring her drink, "yes, indeed. There was one Patrick Bell lunching with an elderly gent. My equally elderly boy friend pointed him out to me. Said he was a comer. Said that his outfit is the biggest, the most strongly entrenched, and has the most political backing. I wasn't interested. I was looking at Mr. Bell. Blue eyes and black hair and a dark skin. Very nice. Shoulders like a truck and hands like hams. My child, watch your step."

"He's swell," said Kathleen.

"I can see that. How about the work?"

"I'm learning."

"That's what I'm afraid of." She set down her glass. "We'll throw a party," she suggested, "in honor of your coming here to dwell beneath my fig tree. That sounds all wrong somehow. We'll throw it tonight. You can ask your boss."

Kathleen laughed. "I'm not on party terms with him, Hannah."

"You will be, you will be. The sooner the better. Eventually, why not now? O. K., we'll throw this one without him. Hand me that telephone book."

"I can't —" began Kathleen.

"What's wrong — break your right arm?"

"Party, I mean. I promised Paul McClure that I'd dine with him tonight."

The living room was quite still for a moment. It was a crazy room, with a certain brittle, cockeyed charm. Hannah regarded her friend reflectively. She ran her hands through her dark-red hair until it stood up all around her head. She said, "Paul. So that's it."

"Mind?" asked Kathleen.

"God, no, why should I? I'm all for it . . . I didn't know you'd been seeing him, that's all."

"I haven't been," said Kathleen truthfully, "not since the night of the Eloise party."

"He took you home."

"Yes, but I didn't ask him in," said Kathleen, "like the gal in the advertisements. No, haven't laid eyes on him since. Then, today, he phoned."

"He's a strange critter," said Hannah. She poured herself a second drink and lay back against the mulberry velvet of the divan. "I was so goofily in love with him that I thought I was fourteen weaving daisy chains in a meadow, believing in Santa Claus, going to church on Sundays, and wishing on loads of hay. That's how crazy I was. But something happened . . . I don't know what. We'd even talked about getting married. Oh, I pretended I wasn't serious, Paul would have been scared to death of the simple creature I'd become, I didn't confess it to him . . . but we did mention the idea. And then we had a quarrel and then after that — Oh, well —" she grinned, and set down her glass — "water under the bridge, muddy water. Only I'm warning you."

"You're full of warnings," said Kathleen. "Perpetual stop light, or what is it they call the yellow one at which traffic hesitates?"

Hannah leaned over to pat her shoulder.

"You'll get along," she prophesied, "and more power to you. I think I'll throw that party, after all . . . you and Paul can wander in when it suits you."

Dressing, Kathleen wondered idly how Paul McClure and Pat Bell would like each other. Not much, she thought; two such entirely different types, they would have absolutely nothing in common, they might even be, in all probability, markedly antagonistic.

McClure called for her at seven, and Hannah, who had been sporadically telephoning all her friends and enemies since the late afternoon, waved to him from the telephone table. "Darling," she was shouting into the instrument, "do drop around . . . tonight.

Oh, any old time . . . I'm tossing a shindig. Of course, it's Saturday, it's been Saturday all day. . . . All right, after the theater then. Naturally I'll be up, when did I ever go to bed?"

She replaced the receiver and swung around. Amelia was beaming at Paul in a proprietary manner. "You see," said Hannah, "even Amelia remembers you but she can't get over the fact that you're not coming to see me."

"I came to see you recently," Paul reminded her.

"Oh, Amelia never remembers further back than tomorrow," said Hannah. "Kate, you look divine. I shouldn't say so, I'm supposed to be wedded to Eloise, but you don't need Eloise, I'll say that much for you."

The taxi was waiting, they drove toward the center of town. McClure said, "I'm tired of intimate little restaurants, they bore me. I thought — the Persian Room?"

When he had ordered he sat back in his chair and smiled at her. "Now," he said, "the job. What do you do?"

"Mr. Bell's personal letters," she said, "and —"

"What Bell?"

"Patrick Bell."

"Never heard of him."

"You wouldn't," she said, stung, "he doesn't drop in at the Racquet Club."

"Come, come," said Paul soothingly, "didn't mean to tread on loyal toes."

"It's a contracting firm," she said, "a big one. He's the head of it since his father's death."

"Personal secretary," said McClure musingly. "Well, that might run to a number of things . . . theater tickets, for instance, and sending flowers to the wrong girls at the right time and writing the letters to his son in boarding school."

"He isn't married," said Kathleen, laughing.

"That's a blow," McClure told her. "What, no nagging wife? No bald head? No elderly waistline?"

"On the contrary," said Kathleen triumphantly.

"It's nice work if you can get it," said McClure.

It was and she had got it. Personal letters, sorting out invitations, looking after the charity budget. He'd said to her, "When you think it's all right, sign me up for whatever's customary." As for the invitations, he remarked, "I'm getting more of these than I can handle. Most of the people want something, I don't fool myself about that. Some of them don't want anything much. I'd like to accept those bids. But how am I to tell? That's one reason I hired you, to separate the sheep from the goats. Would you think badly of me if I told you I'd like to know the right sort of people?"

She said, "Not at all . . . you're honest about it."

"Well, it's a fact," he told her, leaning back in his big chair. "My kid sister — she's pretty, you see, and only eighteen, this is her last year at school — I'd like her to have things. I've never told you much about my people, thought you'd be bored."

"I wouldn't be."

"My old man was — tops. Yelled at the top of his lungs, terrorized people, and had a heart big and soft as a down pillow. My mother . . . you'll see her someday . . . she's fine. I had an older brother, he died in the war, and then two younger than I . . . they died of diphtheria. The kid sister, Carmela, she came along late . . . when my mother had given up expecting any more. I'd like her to have everything I hadn't."

She wasn't going to tell McClure this. She had no right to tell him, it wasn't his business. Besides, she could imagine the sort of thing he'd say.

He said something now. He asked, "From

your crack a while back I gather that your Mr. Bell is what is commonly known as self-made . . . nature's nobleman," he deduced, and laughed.

"What's so amusing?" she demanded.

"You. Your eyes blazed at me. So, I'm right."

She said, "Not altogether. It was his father's business. He could have gone to college — the son, I mean — and had every advantage. He didn't want to, he went into the firm instead."

"Very smart," said McClure, "America's haywire on this college business. Everyone has to go to college, no matter what sacrifice it involves or how poor the material. Your Mr. Bell was probably right. I don't mean," he added hastily, "that he was poor material, so don't jump down my throat . . . I take back the self-made. It's just half self-made. And if you like, I'll retract the nature's noble man."

"You needn't," she said, "I don't think it's so comic."

"Most of nature's noblemen I've met," said McClure, "have been crooks. Dear kindly old natives with accents and simplicity. Lord, you're lucky if you escape with the gold in your teeth."

"Do you believe that or do you just talk that way?"

"Both." He lifted his glass. "Here's to the job" he said. "And now, let's talk about how attractive you are. You know, I've thought about you too much. I haven't wanted to . . . I had to, damn it."

She said, "Your lines are elegant, Mr. McClure. You should save 'em for the next play."

"I've lots more. So you think that's all a line, do you?"

"How could I think anything else?"

Lights flowed about them, music, the scent of perfume and flowers. The big room was crowded. McClure looked straight into her eyes. "Aren't you old enough yet to have learned how to sift the chaff from the grain? I suppose that's a very bad joke."

"It's a good one," she said, delighted. "Tell me, how is the play coming?"

"It's terrible," he said gloomily. "I think I'll shoot myself."

"Why don't you?"

"Woman, don't sit there coolly in ice green and tell me that you would care."

"Is this ice green?" she asked, "I thought it was just green."

"You look like a delightful head of lettuce," he said. "And so you wouldn't care."

"No," she said, "not especially."

"Aha, my proud beauty," he warned her,

"you'll regret this. One day you'll come crawling to me on your hands and knees. You'll say, 'Paul, can you ever forgive me? I have found out that even a stiff shirt can conceal a heart of gold!' "

Kathleen laughed. "You are too utterly absurd. Tell me about the play."

"Terrific in more ways than one."

"Drawing room comedy," she inquired, "with the Coward touch?"

"The hero touch, darling," he said lazily. "You'd hate it, it's all about unions and strikes and other unhappy situations."

She said slowly, "Your first play was about rather dreadful realities, but somehow I can't believe —"

"You think I've lost touch?"

"I'm afraid so, Mr. McClure."

"Paul to you; I don't know you well enough for surnames. Alas, sweet Kate," he said, "at that, you may be right!"

Chapter IV

Hannah's noisy party lasted most of Saturday night and into Sunday morning. Paul and Kathleen returning late, as they had lingered over their coffee, found themselves drawn into a vortex of people all very informal, all very vocal. They hardly saw each other again except across a room, but now and then she found his regard fixed on her, saw an eyebrow go up more crookedly than ever with a dismal I-can't-help-this expression.

Kathleen was too sleepy to pay much attention when Hannah, after the last guest had gone, trailed into her bedroom and stood there rocking, with yawns.

"Am I tired? Why in hell did I do it? I'll sleep all day tomorrow," Hannah said. "Amelia will have a convulsion . . . one rug burned, three highball glass rings, and about a million cigarette butts. What's more dismal than after the aftermath? I had to pay her a fortune to come on Sundays as it is, she'll growl all day."

Kathleen said, "I had a marvelous time."

"I believe you," said Hannah. "Where you

get, how you preserve your capacity for enjoyment, I can't imagine." She turned away. "Oh, by the way," she added, "how was Paul tonight? Amusing?"

"Very," said Kathleen serenely; "he's excellent company."

"If he exerts himself. But I've known him to sit around for eternities in a sort of glum stupor," said Hannah, "and not even know he wasn't alone."

This was a different picture of McClure, thought Kathleen, trying to adjust herself to it. She said, "Oh, the alleged artistic temperament, I suppose, fads and fancies, whims and moods."

"That's what I once thought," said Hannah. "Good night, Kate."

Sunday was boring, people came and went. Kathleen went for a walk to get some fresh air in her lungs. She called up a classmate, and invited herself for tea. In the evening she went around to the apartment to say good-bye to Mary and John and returned early to put herself to bed. Hannah was out, would probably not be home till all hours.

Monday was like rescue. Sunday she felt like something on a raft — Monday was a steamer . . . nearing.

She was to feel that way on successive Mondays. During the weeks which followed she and Pat Bell came to know each other rather well. He said, when she had been there a month:

"Mind if I call you Kathleen?"

"I'd like it," she said instantly.

"Pat then? Two good old Irish names."

She said, "It isn't office procedure."

"But this isn't like most offices."

She hadn't had much experience of offices, but she was inclined to agree with him. It was, like many others, run at top speed, a terrific tempo, and no one wasted time. But a breezy informality prevailed. Bell was never too busy to see any of his men and they wandered in and out of his anteroom all day, sometimes they waited there with her, instead of outside, while Pat finished talking to someone else. Laborers came, foremen came, union delegates, or men who had worked for his father, often shabby and down at the heel, smelling, most likely, of poverty and sometimes of poverty's escape. She grew to know many of them by name, they would linger by her desk and talk with her. They all had the same word for Pat: "a grand boy," they said, "a fine upstanding generous lad," and generous he was, often to a fault, she thought. When one of the old men came in Pat's hand went out to him at once, and then it went into a pocket and came out once more, laden. "There. Buy yourself a shave, a meal and a night's lodging. A drink too. Not more than one. Get some sleep and come back. I think I can find a night watchman job for you somewhere."

Generous but mistaken.

"Did you mean that about the night watchman job for old Joe?" she asked.

"Sure, why not? I've a friend with a string of warehouses."

"But he isn't fit for it, Pat; he's too old, and he's been too afraid. He'd run at the first sign of trouble."

"You wouldn't want him to stay and get plugged, would you, Kathleen?"

"No, of course not! But he drinks . . . he's never been here quite sober."

"Oh, he'll be able to punch a clock and make the round," said Pat carelessly. "Besides, nothing will happen . . . Hateron is heavily insured and pays plenty protection. It will be a made-to-order job. I can't let old Joe down, he worked with the Old Man and he — Why, if I couldn't help him, he'd think the world was at an end."

"Why didn't he come to you before?" she asked.

"He has," said Pat in astonishment, "a dozen times. Damn fool, he's always quitting or being fired."

"Yet you'd try again!"

"Naturally." He looked at her, puzzled, as if she was a little stupid not to see things in his clear light.

Perhaps she was. Perhaps she couldn't believe in people as he did. She spoke of this to Paul McClure the next time she saw him. Hannah was out and he had phoned and asked if he might come around and bring the play. He came without the play.

"Oh, why not?" she wanted to know.

"Cold feet."

"I'll never believe that. What happened to it?"

"The cat ate it, my Jap threw a highball over it — pick your own excuse."

"The truth, out with it."

"I burned the damned thing."

"Paul, not really? But you're crazy." She looked at him in despair. "You had a producer, he'd read the first draft."

"I don't care, it wasn't right," he said, "I pulled my punches. Well, I'll make another stab at it."

That made her think of Bell and she told Paul about him and old Joe. She ended, "He's like that."

He looked at her oddly.

"You think that's fine, don't you?"

"Of course, I do; don't you?"

70

"No, I think it's cowardly."

"Paul!"

"Look here, suppose the warehouse burns up or is robbed because of this old geezer who's half soused most of the time and too old into the bargain to put up a fight. How generous is your gallant employer being to his friend who ovens the warehouse? Lord, he isn't thinking of him at all. He's being Santa Claus, my dear. The big benevolent brother, his father's own son. He couldn't let old Joe down, could he? Hell, that isn't it. He couldn't let himself down, the idea he had of himself. Can't you see, Kate? No, of course, you can't. You're staring at me as if I had uttered blasphemy. . . . It will take a long time to learn that easy generosity is the soul of selfishness."

She was raging with indignation.

"You couldn't possibly understand him, Paul," she said. "He's simple and honest . . . maybe he's mistaken sometimes . . . but he follows his own star."

"Don't we all? Simple and honest! And I'm not?"

She said slowly, "You've a pretty complicated mind . . . as to the rest, I don't know. You're always putting on an act. How can you be honest with yourself or anyone else? You don't care about anything but your own queer, highly colored little world. You don't know what's happening outside and you don't care."

"You must be right," he said, staring at her. "Anyone as beautiful as you are, Kate, has to be right."

She said, "Oh, let's forget it, I was very near quarreling with you."

"Over Patrick Bell, the great unknown? I'd like to meet him."

"All right," said Kathleen on sudden impulse, "why not? I'll give a party and you can all meet him."

"A friendship which extends beyond office hours?" he said.

"What's strange about that?"

"Nothing, according to the best fiction formulas. Throw your party, Kate. I'll wear my social smirk, my diamond gardenia, my white tie and tails and, for safety's sake, my bulletproof vest."

Hannah was delighted at the idea of a party at which Bell would be present. "I thought you weren't on party terms," she said curiously. "It hasn't taken you long."

"Well," said Kathleen sedately, "as a personal secretary —"

"You are growing up," said Hannah with admiration.

Nevertheless, Kathleen regretted her plan

when she entered the office next day. Entering, the mere act of it, had never ceased to amaze her. Astonishing that she, the kid herself, should be speaking with familiarity to the grim receptionist — who wasn't grim at all, but merely suffered from a good-for-nothing brother, his large family, and a touch of arthritis. Amazing that she could walk down between the aisles of desks and call the girls by name. Astonishing that she should have a luncheon date today with the chief engineer's secretary. And magical that this anteroom with its desk and straight chairs was her own, that the door opened into Pat's office.

He came in chuckling and threw a thick white envelope on her desk. "This came to me at home," he explained, "I seem to be stepping out."

She read the invitation. She said, smiling, "It's a charity affair, Pat — you pays your money and you takes your choice."

"Sure, but I got on the sponsor list," he said.

He was a child, greedy for new toys. She was tolerant, but her heart ached for him. She thought, I'd like to give him the moon and the stars with the four hundred thrown in, just for fun. And thinking it she was frightened. She *mustn't* be!

But she was. . . .

That was why the time between nine and five was so short and it was so long until the next nine to five. That was why she was astonished every time she hung up her hat, astonished at her own happiness and her own luck. She was crazy to fall in love with him . . . she'd be crazier not to! And he'd fall in love with her, she thought, setting her little jaw, if she had to blackjack him into it. After all, she had one advantage, she saw him almost every day in the week. She could make herself necessary to him, she believed she had already done so. Propinquity, need . . . and her own attraction. If Paul McClure admitted that attraction . . .

She smiled again. She said, "Of course, you're on the sponsor list. Why shouldn't you be?"

Making out his check for the box afterwards, she wished that she might be there with him, might sit in his box and hold his hand and think, If this is what he wants, I'll help him get it.

Before she left that day she came in with a batch of letters to be signed. While he signed them with sure firm strokes of his stubby pen she looked out the windows and down on the street black with people hurrying home from the offices. She thought of her mother and father and was so still that he swung around and spoke to her.

"Penny for them."

"Worth more. I was thinking of Mother and Father."

"They're all right?"

"The last wireless reported that they were blooming."

"You miss them, don't you, Kathleen?"

"Terribly."

"But you aren't too lonely — with that friend you live with, what's her name?"

"Hannah Arnold. No, not lonely exactly."

"And you go out a good deal."

"A lot . . . sometimes with Hannah, sometimes without her, and people come in . . ."

"I'll bet they do."

"Would you? I'm asking a few for Sunday night. Eight, and don't dress. We'll eat and drink, roll up the rugs and dance. There's a man who plays the piano awfully well and a girl who sings . . . she's on the stage. Would you like to come," she asked, "or wouldn't it be proper?"

"Proper?" he repeated on a great roar.

"I mean . . . nine to five is proper, but after that?"

"I thought we were friends."

"We are."

"Of course. And you bet I'll come . . . don't dress, you said?" and his face fell, a little.

"As you like," she told him, "but the others won't . . . it's an informal sort of gang."

It sounded harmless, child's play, "eat and drink, roll up the rugs and dance." He thought, on his way there in the big sleek car, which despite his broken-nosed chauffeur he almost always drove himself, I'll be bored . . . sounds like a children's party. But he knew as soon as he entered Hannah's apartment, which had certainly not been designed for children, that whatever else happened to him he would not be bored.

His eyes widened at two of the prints on the walls, at a small statue on the table. Hot stuff, he thought uneasily. He liked, he told himself, good clean dirt as much as the next man but he couldn't quite get this sort.

Hannah overpowered him, and he looked down on her from his great height in amazement. Little and vital and high-pitched. She cried, "Where in the world has Kate been keeping you . . . or hasn't she? Come on and meet some of the troupe." Kathleen rescued him then, took him around. The man who played the piano had long hair and a short temper. The girl who sang turned out to be a musical comedy star whom Pat had admired across the footlights for several years. There were other pretty girls. Some in sports clothes, some in long dresses with brief bodices, others in tailored velvet suits. There was a girl with her hair piled on top of her head and leg-of-mutton sleeves. She had slanting eyes, and a full red mouth. Eloise had rushed the fashions. The girl looked like the nineties but she talked like tomorrow.

"Mostly Hannah's friends," Kathleen told him, "I thought they'd amuse you."

McClure came in late, and straight across the room to Kathleen. "Hello, Kate," he cried, "and of course this is Patrick Bell."

They shook hands. They disliked each other at once. Pat thought, It isn't possible, she wouldn't go in for this kind of — He shrugged mentally. And Paul thought, Good God, well, perhaps I'm mistaken!

Kathleen looked from one to the other. "You really ought to like each other, you're so different."

"I'll try," said McClure without a change of expression.

There was food and there was drink. The rugs were rolled up and there was dancing. Viewing it, Pat thought, his hands thrust in his pockets, You couldn't get away with it in a clip joint.

The slant-eyed girl pulled at his sleeve. "Come on, you look as if you could shake a mean leg," she suggested.

He had taken lessons, all last year. He said,

however, "I'm not up to this." He grinned. "I haven't got that far at Murray's."

"Don't let it throw you," she advised.

She dragged him into the middle of the room and before he knew it he was witnessing and indulging in the earliest, pre-St. Regis version of the Lambeth Walk to reach these shores. "Oi, Oi," he shouted with great hilarity.

"He's having a good time," Paul told Kathleen.

"You like him?"

"No. He's very good-looking however."

She said, "Snap judgment . . . you don't know him."

"You asked for it. You like him?"

"Of course."

"How much?"

She flushed and turned away. He said, following, "Not that much. You can't."

"Why not?" she asked defiantly.

He said, low, "You haven't known him long enough. Besides, I love you."

She laughed outright at that. "You haven't known me long enough," she reminded him.

"Kate —"

"Does the length of time matter, then?"

"No, I suppose not and I do love you."

The others were noisy enough, he could say it, standing there with her against Hannah's bedroom door. Hannah saw them and her narrow eyes almost disappeared from her smooth face. She was dancing with Pat now. She said, as if casually, "Witness your secretary and her boy friend. Too proud to fight."

He said, "Boy friend — him?"

"Yes, him," said Hannah, discarding syntax. "He has a way with him . . . I ought to know, I was in love with him once, and since then I've worn my heart on my sleeve."

She displayed it, a red satin heart stitched to a long black velvet sleeve. The bodice was heart-shaped too. The heart on the sleeve had an arrow through it and it had bled embroidered drops of blood.

He did not look, he was not interested. His puzzled eyes were on Kathleen and Pearl.

Well, thought Hannah, maybe I've done her a good turn at that.

The telephone rang shrilly. She went to answer it presently, and shouted into it, then turning she said in surprise, "It's for you, Pat Bell."

He took her place, listened, and then said, "I can't hear." He turned and held up one big hand. "Be quiet, all of you," he shouted, "I can't hear a word."

They were quiet, stunned into silence.

79

Kathleen moved forward and stood beside him. His face was perfectly ashen. He asked, "When? I see. No one there? Just the watchman. My God, if it had happened on a weekday. All right, I'll go up."

He slammed down the telephone. Then, as the noise began and the dancing, as Hannah came forward to ask, "Is anything wrong?" he said, "I've got to get out of here."

Kathleen followed him into the square foyer.

"What is it, Pat?"

"A school building," he said briefly. "We built it, last year. A wall has collapsed."

"Pat!"

"Collapsed," he repeated. "The watchman was in there. No one else. Sunday, of course, no kids." He breathed deeply and his forehead was covered with sweat. "I've got to go," he said again.

She said instantly, "I'll go with you."

Chapter V

Kathleen ran back to her room, evading questions, exclamations and clutching hands, and emerged with her beaver coat, over her arm. She cried, "Sorry, everyone!" to her startled guests and swept Hannah with her out into the hall. "You carry on for me," she said, "we'll be back." Hannah stared at her. She said, "I don't know what it's all about but you certainly take your duties seriously."

"If you're coming —" began Pat impatiently.

She fished in the pocket of her coat, pulled out a scarf, tied it around her head. "I'm ready," she said. The door closed after them and Hannah stood there looking at it thoughtfully. Paul McClure came out. He asked, "What happened?"

"God knows," said Hannah. "He probably said, 'Take a letter!' "

"Must be air mail," said Paul. He laughed but he did not look as if he saw the humor of the situation. Hannah slid her arm through his. "Paul, you're really more attractive than you used to be. And that's saying something. Let's go back to the ravening horde, find some sandwiches, two bottles of beer, and a nice dark corner where we can rake over the ashes of our dead love."

He advised, smiling, "We'd better wear gloves."

He left her, to paw through a heap of overcoats and returned with his gloves on. Hannah went into her bedroom and came back, her hands hidden in pigskin, to the amazement of the beholders. They found the beer, the sandwiches and, by ousting incumbents, "last come, first served," they said, the corner. Their friends looked at them in astonishment. But then this was a screwy place anyway, your hostess dashing off with a strange man, and her proxy sitting in corners with Paul McClure, both meticulously gloved.

Pat did not speak to Kathleen in the elevator. Once he said something under his breath but she was aware that he was not addressing her. He was merely swearing, expertly.

She got into the front seat of his car and they shot away from the curb. They were traveling downtown, still on the East Side. They were also traveling at a high, illegal rate of speed. A policeman blew a whistle sharply and Pat slid to the curb and stopped. The officer came up. He asked, "Where's the fire?"

Pat responded evenly, "It isn't a fire, it's an accident."

He handed over his license. Kathleen saw a flash of something green. The officer looked at the license. He said, "Oh, it's you, Mr. Bell . . . didn't recognize you. O. K., go ahead. You can pick up an escort, if you want to."

They went on. And Kathleen asked after a moment, "Do you always keep a bill in with your license?"

"Yes."

"But, Pat, surely sometimes . . ."

"There are plenty who don't or won't accept it," he said carelessly, "but in that case I don't worry either. I take the ticket and get it fixed."

She said slowly, "That's obstructing justice . . . either way."

He laughed shortly. "Not so much . . . parking, a fire hydrant, a little speeding. Other men get away with it, why shouldn't I?"

Other men did get away with it, but that didn't make it any better, she thought. But perhaps there was an excuse tonight. A real excuse.

A motorcycle roared up behind them and

the man in the saddle slowed up alongside. Pat slowed also and leaned out. The officer yelled, "It's all right, Mr. Bell — Ryan told me. Where to?"

Pat told him, the cycle pulled out ahead, and with its siren sounding, blazed a trail.

Kathleen held fast to her courage. She had never driven like this, in a city or out of it.

When they reached the school building several policemen were holding back the crowds. The motorcycle officer cleared a place for them, and found a parking spot. "You'd better stay in the car," Pat told Kathleen, jumping out. But she shook her head. "I'll tag along," she told him, "if you don't mind."

The street was in chaos . . . an entire wall had fallen in. Hundreds of people had gathered. Some were women, who stood in groups and talked together, in a continuous angry murmur. One screamed shrilly, "It's God's mercy our kids wasn't in there when this happened. I'd like to get my hands on the people who built this rattrap!"

Kathleen shuddered. But Pat made no sign that he had heard, pushing his way to the front, talking to the policemen, to another man who seemed to have some authority.

"That's him," said a big man, "that's Bell."

The crowd swayed, drew nearer.

Pat spoke. He raised his voice, and it quieted and held them. "You people all go home. You can't do any good here. Your kids are all right, they weren't in the building. There's that to be thankful for. And you must remember that this building was passed by the inspectors. It was no one's fault."

The people murmured and then were quiet. But a woman pushed herself through the lines and reached him, beating at him with her clenched fists. She was an old woman, but wiry and strong. She cried, "What about my poor George, what about him . . . you — you murderer!"

Pat shook her off, gently enough. A policeman standing beside him explained, "Her husband was the watchman, Mr. Bell."

"*Was?*"

"He's in there, somewhere."

Pat caught the woman's fists in his and drew her away. He spoke to her, low, his tall head bent. After a while she listened. Then she began to cry.

He put his arm around her and asked the officer, "Isn't there a woman here who'll take her home and stay with her?"

"I will," offered a big stolid Polish woman,

85

making her way forward, "I'm a neighbor."

Pat had taken a notebook and a gold pencil from his pocket. He asked the woman, "Where does she live?" He wrote down the address and added, "She isn't to worry about anything."

After a while they left, driving at a more sedate rate of speed and without their former escort. And Kathleen asked, "Pat, what happened?"

"God knows. A fault somewhere, of course. One of those things you can't foresee."

"But," she said, "how awful! You feel that no one's safe."

"Nonsense!" he said. "It doesn't happen once in twenty years." He breathed deeply of the still frosty air. "We should be down on our knees thanking God that it didn't happen tomorrow."

"I suppose so. . . . Pat, you're going to help the watchman's wife?"

"Sure, I got the old fellow the job," he said, "he wasn't insured . . . so we'll take care of all the expenses for her."

He was so good, she thought, with a leaping heart. You could forgive the folded bill in the license . . . arrogant, as a little boy is arrogant, bribing his way out of a ticket. But taking measures to bury the poor old man in decent earth, and to look after the widow! She put her hand over his on the wheel, impulsively, and then took it away, flushing.

"What's that for?" he demanded curiously.

"Nothing. . . . Perhaps you'd rather not go back to the party," she went on hastily, "after this? I'll understand. You just drop me off and —"

"Don't you want me to come back?"

"Of course, I just thought —"

"Let me do the thinking. I could do with some music and a drink," he told her. "Who's this McClure?"

"Who?" She wrenched her thoughts back. "Oh, Paul? Why, he's a friend of Hannah's," she said, "a playwright."

"Never heard of him," said Pat.

"That's what he said about you!" said Kathleen, laughing.

"He did, did he? Makes us even." Pat laughed too. He added, "Smooth guy, isn't he? Looks like an actor."

"I believe he was on the stage for a time after leaving college," Kathleen said, "but I don't suppose he was much of an actor. He wanted the backstage experience . . . to help him in his work."

"What's he ever done?"

"Oh, several plays . . . one, his first, was a great success. It was a fine play, Pat, it was called *Nothing Is Lost.*"

"Oh," said Pat slowly, "I remember that. Full of high ideals, wasn't it?"

She reflected. "It was fine. Since then, while he's had three produced, they haven't been much good. One was a failure, one was just so-so, the other ran a long time but it lacked something. He's been out in Hollywood."

"There's the place!" said Pat enthusiastically. "I'd like to go there!"

"Why?" she asked, amused.

"Don't you like the movies?" he inquired, astonished. "I eat 'em up. I'd like to meet some of those girls."

"The glamour girls?" she said teasingly. "Crawford and Garbo and Dietrich and the others?"

"I like Ginger Rogers," he confessed, like a small boy. They laughed together. Then he returned to the subject of McClure.

"Known him long?"

"Who?"

"McClure."

"Oh, you do skip about! No, I met him, in fact, just the day before I met you."

"He's pretty attentive."

"That's his line," said Kathleen. "He's attentive to all women."

"I don't mind," said Pat, "whatever *other* women he's attentive to."

Her heart raced, happiness ran along her veins like quicksilver. She tried to answer casually. "I wouldn't worry."

"Has he money?" Pat asked bluntly.

"He's made it," she responded, "especially in Hollywood, and he has a private income, enough to live on at all events."

"That's too bad. Does he want to marry you?"

"What a question!"

"I suppose it's none of my business?"

"Of course, it isn't," she told him spiritedly, "but the answer is No. I doubt if he wants to marry anyone."

"Good," said Pat heartily.

They slid up before the apartment house. He said, helping her out, "I'll pull up and park. Wait for me."

When he joined her, he took her arm. "I've never asked you how you liked your job."

"I love it," said Kathleen.

"All right. Remember that."

"You haven't ever said," she countered, "whether I'm satisfactory."

"You're doing all right," he told her, "don't know how I got along without you all these years."

They went up in the elevator but it was crowded, and they did not speak. They stood at the back, and she was aware of his strength and nearness to her. She looked at him and looked away. He did not look like the same man who had answered the telephone a little while ago. His color was healthy and normal under the olive skin, which she had seen pale to gray, his blue eyes were clear, as untroubled as a child's. He was whistling under his breath. He looked solid and strong, prosperous, self-confident, and without a care in the world.

She thought, How *can* he look like that? But her new allegiance to him hurried to his defense, to explain, It's over and done with, it wasn't his fault, and he will remedy what he can . . . besides, no one was hurt except the watchman. If the children had been there it would have been different.

The party was still in full swing. The door was unlocked, they walked in, and Hannah rushed forward. She cried, "For heaven's sake, will you come in and tell us what it's all about?"

Pat said, "Read the papers. They'll take me for a ride. Could I have a drink?"

"Ask Kate, it's her liquor," said Hannah. "I think there's something left over . . . beer?"

He shook his head. "Something with a real kick."

"Bourbon," decided Hannah, "not Kate's. My private stock. At your disposal."

Kathleen asked, shedding her coat, "Why in the world are you wearing those?"

Hannah pulled off the pigskins. She answered, "It isn't the first time I've put on the gloves with Paul!"

He was coming toward them, his gloves in his hand. Pat looked from one to the other. He said, shrugging, to Kathleen, "It's a private gag, I guess. They don't like to be questioned."

Hannah went off to get the bourbon and Pat, a hand under Kathleen's elbow, steered her to a love seat on the far side of the room. When Hannah arrived with bottle, glass, and ice he took them from her gratefully.

"I always wanted to lie back," he said, "and be served good whisky by a beautiful woman."

Hannah made large eyes. She commented, "Pretty speeches from predatory Pat . . . this wants looking into. Get up there, Kate, and leave me look into it!"

Kathleen surrendered her place by Pat and McClure drew her aside.

"Well?"

"What?"

"Didn't you depart on an errand of mercy?"

She said coolly, "A wall of a school building collapsed. Naturally he'd go right down."

"And how!" said McClure. "He seemed pretty upset when he left . . . but now, now."

"After all," said Kathleen hotly, "it wasn't his doing, the building was passed by the inspectors."

"Is that always according to Hoyle?" he murmured.

She looked at him with blazing eyes. "That's a pretty rotten thing to say, Paul!" she told him.

"Sorry . . . he looked pretty much on the chipper side when he returned," he said.

"Well, it's Sunday," she said, "and no one was there but a watchman."

"No one but a watchman! Of course, the loss of one life is preferable to the loss of several hundred, but aren't you pretty callous?"

To her horror tears filled her eyes without warning. She stammered, "I'm not callous, Paul, how can you think it? I saw the man's wife . . . but — Oh," she said, the tears drying, "you're being so unfair to Pat. He was wonderful with the poor creature . . .

she'll be taken care of, always."

"Croesus and Sir Galahad rolled into one," said Paul. "Sorry again. But he gets under my skin." He took her hand and pulled her to the windows. "Look down there," he said, and she looked, startled, at the street and river below. "I'd like to ask him to take a running jump in that," he told her, "but I won't. Because you love him . . . and because I love you."

"No, Paul —" she began but her protest died at his interruption.

"Yes," he mocked her, "yes, Paul. Of course, you do. But don't think for a moment that I'm licked. I'll be around, underfoot. You can't get rid of me. Even if you marry him you can't. No matter if he forbids me the house like the stern husbands in the drama! Because I'll be there, waiting. Loving you, wanting you . . ."

"You can't mean it," she said breathlessly, "you haven't it in you to mean it!"

For a moment his gay, mocking eyes were still and grave, and something looked out at her from them, something she tried to define but could not.

"No," he asked, "can't I? You wait and see!"

"Kathleen," called Pat, turning his head. "Come over here and settle an argument

. . . I'm getting the worst of it."

"Your master's voice," said Paul with a courtly bow, from the waist.

Chapter VI

Kathleen always dated the most exciting and eventful period of her life from the night of her party. For a few days following it the newspapers were busy with the Bell Construction Company and reporters haunted the office. Several of them evinced a personal interest in Kathleen herself and asked her innumerable questions, many of them entirely unrelated to the matter of the school building. Some tried to make dates with her. And it wasn't long, naturally, before it was learned and printed who she was. "Society Girl Secretary" was the label she most often received and she said to Pat, in resignation, "Every girl who has ever had a high school education and can afford a new pair of silk stockings a week is a society girl to the newspapers! By that token my four years at college makes me eligible to add society girl *and* intellectual on my calling cards."

Socialite in the strictest sense she might not be but she was Lawson Roberts's daughter and they made a good deal of that indubitable fact also. They discovered where she lived and came around there evenings, but they saw Hannah instead and she was more than a match for them. One determined young man found himself taking Hannah out to dinner — and what a dinner! — and wondering glumly while she ordered, or rather smiled at the captain, "I'll leave it to you, Henri . . . something very special" — how in hell he could put her on his expense account, as even he could see that she was a trifle irrelevant to the business in hand. But Hannah had a wonderful time. She was fed up with her Georgian prince who, moreover, had struck a gold mine in the bucktoothed daughter of oil millions, and the gentlemen of the press were always interesting. Besides, she might manage a plug for Eloise, Inc., she explained to the skeptical Kathleen.

Some of the more sensational papers muttered darkly about an Ethiopian in the woodpile and asked in the headlined horrow, "Shall We Continue to Expose Our Children to Danger?" They interviewed the widow of the watchman, sending a sympathetic sob sister to wrest from her the story of her ideal life with her George and her grief at his untimely demise. The sob sister did a good job in describing the "hovel" in which the widow resided — not a bad little place, as it happened, a clean small walkup with hot water — but was rather balked in her search for sensationalism when Mrs. George told her vociferously what a wonderful man Pat Bell was. He'd got George the job and now that, so to speak, the job had got George, Mr. Bell had given him a beautiful funeral and herself an allowance.

The more serious press confined itself to grave speculations and a well-written editorial sprinkled with a number of "allegedlys" and both factions kept well this side the libel law.

But it got on Kathleen's nerves, she was unaccustomed to the goldfish-bowl life. She was inclined to be rather short with the first batch of charming vultures, but Pat set her straight. "Doesn't pay. Tell 'em what they want to know. Be pleasant — that's the best policy. Kicking a reporter downstairs is a direct invitation to break your own leg," he said.

So she smiled and was amiable and Pat handed out cigars, opened the cellarette in his new, larger, more elaborate office, and broke out a new bottle. And everyone was very very "happy about the whole thing."

Also the sob sister had a setback when the neighbors of Mrs. George crowded in to tell her, confidentially, that the two had led a dog's life, that George was drunk more often than sober and that she was well shut of him and had said so, on more than one occasion, the first shock of his violent passing over. Moreover, would she not be more comfortable than she had ever been in her life . . . as George's working days had been limited and indeed curtailed whenever they interfered with his thirst. His tenure of the watchman job had not been long. Yes, his widow was really very well off. She could be sure of her money from Mr. Bell. Her son, who had given her so much trouble, that bad boy, the very spit of the old man, was safe in jail for several years to come because of a little misunderstanding with the police and her daughter was married to a fellow with steady work.

And so the collapse of the school wall was by no means a nine days' wonder. Other things happened. A racketeer carelessly forgot to pay his income tax, a hotheaded young man murdered his landlady because she called him a dead beat, and a couple of politicians had a fist fight on the corner of Forty-fifth Street and Broadway. Also Europe was in an unsettled state and a WPA worker was found to be supporting two wives, in moderate affluence, and two cars.

Once that flurry had passed, life settled down into its new routine. For a time after the disaster Pat was in and out of the office a good deal. When he was in he was closeted with men Kathleen had never seen before and the door was closed to the anteroom. And he did a good deal of telephoning, also behind closed doors. But now and then she heard him shouting, at the men or over the wire. And the burden of his song seemed to be that something was wrong and he would not have it. She was, as it happened, in the room when he rang up a gentleman powerful in city politics. She heard him say, "I'm getting tired of this newspaper stuff. They've had their fun. Now they can lay off. O. K., Dan, I'll leave it to you."

He hung up, swung around, and smiled at her. "We won't be bothered any more."

"But what can he do?" asked Kathleen, who knew the formidable Dan by name and had even seen him once or twice.

"Plenty. He knows some heavy advertisers."

She gave that up, because if she looked into it too closely she might not like what she saw. And she wanted to like everything, everything.

One thing she didn't especially like about the office was Jim Haines. Haines was the "business" secretary. He was a lean man, in his forties, with a hard, unrevealing face. He had sharp gray eyes and narrow shoulders and he looked always a little dingy. He had the run of his chief's office and was a repository for all the Bell business secrets. He was courteous enough to Kathleen and had been helpful to her, particularly at first when things were new and strange. Whether he liked or disliked her she did not know but she realized that she definitely disliked and distrusted him although she was fair enough to admit that she had no real reason for her reactions. She discussed him with Pat one day shortly after the school building affair had become a thing of the past.

Pat started it. He said, "I'm afraid you'll have overtime to do — Kathleen. Jim's off, for a few days, but there won't be anything you can't handle. Some letters in regard to the closing of the sea wall contract . . . that's all."

She said, "You give him a lot of latitude. That's the second vacation he's had since I've been here."

"He had the grippe the first time," explained Pat carelessly; "this time it's his bi-annual bat."

"Bat?"

He smiled at her. "He's a periodic drinker," he said patiently. "Twice a year he takes about three days off. I can always tell when it's coming . . . and I give him the free

100

time before he asks for it, to save his face."

"But, Pat!" She stared at him in horror. "You can't afford to have that type of man around!"

His face became still, a little sullen. Then he smiled again, swift and warm as sunlight. He said gently, "You don't understand. Jim's a good man, he's my right hand. There are always men like him. Any engineer on a big construction job will tell you that. You're forewarned, however, and you know your man's worth. Jim always returns, sober and quite remorseful. And it doesn't happen more than twice a year. Also when he drinks he doesn't talk — which is important. He simply drinks and gets more and more quiet. Then he sobers up and comes back. He's loyal and hardworking. He was with my father, as you know, in this same capacity and the Old Man knew how to handle him and passed him along to me as a sort of legacy."

Kathleen digested this without comment. On her next luncheon engagement with Sadie Fischer, the chief engineer's secretary, she asked a timid question and Sadie, a smart dark girl, laughed.

"Oh, don't let Jim get in your hair. Everyone knows about him, we're all sorry for him. He's all right . . . he adores the ground Pat

Bell walks on . . . he'd cut himself in two for him."

"But he couldn't stop drinking for him?" asked Kathleen scornfully. "He can't have an ounce of will power!"

Sadie's bright dark eyes regarded her tolerantly. She said, "You haven't been around much. It's a disease — really. Old Frank Bell had him take a cure several times. It nearly killed him but he took it, and it didn't stick. There's a reason for the drinking; you see, he can go just so long and then when he gets remembering — it happens twice a year or so — he has to drink."

"Remembering what?" asked Kathleen.

"Didn't you know? When he was a young man, in his twenties, just out of college he married a girl from his own neighborhood, he'd been crazy about her for years. She was some distant relation of the Bells — a pretty Italian girl, they say, with a beautiful voice. She was studying for opera, but she fell in love with Jim and married him. They had a baby, and she, Jim's wife, went insane after its birth and Jim nearly lost his mind too, worrying. They took the baby away from her and Jim's mother kept it. Then they sent Mrs. Haines home for cured, and she was cured as far as anyone knew. Things went along all right for several months and then

one day while Jim was away on the road —
he was a salesman then — and the grandmother had slipped out to see some of the
neighbors, she killed the baby. Strangled it."

"Oh!" said Kathleen, looking with distaste
at her luncheon plate. "How utterly horrible!" She pushed the plate away and felt as
if she never wanted to eat again.

"She's gone off again," said Sadie, "and
this time for good. She's been in an institution for years. He goes to see her, he feels
that he must. It's after he sees her that this
— happens. The really terrible thing is that,
afterwards, he found out that her mother had
been the same way . . . and they didn't tell
him. She never should have been permitted
to marry. After it was over he went to pieces.
He lost his job. Frank Bell heard about it,
and gave him a job in the office. He worked
up into what he's doing now, at first they
just called it confidential clerk . . . now he's
confidential secretary. He gets a very big
salary, lives alone somewhere on Long Island; his mother's dead now and he has no
one. And he hates all women . . . he's a my
— my — what's-its-name?"

"Misogynist?" suggested Kathleen.

"That's it. Anyway, he doesn't like 'em."

She said thoughtfully, "That makes me
feel differently toward him."

Later she asked Pat:

"Why didn't you tell me about Jim Haines? That tragedy . . . it makes me see him in quite another light."

"I thought you knew," he answered; "everyone knows everything in this office. Besides, it was so long ago. I don't suppose he thinks of it . . . more than twice a year."

"Poor devil," said Kathleen, "he's thinking of it now."

Pat shrugged. "My Old Man made allowances for him. Me too. Of course, I can't see it. What's done is done. Cut it out of your life, discard it, and go on. The other is a weak way. Brooding, remembering. I don't believe," he added thoughtfully, "that anything could get me. Not really." He waved his hand around the office. "Take this, I love it. I've been part of it ever since I was a kid. But if I lost it tomorrow . . . hell, I could always go to work and build something up again. I like a fight."

He was like that, never looking back, washing his hands cleanly of the past. A very strong man, she thought. But she said, "You're hard, Pat, did you know that?"

"I have to be," he told her. "You don't get anywhere unless you are."

But he wasn't always hard. Take the good-for-nothings who came around for money, for work; take George's widow; take the crippled newsboy down on the corner. He got his dollar a day regularly and sometimes when Pat looked at him there were actually tears in his eyes. He'd even had the boy to the best orthopedic surgeons and had cursed like a stevedore when they told him that it was too late, nothing could be done. Hard and shrewd. He could drive a bitter bargain. He could throw away money, he could be generous, but when it came to business deals, a matter of lending money to someone who could afford to return it, he saw to it that it was returned . . . at interest.

Kathleen was learning these things about him. She had fallen in love with him, she sometimes thought, trying to consider the matter dispassionately, because of the way he looked . . . the surface things. The set of his shoulders, the way he carried himself, his unruly thick black hair, the astonishing contrast of his blue eyes. She had fallen in love with him because when he touched her by accident or design she felt faint, her knees shook, and there was a singing in her blood. She had fallen in love with him because he was utterly unlike anyone she had ever known, because he had the drive and vitality of six men, because he could be boyish and disarming, because he could be hard and profane and bitter. Because he could knock a man down one minute and the next pick him up, dust him off, and stake him to a good dinner.

She was learning more about him every day, and falling deeper in love.

She was seeing him, too, out of office hours. They never lunched together. As a rule he had lunch sent in to him, a bottle of milk, a roast beef sandwich, an apple, or an enormous dish of ice cream. He was like a child in his passion for ice cream. But they often dined together, sometimes when she worked overtime with him on the less important mail which he couldn't clean up during a busy day, and sometimes in a purely social fashion. "I'll pick you up at seven-thirty and we'll have dinner and do a show," he'd say.

She was always ready, and she was, she found, spending more of her own income on clothes than ever before, since he liked her to dress, to have new frocks, pretty and extreme. She even thought, Perhaps I'll splurge and get an Eloise for a New Year's present. He liked to dress himself, and to walk into a restaurant and bully the waiters in a genial fashion, liked to feel that people were looking at him, admiring his girl and possibly himself.

He demanded service and got it. Sometimes Kathleen went hot with embarrass-
ment at the methods he used, at the dishes
he sent back, at the tables he refused. But
he said calmly, "You can't let them get the
upper hand . . . they'll always stick you behind a post if it's humanly possible. You have
to kick . . . or be kicked."

He overtipped, of course, and the waiters
scurried around him. But if his reservation
was not to his liking there were fireworks.

He liked to go to places frequented by
well-known people, he liked to have them
pointed out to him by the captains or to
recognize them himself. He took a mild interest in the stars of screen and stage, in the
newest novelist, but his real attention was
given to those whose names appeared often
in the society columns. "Is that Mrs. So-and-
so?" he would ask with curiosity. "You
know, she just divorced her husband and
she's marrying Wyck, the yachtsman."

It would have been tiresome, it would have
been a little revolting if he hadn't been so
perfectly frank about it . . . and if she hadn't
loved him so much.

Now and then Kathleen ran into people
she knew, well or slightly. One of the latter
was Mrs. Doringford-Carter, a client of her
father's, very social register. Mrs. Doring-

ford-Carter swept up to their table, an amorphous mass of sables, with a hard, weather-beaten face, priceless pearls, and an impediment in her speech. She was enchanted to see Kathleen, and how was her darling father and her sweet mother?

Pat sprang to his feet, Kathleen presented him, Mrs. Hyphenated Carter looked him over with the approval she would bestow upon a fine horse; she liked big hulking personable men, possibly because the only man for whom she had really cared had been her father's groom . . . a youthful indiscretion which had been rudely broken up by the adults in authority.

Kathleen reported, as Mrs. Doringford-Carter waved her escort over impatiently and sat down with him at the Bell table, that her parents were well, they were having a marvelous trip. They had decided to leave the cruise ship in Italy and stay there for a little while before going on to England.

"Ah, England!" cried Mrs. Doringford-Carter and launched into an explanation of why she hadn't gone over for the grouse shooting this past season. "But we're poverty-stricken," she said dramatically, "absolutely on our uppers. And, after all, your father did for me too, breaking that absurd will! I tried to persuade Carter" — she always referred to her legendary husband by the last part of his surname — "to rent a moor again but he wouldn't. He said it was out of the question. I suppose your mother and father will visit Elsie?"

"They plan to stop with her," said Kathleen, "for several months."

Mrs. Doringford-Carter turned a bright, meaningless smile upon her escort, a chinless young man, who played beautiful polo. "Her father's sister," she explained, "the Duchess of Ainslee."

She rose and swept on, shouting over her shoulder, "Do come see me . . . we'll be in town after Christmas for a bit — bring your young man to tea."

She departed.

"Horrible woman," said Kathleen apologetically, "but she was one of Father's practical moments. I mean, as a rule he interests himself in the downtrodden, but every so often he has to take a job like that. A will, in her case, that of an eccentric aunt. Legally she was entitled to it — Mrs. Doringford-Carter, I mean. The aunt had willed most of the money to establish a foundation to study the habits of goldfish!"

"I thought she was all right," said Pat. "Look here, what was that crack about the Duchess of something?"

"Oh," said Kathleen, "that. It wasn't a crack. She is . . . I mean, you know, my father's sister . . . she married Butch ages ago when he hadn't a ghost's chance of coming into the title. Then a whole raft of relatives died . . . war, flu, big-game hunting, and a boating disaster. A holocaust. So he came into the title and property. The title bores him and the property is something terrific to keep up."

"But why didn't you tell me?" he demanded.

She said, "There wasn't anything to tell, Pat. Aunt Elsie is just Aunt Elsie. She's vague and sweet on the surface but a good businesswoman really. The tenants adore her, everyone does. She's lived over there for over thirty years and is very British. Funny shoes and hats and shouts 'Ha!' at you at odd intervals. Carries a shooting stick and has lots of dogs. . . . They've a daughter, married in South America, and one son — he's married to an American girl, a friend of mine . . . he met her through us."

He considered that in silence. He said, after a moment, "I hope you're going to take me there for tea someday."

"Where?"

"To Mrs. Doringford-Carter's."

"Of course, if you like," said Kathleen,

110

"but you'd be bored stiff. All she thinks about is horses. Her butler even looks like one. I was there for dinner one night and I couldn't eat. It was all too too stables. You expected the roast to rise up and shout 'Yoicks!' "

She thought briefly of Paul McClure. Paul would adore to meet Mrs. Doringford-Carter, he'd think her a riot. He'd like a roast to shout "Yoicks!" . . . she must tell him of this encounter. She was seeing him now and then at Hannah's, but since the night of her party she had refused to go out with him or to see him alone. She had told him so: "It's too uncomfortable until you get over this — this notion."

Pat said thoughtfully, "I wouldn't be bored. Do you ride?"

"Why, yes," she replied, "but not much recently. I gave up my horse when I started business school. Summers — we've a very tiny place in Connecticut — I rent a horse now and then. Sometimes visiting, of course, your hostess will lend you one."

He said, "I never learned, hadn't time. I might take it up."

"Why don't you? You don't get any exercise, you don't golf or tennis . . . it would be good for you."

"I suppose I'd have to wait till spring."

"No," Kathleen told him, "you can ride in a ring all winter . . . by spring you'd be pretty good."

"And would you ride with me?" he asked her.

"You'd never get up that early," she declared. "Have you forgotten I've a nine-o'clock job?"

"We'll see about that," he declared.

Just before Christmas Kathleen was alone in her anteroom. Pat was out, she had not seen him all day except for a brief glimpse when she came to work. The door to the anteroom opened and she looked up. An extraordinary little person marched in. She was completely muffled in a fur coat. She wore an old-fashioned toque. Pinned to her lapel was a bunch of fresh violets. She had a round firm face like a winter apple, with very few lines. She might have been an aging forty or a well-preserved sixty. She walked with a slight limp and carried a man's old-fashioned, gold-headed cane. On her glove-less hands were a quantity of good diamonds. When she spoke she had an accent, not a brogue, not enough for that, but a coloring, a softening.

She asked, "Are you Kathleen Roberts?"

"Yes," said Kathleen, who had risen. She started to say "What can I do for you . . ."

and then she saw the older woman's eyes. She knew those eyes, she knew them by heart, awake or sleeping. She cried, and her heart pounded, "Why . . . you're Pat's — I mean you're Mr. Bell's mother!"

Mrs. Bell looked pleased. She said, "I'm Pat's mother, all right. Is the rapscallion here?"

"No," said Kathleen, distressed, "I'm so sorry, he won't return until late. He didn't come back at luncheon and he left me no word where I could reach him. Mr. Haines would know. I'll call him."

"Never mind Jim," ordered the old lady, "I don't want to see him *or* Pat. It was you I came to see. I would have been here sooner but I've been away . . . on a fool trip."

"Yes," said Kathleen, "I know. Did you like Virginia?"

"It was all right," said Mrs. Bell, "a lot of old women in rocking chairs and young ones running loose. And some that weren't so young exposing themselves disgracefully in shorts. Pat thought I needed the change . . . but I'm back now. I suppose it was you that wrote me the letters he signed?"

"Well, not exactly," began Kathleen cautiously.

Mrs. Bell chuckled. "Don't lie to me, young woman, I know. That boy of mine couldn't write a decent letter to save his worthless neck. 'Dear Mom, I'm well, I hope this finds you as it leaves me . . .' Look here, isn't there a quiet place we could go and have a cup of tea?"

Half an hour later, bewildered but delighted, Kathleen faced Mrs. Bell across a table in an almost empty tearoom. Mrs. Bell was as fussy about tea as Pat about wine. Strong she wanted it, black and strong, with a drop of milk. None of your silly lemons or heavy-bodied creams. She stirred it, drank it, smacked her lips, and set down the cup. She said:

"You're a pretty girl, Kathleen."

"Thank you," said Kathleen, entertained.

"I've been thinking," said Mrs. Bell, "that my son is falling in love with you. When I saw him, last night, I was sure of it. So I made up my mind I'd have a look at you and I'd ask you straight out, are you in love with him . . . and if so, what are the two of you going to do about it?"

Chapter VII

Kathleen set down her cup very carefully. She had an illusion that it was made of crystal and if she was not exceedingly cautious it would shatter. She experienced a second illusion, which was that the cup could not have contained the tea she was sure she had heard herself order, but champagne . . . for she was suddenly quite lightheaded, dizzy. She wanted to laugh, she wanted to cry.

The cup achieved the saucer without mishap. The tea spilled only a little. The room in which they sat was almost empty, only three or four tables occupied on the other side. Their waitress passed and whisked water into the glasses, and departed again. Mrs. Bell was smiling.

"Well, speak up, girl," she said, with controlled impatience.

Kathleen tried to obey. She tried to say "Nonsense!" She could see it all with great mental clarity . . . she could see herself, sitting there opposite Pat's mother, very restrained, very calm, tossing her head, like the heroine of an old-fashioned comedy and saying "Nonsense!" in a most convincing way.

115

But she couldn't toss her head and she couldn't say nonsense to save her life.

She said, finally, "I don't know, Mrs. Bell," with great humility.

It dawned upon her abruptly what Mrs. Bell had really said before she asked her questions. She had said that she was sure that her son was in love with his secretary. Remembering that, like a sword of light cutting through the confusion, Kathleen began to color. The scarlet flooded up almost under her eyes. The blood, tingling, rushing like that made her regard brilliant, and her breath came quickly. Mrs. Bell nodded. She said, "You're a pretty creature. And a lady. I always wanted Pat to marry a lady." Somehow from her mouth the words didn't sound so awful, so impossible as they should have sounded. She concluded sharply, "What do you mean, you don't know whether you're in love with him or not, or do you mean that you don't know what you're going to do about it, the two of you?"

Kathleen swallowed. Sanity in a measure had returned to her. She answered Mrs. Bell's piercing blue look gravely. She replied, with an attempt at smiling, "Yes, I'm in love with him, Mrs. Bell."

"Good," said the old lady with satisfaction. She poured herself another cup of tea, blew into it with delicacy to cool it, and drank down half the cup. Then she set it aside and wiped her lips. "That's all I wanted to know," she remarked.

Kathleen suppressed a wild desire to inquire in her turn, "And what are you going to do about it?" She said, instead, "I haven't known just how I felt for very long, Mrs. Bell. I haven't been absolutely sure." She had regained her poise, she felt comfortable and at home with this round little woman with her winter-apple cheeks and her snapping eyes. If only the eyes weren't quite so much like Pat's! She added thoughtfully, "There's the legend, you know."

"Legend?" repeated Mrs. Bell, startled. "What's got into you?"

"Oh, secretary-boss," explained Kathleen, smiling. "You know . . . stories, novels, movies . . . just one of those things. But there's something in it, isn't there? You work day in day out with a successful man . . . a man who's rather like a dynamo — so other men seem tepid and pale to you. Then there's that old debbil propinquity — being with him all the time. So, how much is love, Mrs. Bell, and how much is legend?"

"Stuff," said the old lady. "Fiddlesticks," she added after a slight pause. "Either you're in love or you're not. No two ways about it.

Of course," she added thoughtfully, "you can be in love more than once, no matter what the books tell you."

"I haven't been," said Kathleen with pride.

"You haven't been? How old are you?"

Kathleen told her. She shook her head. "Must have been something wrong. Before I was sixteen, in the old country, I thought I would die for a man. He was in love with my sister. Married her too, and made her a very bad husband. He wasn't the only one I fancied. But when I came over here to visit my aunt, whose husband had made good money in the contracting business, and met my old Frank — Francesco, he called himself then — Pat's father, I forgot the others."

"Rehearsal," said Kathleen, smiling.

"Eh, what's that? That's it . . . rehearsal . . . rehearsal for love," said the old lady. She laughed heartily, as a man laughs, and Kathleen laughed with her. Then she beckoned the waitress imperiously. She said, "I should be getting home."

Kathleen felt frightened. She had told her . . . what had she told her? She had said, in effect, "I'm in love with your son. There. Now what?"

Mrs. Bell looked at her. She said, "I've worried you, coming out with it like that. I didn't mean to. I like you. If I hadn't do you suppose I would have asked you to drink a cup of tea with me? Not Molly Bell! I would have said, 'And so my son isn't in? Thank you, young woman and I won't wait and a very good day to you.' "

"I'm glad you like me," said Kathleen. She regarded the older woman with sweetness and gratitude, and added simply, "I like you too."

"Well," said Molly Bell, "that's a step in the right direction. I'd make a very nasty mother-in-law to a woman I didn't like!"

That was Kathleen's chance. She said, a little breathlessly:

"But he hasn't said . . . he doesn't know . . . I mean . . ."

"You mean," interpreted Mrs. Bell, "that you'd die of shame if I should tell him. That's right. That's modest and ladylike. The girls today, most of 'em, don't know the meaning of the word 'modest.' Where I come from, the north of Ireland — and it's beautiful there, Kathleen, it's lovely, someday I'll be going back — girls were modest. Not that they didn't see to it that they got their men, only, to my way of thinking they went after them without advertising . . . You can't tell me that you haven't said to yourself, That man's mine and I'll have him . . ."

"Perhaps I have," said Kathleen flushing again.

The waitress returned, Mrs. Bell waved aside the change. She said:

"You're not to worry about me. I'll tell the boy that I came to the office to see him and he was away, that I was tired and needed a cup of tea to warm my bones, and that I took you along. I'll say, 'She's a fine young woman, Pat; ask her to have Christmas dinner with us at the house, her mother and father being away, poor girl.' Have you told them anything?"

Kathleen shook her head. "No, I haven't. There wasn't anything to tell, Mrs. Bell, not really. If I wrote them, 'I've fallen in love with the boss,' it might scare them to death, they might come rushing home. They mustn't, they deserve this trip. They need it. My father's been very ill," she added and because of her emotional confusion her eyes filled with quick bright tears.

Mrs. Bell nodded.

"Pat told me about your people," she said, "they sounded just fine. Why would they be scared? Wouldn't my Pat be good enough for them?" she demanded with a certain amount of severity, and Kathleen thought, I'd hate to see her in a temper!

"Of course," said Kathleen eagerly, "of

course. Only, being away and all — oh, you know how it would be yourself." She went on: "Look here," and her eyes danced, the tears dried, "weren't you just a little scared yourself? If you hadn't been, would you have come to see what I was like?"

"You're smart," said Mrs. Bell with admiration, "and you're sensible. Of course, I was. I was scared out of my wits. I said to myself, 'If some flibbertigibbet has got hold of him!' " She laughed and rose and Kathleen went around to help her into her coat. And Mrs. Bell asked, "Do you go back to the office now?"

"I think I'd better. There's always someone there, until late. There might have been a message."

"I'll come with you," said Mrs. Bell.

The office was empty except for a couple of clerks. No message, they said, and Kathleen looked at Mrs. Bell and shrugged. The old lady said, "Well, that's that. He'll come walking in at all hours. We'll get a taxi and I'll take you home."

"It's out of your way," protested Kathleen, knowing that Pat lived with his mother and sister on Riverside Drive.

"Of course, it is; but it will give us longer together. If Pat had been here," said his mother with relish, "he would have raised the devil with me. He'd say, 'And where's the grand fine car I gave you and the lad to drive it?' and I'd have to tell him that I let Pete off for the day, his wife's having a baby . . . I'd be frightened out of my skin to drive with him and that's a fact . . . he's been running me into trucks and up on curbs, his mind not being on his work."

To Kathleen's amusement and delight as they stood on the curb together Mrs. Bell put her fingers in her mouth and whistled like any street boy for a cab. When one drew up the driver looked amazed and unbelieving. Two women, an old woman and a young one. A pretty young woman in smart, unobtrusive clothes and an old woman with a bonnet and a mink coat. He must have been hearing things.

On the long drive uptown Mrs. Bell did most of the talking. "You needn't be afraid that I'd interfere. Not now. When I interfere it's bad. People stay interfered with . . . only maybe not Pat. He's had a will of his own ever since he was small. He's a good boy, Kathleen, impatient sometimes and stubborn as a donkey. Sometimes I think he's got too much push . . . it burns him out. He can ride roughshod too. He hates to be crossed. That's my advice: don't cross him, not in the little things, not in the things that

122

don't matter very much to you. When big things come you can talk 'em out, maybe reason with him. Not," she added thoughtfully, "that I've ever been able to, at all."

Kathleen said, no longer embarrassed but feeling marvelously at home, "You talk as if everything was settled."

"Well, won't it be, now? Can you sit there and look me in the eye, girl, and tell me that you haven't made up your mind?"

"No," said Kathleen, "I can't."

"Good." Mrs. Bell put out her firm, astonishingly unwithered hand and patted Kathleen's round slim knee. "Good, I like that in you. No quibbling, no 'Oh, Mrs. Bell.'" Her mimicry was wonderful and Kathleen shouted with laughter. The taxi driver looked around smiling . . . he wanted to share the joke.

"Good luck," she said, as the taxi stopped in front of Hannah's, "I'm on your side, you know."

Kathleen turned back to pop her head in at the door. She said anxiously, "I hope you won't tell him that."

"Never fear. Not till the time comes. Run along. Remember, you've a date for Christmas dinner. And I'm an old hand at keeping a secret . . . I can talk more than most women but I can shut my mouth too. I wish Pat

123

could," added his mother, sighing and waved her hand at the driver. "Get along with you," she ordered.

Kathleen was still smiling when she let herself in with her latchkey. She could hear Amelia whistling her doleful spirituals in the kitchen. That meant that she was happy too. But she wasn't prepared for Paul McClure. He was sitting on the divan, a coffee table pulled up, a Scotch-and-soda upon it. Cigarette butts smoked in the ash tray. He was reading a magazine.

"Paul, for heaven's sake!" she cried, disconcerted, her holiday mood gone.

"You didn't mean heaven. You thought — what the hell!" he retorted. "Try to look glad to see me."

"But — where's Hannah?"

"Out, to dinner. You and I are dining at home, my angel. Amelia has it all fixed up."

She said, "I hadn't asked you."

She thought of her budget. She had an arrangement with Hannah by which she paid Amelia extra when she entertained, and she paid for the food. Damn!

"You are pretty exasperating," she remarked, standing by the couch looking down at him, her eyes bright with anger.

"I know it. You are exasperating too," he said calmly, "and a lot prettier than I am.

I'm here, I brought in the steaks. There is nothing you can do about it. Amelia dotes on me."

"That's more than I do," said Kathleen. She had wanted to be alone this evening. She had been glad, remembering Hannah would be out. She had thought she could have something to eat on a tray. She'd wash and set her hair, listen to the radio, read a little, take a long scented bath in a boiling-hot tub and then tumble into bed to think over all that had happened since teatime.

Her heart sang, even Paul could not deflect the melody. Pat was in love with her. His mother had said so . . . in love, in love, in love . . .

"You look like a pretty little Cheshire cat," said Paul, "who has devoured the entire aviary and the cream on the milk bottle too. And yet you are cross with me," he concluded in wonder. "But I had to do something. I can't go on imploring you — dine with me, come for a drive, let's go to a play, a movie, let me come sit by your fire. You've only one answer. So I have to take matters into my own hands. Remember the old song, 'Madame will you walk, Madame will you talk?' "

No, he couldn't spoil this day for her. Perhaps this wouldn't be such a bad evening.

She could tuck her knowledge away like a jewel in the secret places of her heart, she could pretend it wasn't there. When Paul had gone she could take it out and turn it in the new light, she could watch it sparkle, she could hold it in the hands of her mind . . .

She said, "I'm resigned. Give me a few minutes to shower and change, will you?"

"As long as you wish, if the steaks won't be overdone," he responded, "and you're in for an evening, my lass. A long one. After midnight." Should she ask him to leave? "By the way, what news of your family?"

"They're fine."

She disappeared into the bedroom, tore off her clothes and left them in a heap on the floor. Remorsefully, as an exercise in discipline, she picked them up again. She stood under the shower and wished that she could sing. Her skin tingled, her hair was damp, she rubbed it with a towel. Then she pressed the waves back where they belonged, and put a touch of cream, a dusting of powder on her clean scrubbed face. Her eyes shone, her lips were so red she didn't need lipstick. She used it, nevertheless. She put on the hostess gown her mother had given her last Christmas. It was blue quilted velvet, beautifully fitted. She looked tall in it. Impulsively she drew her hair back from her ears and pinned it high, like the girl at Hannah's party.

Amelia had made sidecars. "And why not?" asked Paul when Kathleen exclaimed. "I brought the makings. Your private stock, as it were." The appetizer was new and delicious, the steaks and salad perfection, the little meringues as light as a cloud . . . a good dinner, with Amelia beaming fatly.

Afterwards . . .

Paul set down his coffee cup. Amelia clattered around the kitchen. The fire burned low, the lights were rosy and flickering. He asked:

"May I tell you that I love you?"

"Paul," she said, "it's no use."

"Of course not. Not yet. Someday it will be. Remember that. I love you, I want to marry you. Look, my dear, I'll make a bargain with you. Let me come to see you, like this. Let me take you out and watch the envy in other men's eyes. And I promise I'll never say this again, not a word of it. I'll not say it until you ask me to . . . and if you never ask me . . ."

She said proudly, "I never will."

"Don't be too sure. There are stars in your absurdly lovely eyes tonight."

"Paul, stop talking like a play. Isn't that what's the matter with you? I'm a peg on which to hang your emotions, a new heroine in a new play you're writing. Do believe that."

"I'll pretend it if you want me too. The new play's started," he told her abruptly. "No one will like it. But at least it's honest."

"But the other, Paul, you really destroyed it?"

"I did."

"No copy? I thought it was a gesture. You would have had a production."

"I think so, and most likely a hit." His lean face hardened. He looked older, he looked a stranger, no longer gay, no longer casual. "Can't you see I've got to be honest? I wasn't for a time. I didn't like it. I didn't like myself. I liked myself least of all. I've enough money to live on. Enough for us both to live simply if it comes to that. Sorry, I won't offend again. And I'm not going to weaken again, not going to do the shoddy makeshift thing in order to make the extra dollars. Not again, sweet Kate."

She looked at him with new respect.

"I didn't know you felt like that."

"Well, I do," he told her more lightly, "and it can't be helped. No star danced when I was born. One fell, I think, or it had St. Vitus. I'm screwy probably. Nuts . . . but there it is. How's your dear boss?" he asked suddenly.

"Fine."

"Too bad," said Paul.

"Really, Paul!"

Paul said calmly, "Would it shock you if I said that if by pressing a button I could contrive that one Patrick Bell fell and broke his handsome neck I'd not only press it, I'd stand on it."

"That's not fair, you don't know him!"

"A case of Dr. Fell," he said glumly, "yet there is a reason . . . you know it, I swore not to discuss it. But even if you were not in the picture, my dear, I'd feel the same way."

Hannah came in. She was frowning. She had had dinner with the newest beau. He had bored her. So she had produced a silver box of aspirin, sighed at him prettily, permitted him to kiss her gently in the taxi. That was that. She cried, entering:

"Well! You two!"

"A fine greeting," Paul told her. "You're just in time to save Kate's reason. She's bored to death with me."

Hannah emerged presently from her bedroom. She said, "It's early yet, shall I call up someone and set up the card table?"

"No," said Paul, "sit where you are, quite still. It isn't often I am surrounded by wit and beauty after a superb dinner."

"Where did you dine?"

"Here," said Paul. "Kate invited me."

"I did not," said Kathleen.

"Amelia did, then."

"Who's to pay for it?" asked Hannah and looked at Kathleen obliquely. She laughed when she said it, but her eyes did not.

Kathleen's face grew hot and Paul said lazily, "I did, my angel, be not distressed. I went forth with a basket on my arm like any good little housewife and bought all the makings."

The telephone rang and Kathleen, nearest to it, answered. Her voice was cool and indifferent. "Yes," she said. Then her voice was colored with warmth and personality. Hannah grinned at Paul and raised a dark eyebrow. He said nothing, his face was a mask. But he lighted one cigarette from the stub of the last.

"Yes. Of course, Pat," answered Kathleen, "where would I be?"

Pat said, "Look. I got back to the office at all hours and you'd gone."

"I didn't think you'd return. There was no message."

"I know, my mother told me. She's taken a great fancy to you, Kathleen."

"No more than I to her."

"Then you'll come Christmas?"

"Of course, but I'll see you before that!"

"Tomorrow," he said caressingly, "tomorrow."

"Good night," said Kathleen softly, and hung up.

Paul was on his feet. He said, "I just remembered I have to see a dog about a man! Good night, girls, and thanks for a lovely evening."

He kissed the top of Hannah's head lightly and waved to Kathleen. And the door closed after him.

Hannah asked softly, a little later, "Where are you going, Kate?"

"To bed . . . and to do a few chores first, that Paul interrupted. When I reached home he was here. I had no idea —"

"You don't want him, do you?" asked Hannah.

"Of course not!" said Kathleen.

"He wants you," Hannah told her.

"He just thinks so," retorted Kathleen, going into her bedroom.

Hannah followed. She stood against the door, smoking reflectively, looking very smart in her tailored black dinner suit with the sequined blouse. She said:

"Then you won't mind if I try to get him back. It won't be easy . . . but —" her jaw hardened — "things have never been the same. There must be a way," she said des-

131

perately, "there must be!" She stared at Kathleen, her narrow eyes filled with a curious light. "I like you so much, Kate. You're the only woman I could ever stand around me for long. We go our own ways, we let each other alone. You're swell. I thought, tonight, when he went like that, that I ought to hate you. Yet how silly that is. I let him go, I didn't put up a fight. It isn't your fault . . . I wish to God I'd never set eyes on the man. You don't know what it's like."

"Yes," said Kathleen, "in a way I do . . . good luck, Hannah."

"Do you mean that . . . then Pat Bell —" She broke off. "I shouldn't say this, I'm being too damned honest for my own good. Pat's not your man, Kate."

"You don't know him."

"I dare say not. Has Paul asked you to marry him, ever?"

She could do one thing for Hannah. She could lie. She did lie steadily. She said, and laughed, "Of course not, Hannah," and turned away in order not to see the stark, overwhelming relief on Hannah's little face.

Chapter VIII

A few days later Paul called Kathleen at the office. It was the first time he had done so and she was frightened, hearing his voice. Perhaps something had happened to Hannah? Or had a cable come, and Hannah, notoriously unwilling to impart bad news, had delegated the job to Paul?

"Is anything the matter?" she asked, her voice catching.

"Certainly not, unless you say No. Oh," his voice changed perceptibly, "I frightened you, I'm sorry."

"That's all right, Paul, only you've never called me at the office . . . and I thought something was wrong."

"Forgive me," he said, "it's just that I have tickets to the opening tonight, will you come?"

She said instantly, "I'm sorry, Paul, it isn't possible. Hannah was talking about the opening this morning — it's the Fontanne-Lunt, isn't it? She'd adore to go."

"Look," said Paul, "I thought we made a bargain."

"I don't remember that I made it," she said.

"But you were willing. I'd swear that you were," he said eagerly.

"Perhaps I was then," she said slowly, "but not now."

"What changed your mind . . . big business?" he inquired sharply.

"No. Oh, don't let's discuss it now, Paul, I haven't time. I'm sorry about tonight."

She hung up and swung around to see Pat standing by the windows with his back to her. She had not heard him come in. For a big man he was as light on his feet as a cat.

"I didn't hear you," she said.

"So I observed. Quarreled with McClure?"

"No, of course not. Why should we quarrel? He called up to ask me to go to the opening tonight."

"And you refused?"

"Well, you must have heard me."

"Why?"

She said hesitantly, "Hannah wants to go."

"None of that girl scout business . . . why?"

He came over and stood by her desk, looking down, smiling. His eyes were very bright. She said evasively, "Perhaps I had a previous engagement."

"Of course, you had. You're going with me!" he said.

She laughed. "You just thought of that one, admit it."

"I can get tickets," he said, "pick you up at seven-thirty, we'll have dinner. How about it? Supper after, perhaps your little friend and McClure would join us?"

She said, "I don't know, I don't even know that they'll be going together. Pat, you are terribly roughshod."

He looked down at his feet encased in expensive leather. He said, "That's the way to go about things. Besides, we rate a celebration."

"For what?"

"You forget that jobs have been coming in fast and furious. And after the first of the year the new city subway contract."

"You're pretty sure of getting it," she told him.

He said carelessly, "I've reason to be sure. No nonsense, Kathleen. Best bib and tucker and we'll go out tonight and do the town."

On reaching home she found Hannah burrowing in a clothes closet flinging heaps of rosy chiffons, stiff damask, and cream smooth satin to the floor.

"What in the world!" Kathleen exclaimed, on the threshold.

"Haven't a rag to wear," said Hannah frantically. "Well, maybe . . ." She regarded a full-skirted sage-green velvet with a necklace of pale-pink camellias at the low bodice line. It was one of the very first of the strapless dresses and Eloise, Inc. had made it. "That's new," she said, frowning, "but I hate the color."

"You've never worn it," said Kathleen, "it will be lovely . . . what's up?"

"Oh," said Hannah overcarelessly, "nothing except that Paul has asked me to go to the Lunt-Fontanne opening tonight . . . I was never more astonished." She darted into the little room off her bedroom in which she did her sketching, knocked down two drawing boards, stepped on a thumbtack, swore, and emerged with a battered pack of cigarettes. She said, "I thought he'd ask you."

"I'm going with Pat," said Kathleen, turning away to go into her own bedroom and inspect her wardrobe. She couldn't compete with Hannah, but as far as that went, she didn't want to. She thought, I've never worn the lamé . . . too formal. It won't be tonight. He's never seen it. She took it down, a slim russet-colored frock with simple clean lines and heavy glints of gold, it matched her hair. It had been a great extravagance when she bought it. Now she was glad.

She said, sticking her head out the door, "If you and Paul haven't any plans Pat proposes to throw a party afterwards."

"Frankly," said Hannah, "I'd like to get Paul to myself over a bottle and a small table. But if worst comes to worst . . . you understand, don't you?"

"Perfectly," said Kathleen with relief. She had not looked forward to the proposed foursome with any great enthusiasm. Silently she wished Hannah luck and congratulated herself that she had not been forced to lie.

Paul came first. Hannah was ready, enveloped in the circular ermine wrap she had bought from Eloise when a client had thrown it back on their hands. She looked smart and prettier than usual. Her eyes had topaz lights, with excitement. She said, "Regard . . . and if you don't tell me I'm the last word in what the well-dressed woman can get on credit, you're crazy."

Paul said perfunctorily, "You're always charming, Hannah." He added, "Where's Kate?"

"Oh, around dressing for the heavy beau . . . and wondering if she can bear up under twelve tons of orchids," Hannah answered. Then, "Kate," she called, "look who's here!"

"Sorry," replied Kathleen, muffled, "busy. Have a good time."

She was dressed, in the gold and russet frock. The orchids were brown and green and yellow. She stood before the mirror and pinned them at her shoulder and let the long spray fall downward. Very effective. She stood back, smiling, and waiting until she heard the door close.

Amelia waddled out. She said, " 'Fore the Lord, Miss Kate, I never seen you look handsomer."

Pat said so too, arriving. He said, as Amelia let him in:

"Met Hannah and McClure downstairs. Why didn't they wait?"

"Hungry, I suppose."

He said, staring at her, "You look like a million dollars. Come on, let's go."

They were chauffeur-driven tonight. Leaning back in the big car on the way to the Colony, Pat asked:

"Did you ask 'em for after the show?"

"I spoke to Hannah . . . I didn't see Paul."

He commented after a moment, "How in hell can she afford ermine?"

"Don't get any notions," said Kathleen a little sharply. "Hannah makes a good income. Her things come from Eloise — cost price, practically. And she has something of her own besides. Pat, don't you think of anything except money and how to get it and how other people get it?"

"Not too often," he admitted cheerfully.

"What else is there to think about — that's important, I mean?"

"Lots of things," said Kathleen with energy; "books and flowers — and yours are lovely, by the way — and people. Gardens and sunsets, mountains and the sea. And where we're going from here and why. And what directs us. That's all very important, Pat."

"You are," he said, "too important. You worry me, Kathleen, I think about you too much. So there is something besides money, after all."

She touched his hand with hers in warning. The window between them and Garman, the broken-nosed driver, had been rolled down. And Pat said casually, "Oh, what difference does that make? You look marvelous," he added boyishly, "like a — a duchess —"

"Oh, no," she denied, laughing, "not like the average. Wait until you see my aunt!"

"I'd like to," said Pat. "Why don't she and her husband come on over when your people return? We'd show 'em a time."

"They'd hate it," Kathleen told him. "Now, there are people who *have* to think of money. They're land poor, Pat, and they have responsibilities and obligations toward the many people dependent on them. It was a blessing when my cousin — John — married a girl with money. He was in love with her too, which is something else to be thankful for. But aside from worry and income tax and all that, Butch and Aunt Elsie are the most contented people you ever saw. She putters around with dogs, roses and tenants, and he putters with farms, books, horses and, of course, politics. They have great arguments, they wrangle and quarrel and make up. They're swell. I don't suppose they've been to a night club in years. Or to a first night. They rarely open the town house. They don't like it, they can't afford it. But —"

He asked, "What's wrong with their picture? I thought people in their position always had money."

"Tell them that," said Kathleen, "and see what they'd answer. You're still believing fairy tales and the novels of the nineties . . . here we are!"

They dined, very well, they were only a little late at the theater, but so was almost everyone else. Those who had come early in order to see were walked upon by those who had come in order to be seen. There were autograph collectors, and the usual dinner parties, annoyed at having to stand after the curtain was up . . .

Pat's seats were very good, better than Paul's which, while down front, were on the side. During the entr'acte Pat suggested, stretching, "Let's get out of here."

Kathleen would rather have remained where she was. She was still under the spell of the play and its actors. She did not want to go out and smoke and walk about the lobby. But everyone else was going and she was being stepped upon. So she rose reluctantly.

"Have to show you off," said Pat in her ear.

People looked at them, looked, she believed, mostly at him, he was extraordinarily striking in evening clothes, his height, his broad shoulders, the curly black hair and the blue eyes blazing in contrast with his olive skin. She thought humbly, He should be with the most beautiful woman in New York.

He was having a good time. He liked being stared at, he was thrilled as a kid at the circus when someone recognized him, as happened once or twice, and turned aside to hiss his name audibly to a companion.

In the lobby they encountered Paul and Hannah. And Pat demanded:

"Well, how about it?"

"How about what?" asked Paul, and Hannah said quickly, "I forgot to tell him, that is —"

"Forgot what?" Paul asked her, puzzled.

"Pat wants you to have supper with us," Kathleen broke in. The moment seemed awkward. Hannah looked anxious under her rouge and not especially happy. Paul seemed morose and disagreeable. But Pat was like a triumphant army, complete with banners.

Paul said slowly, "It seems like a very sound idea."

Kathleen returned to her seat disappointed, as she was aware Hannah was disappointed. But if it made Pat any happier . . . He was gregarious, he liked lights and music and people around him. He liked admiration and ordering waiters about, he liked seeing people and being seen.

The rustle was subsiding, the people were taking their places, there was a faint odor of tobacco, of perfume . . . the house darkened and the curtain rose.

Afterwards, while they were waiting for Paul and Hannah, Mrs. Doringford-Carter came wandering up to them, clad in a most unbecoming frock, her weather-beaten face rising from masses of sapphire tulle, striped with silver. She was covered with a quart or two of sapphires and a diamond and sapphire feather was fastened to a tulle band around her head. She said, screaming, "Wasn't it divine? And who's that with you, Kathleen? Oh, don't tell me, let me guess. When are you going to bring him to tea?"

Pat beamed, glad that she had remembered him. He said something and Mrs. Doringford-Carter laughed. She said, "Too amusing. Come, Carter," and drifted on, towing her mild as junket little husband in her wake.

Hannah came up panting. "Thought we'd lost you," she said. "Did you see the Carter woman? A spectacle, my dear. How Eloise can bear . . . Oh, there you are, Paul."

Presently they were in Pat's car headed for the Stork Club, at which Pat had had the foresight to engage a table. Kathleen hoped it would be satisfactory. And was relieved when it proved to be.

She danced with him after they had ordered. He held her close, dancing very well, humming to the music. He asked, "Having a good time?"

"Elegant. And you?"

"Of course!"

Later she danced with Paul. And she was aware that, well as Pat had guided her, Paul was the perfect partner. He said:

"So you lied to me, sweet Kate."

"No," she said . . . and then caught herself

143

back. Which was worse, to say "Yes, I lied, I was going out with Pat all the time" or to say "No, I turned you down and then accepted his invitation?"

"It doesn't matter," said Paul, "one way or the other. And I promised I wouldn't talk about subjects which are tabu. You are wearing very lovely orchids, Kate, you look . . . as always . . . radiant. Am I to congratulate Mr. Bell?"

She asked, "Haven't you been drinking too much?"

"Not nearly enough."

They were passing Pat and Hannah now; Hannah waved and smiled and Pat called, "How goes it?" The floor was crowded, they were caught there together dancing on their separate dime-sized spaces, almost touching.

"Swell," said Kathleen, but Paul did not seem to see the others. He said, "You fixed it all up nicely, didn't you . . . me and Hannah, you and the tycoon?"

They returned to their table, ate, drank, and talked. Pat did most of the talking. Had they seen so-and-so across the room? Who was that, just coming in? He recognized an ex-ring champion, three actresses, a banker. He was in his element.

He and Kathleen danced again and when they returned to the table Paul was there, alone. He said, as they came up, "Sorry, Hannah has a headache . . . I'm taking her home."

"I'll go see her," said Kathleen, moving away from the table, but Paul raised an eyebrow. He said, "She's all right. Better not."

So she had overheard then, or they had quarreled and Paul had told her. Kathleen took a deep breath. She said, "Tell her we'll be right along — why don't we go now, Pat?"

Pat looked like a child whose toy is about to be snatched from him, but said promptly, "Of course, if you wish, Kathleen."

"No, better not," advised Paul. "Stay and have yourselves a good time. I'll look after her . . . Florence Nightingale, that's me."

Kathleen was silent the rest of the evening and distracted and Pat tried to rally her. He asked, "What's the matter?"

"I'm worried about Hannah."

"Women always have headaches," he said, "don't be silly. Here, drink up and let's have another bottle."

"No, I've had enough," she said, "and it's getting very late. It's been such a nice party, Pat, let's go home."

He took her out without further demur. In the car, she leaned back gratefully. Presently, she felt his arm around her, and he pulled her toward him. She asked sleepily,

"What's that for?"

The window was rolled up between them and Garman now. And Pat said, "For luck. Good luck. Mine and yours."

He drew her closer, put his hand under her chin and bent to kiss her without another word. That was right, she thought, wide awake now and alive from head to foot, every nerve tingling, that was where she belonged, here, in Pat Bell's arms.

She drew away and tried to laugh, put her hands to her disheveled hair. She said, "No nice girl gets herself kissed in cars . . . *Oh!*"

Garman had been driving rather fast. But he was a good driver and there wasn't much traffic. He did not see it in time to avoid the taxi swinging around the corner.

She heard Pat curse . . . and then she heard nothing else for a moment or so. She was flung forward violently, her head struck something unyielding . . . there were stars and singing darkness and then silence.

When a little later she opened her eyes she found herself in Pat's arms again. He was saying savagely, "Clumsy fool." He was saying, heedless of the group of spectators, the two policemen, of Garman arguing with the taxi driver, "Are you hurt, Kathleen darling, are you hurt?"

"I'm fine," she assured him, sitting up

dizzily, "it's just a bump. Please don't bother, Pat."

The fender was dented, the steering wheel twisted. Pat got out of the car and talked to the policemen. The taxi driver and Garman were separated before they came to blows. Names, addresses, questions, witnesses. "O. K.," said Pat to the officers. "The insurance company will handle it. Get me a taxi, a safe one."

In the taxi he asked anxiously, "Sure you won't go to the hospital? The cops wanted to call an ambulance."

She said, feeling her head gingerly, "It's just a bump, as I told you, I hope to heaven it won't be in the papers. A garbled version might reach Mother and Father, they'd be wild."

He said savagely, "How do you suppose I felt? For a crazy moment I thought you were dead! I didn't realize how much I loved you, darling, until I thought I might never be able to tell you."

Chapter IX

Kathleen held both hands to her head. It ached, it was a stupendous, a colossal head. It was like fourteen mornings after. She complained, when she could speak:

"Of all the times to tell me!"

He took her in his arms and she said, "Ouch!" involuntarily, but when he kissed her, as he did promptly and with great ability, she forgot the ache and her general sensation of being battered and bruised.

Presently she drew away and laughed, a little shakily. She said, "If I go home with a headache Hannah will think I'm stealing her thunder."

He said promptly, "You're not going to Hannah's. You're going home with me . . . Ma will look after you."

"Pat! What an idea." She put her hand in his and sighed contentedly, despite the throbbing in her skull. "I can't turn up like this — something no self-respecting cat would bring in. And in evening clothes. Besides, there's tomorrow and the office."

"You aren't going to the office tomorrow. Hannah will pack a suitcase for you. I told the driver where to go," he said calmly. "Here, lean back against me and don't try to talk. I've got you now . . . for always." His arm tightened and she leaned back docilely. Her faintness had passed. Except for the ache in her head she felt as if she could lick her weight in wildcats. It was marvelous to submit, to do as you were told. She said, "It all sounds insane to me, but it's all right if you say so. Pat, do you really love me?"

"I'm crazy about you. When are you going to marry me? Tomorrow? The day after?"

She tried to sit up and decided it was not such a good idea. She reminded him, subsiding, "You haven't asked me."

"I'm asking you now!"

"Not tomorrow, not next day. I — oh, Pat, don't talk," she begged, "I'm so happy . . ."

Half a block farther on she remembered something. She said indignantly:

"It seems to me that you take it pretty much for granted that I'm in love with you too."

"Well, aren't you?" he asked mildly.

"Of course," she admitted. "But how did you — ?"

He said, "I didn't . . . but when I saw you there, limp, knocked out, it was like the end of the world for me. And I knew that I loved

149

you so much that you *had* to love me, Kathleen."

It sounded logical, at least at the moment. She said, sighing, "Well, there's no use trying to be coy and keep you guessing . . . you took me, quite literally, off my feet."

"I'll fire that fool tomorrow!" said Pat grimly.

"What fool? — oh, Garman? — Pat, you mustn't. Promise me. He's been with you so long. And it wasn't his fault . . . it was the other man's."

"We'll see to him too."

She said, "Don't go off at a tangent. It's all right. The insurance people will take care of the car. The only thing that worries me is the papers."

He said, "Forget it, I'll fix it. If it sets in at all it will be such a little item that no one will pick it up. I can keep your name out of it, Kathleen."

She asked, feeling beautifully relaxed, although her head still throbbed, "You get everything you want, don't you, darling?"

His arm tightened. "Why not? If you want anything badly enough and know how to go out after it."

When they reached Riverside Drive and the big apartment house she was half asleep, and he had to lift her from the cab.

He helped her across the lobby, the door-man hovering by, and they got her into the elevator, which was empty. He spoke to the boy who ran it and they shot upward and did not stop until they reached the top. Once there, she was able to walk to the door which Pat opened with his key. Half supporting her as they stood in a brilliantly lighted foyer, he shouted "Ma!" at the top of his lungs.

The apartment was a duplex. Mrs. Bell appeared at the head of the stairs, a funny little figure in a voluminous flannel wrapper, her hair skewered with curlers. She said, "What on earth . . . shouting fit to wake the dead!" Then she saw Kathleen. "What's happened?" she asked quickly.

"Accident," said Pat briefly. "She's all right. Got a bump on her head, so I brought her home."

"Well, don't stand there talking," said his mother testily, and began to issue orders.

Almost before she knew it Kathleen was installed in a guest room, undressed and put into one of Carmela's nightgowns. Mrs. Bell and a spare, competent maid officiated. Pat was downstairs telephoning. Presently he came tiptoeing in and looked down at her. He said, "I called Hannah. I'll have someone fetch a bag for you tomorrow."

"How is she?" asked Kathleen.

"I didn't ask," said Pat. "I simply said we'd had an accident, I'd brought you here. When she wanted to know why I hadn't brought you home, I said you belonged here, seeing that you're going to marry me."

Mrs. Bell exclaimed and Kathleen tried to sit up. She said, "But — but — Oh, Pat, you *are* crazy! Nothing's settled."

"Everything's settled but the date," said Pat, "deny it if you can."

Mrs. Bell said, beaming impartially, "It took an accident to wake him up. Get out of here, Patrick Bell . . . did you phone the doctor?"

"I did."

"I don't need a doctor," said Kathleen, "all I want is a good night's sleep."

"You'll have both," said Pat.

He bent to kiss her and she put her arms around his neck. Mrs. Bell cleared her throat and shooed the maid from the room. She stayed, however, her hands folded on her round little stomach and regarded her son and Kathleen with approval.

"What did Hannah say?" asked Kathleen as Pat was leaving.

"I didn't listen," said Pat, "she made so much noise about it. She was squealing. She'll be up to see you sometime tomorrow."

"But, Pat," wailed Kathleen, "I want to go to the office."

"Not you."

"Are you firing me?" she demanded.

"Think I want my wife working?" he asked.

"But I'm not your wife." Her head was aching again, and she looked piteously at Mrs. Bell. "Oh, do get him out of here," she implored.

"Scat!" said his mother firmly and escorted him to the door. He stayed there a moment looking very gay, very triumphant, very handsome. He blew a kiss in Kathleen's direction. "Sleep well," he said. "I'll be right outside waiting to hear what the doctor has to say."

The door shut. Kathleen said ruefully:

"I didn't mean it to happen that way. So — so suddenly."

"That's Pat," said his mother complacently.

"I know, but . . ."

She couldn't explain it, the feeling of sorrow which was interwoven with her happiness. It was too soon; perhaps, as she had said, too sudden. She had so loved things as they were, the daily excitement, the wondering, the tiptoe expectancy. She had thought that they would grow into love naturally as a flower opens to the sun. She had not been sure of his love for her, and yet she had liked not being quite sure, the excitement of it, the living from day to day.

The doctor came, a grave young man. He gave her something to lessen the pain in her head, to make her sleep. He could find no other injury but would arrange for an X-ray, he said, the first thing in the morning. Yet he was perfectly certain that there was nothing more serious than a bad bump and shock — no fracture, no concussion.

After he had gone Mrs. Bell tucked her in and opened her windows and kissed her on the cheek. And Kathleen smiled up at her, apologetically.

"I'm such a nuisance," she murmured, "but he would bring me here."

"Where else would he bring you?" demanded Pat's mother. "I'll be next door. You're to call me. And Emily will sleep in the little dressing room . . . she'll hear you if you as much as stir. Try to get some sleep now."

She did not want to sleep, she wanted to think over the evening, every minute of it. She wanted to remember the first glimpse of Pat's face bending over her as she awoke from her brief unconsciousness. But her eyes would not stay open, the pain had lessened and she slept presently and woke only once in the night when Emily, an attenuated wraith in a long gray Mother Hubbard, was instantly beside her, to turn her pillows, bring her water, and smooth out the crumpled sheets.

She was sleeping when Pat went to the office next day and did not see him. Breakfast was ordered when she waked and Mrs. Bell came in with a basin of warm water, a washcloth, and a new toothbrush, and proceeded to guide her through her ablutions as if she had been a child. One of Carmela's bed jackets was put around her shoulders and presently she was able to sit up, drink some coffee and fruit juice. She felt much better. Her head was sore to the touch but it no longer throbbed and made her feel sick and giddy. She felt refreshed and rested, but confessed she had no inclination to get out of bed.

The doctor returned early with a portable X-ray machine and a technician, and the plates were made. He told her when she asked him if she could not get up, that it would be best if she remained in bed for the day. "It has been a shock," he informed her severely.

"You're telling me?" she murmured with a sidelong glance at Mrs. Bell, who hooted instantly with her full-bodied laughter.

They were alone together that morning.

"I mustn't keep you from anything," said Kathleen remorsefully, "you're so good to me, Mrs. Bell."

"Could you call me Molly?" asked the older woman. "I'd like that."

"Of course, I'd like it too — Molly," said Kathleen, smiling. "But don't put me off like that. Won't you just try to forget I'm here?"

"I haven't a thing to do, in the world," said Mrs. Bell, "until the afternoon when some of my old cronies are coming in for a cup of tea. Pat told me that he wants to be married right away."

Kathleen shook her head. "Golly, I won't do that again," she said. "Yes, I know, he said so last night. But I can't, Molly."

"Why not? Your mother and father?"

"Of course. I wouldn't dream of it . . . not until they come home. And I don't want to tell them that we're engaged, even, until they come back."

"Now why?" inquired Molly.

"Because I know them. They'd cut the trip short, come home by the next boat. I don't want them to do that. I want to persuade Pat to let me go on working in the office and not tell a soul — except you, of course, and Hannah. And then when my mother and father return we'll announce it and be married as soon as possible."

"Pat's not a very good waiter," said his mother.

"I know," said Kathleen, "if what goes on in the office is any evidence. But this is one case where he'll have to wait. And, oh," she said anxiously, "I hope you'll stand by me."

"Of course," agreed Molly instantly, "he won't have a chance, poor lad, with two strong-minded women against him."

A messenger from the office arrived with a bag which Hannah had packed and with an enormous box of gardenias from Pat. Mrs. Bell put them in a silver bowl, and set them on the bedside table. Their heavy fragrance made Kathleen's head ache again but she wouldn't have said so for anything. Pat called up half a dozen times. Hannah arrived in the afternoon with more flowers and Mrs. Bell left them alone together. Her own callers had come and she would send up tea. She measured Hannah with unsmiling eyes before she departed.

"Quaint little number," said Hannah, "looks like a plum pudding."

"She's a darling," said Kathleen warningly.

"Oh, of course," said Hannah. "For heaven's sake, tell me about last night . . . I was sorry to run out on you but I had a tearing headache."

"It was catching," said Kathleen, with a faint smile. "There isn't any more to it than Pat told you over the phone. We stayed late, left, and got hit . . . and I bumped my head. Pat insisted on my coming here and I was too darned sick to dispute him."

"I'm glad he did," said Hannah, "I would have dropped dead with fright if he'd brought you in all limp and bleeding."

"I didn't bleed," said Kathleen.

"Look," said Hannah, paying no attention, "is it true — what he told me — that you're going to marry him?"

"It's true," said Kathleen.

"Oh, darling!" Hannah flung herself on the bed and kissed Kathleen warmly. "Sorry. Hurt?" She straightened up and regarded her friend with beaming eyes. "It's marvelous. Aren't you awfully happy?"

"Of course. It all happened so quickly," Kathleen said, "that I haven't had time to realize it yet."

"When?"

"When what?"

"When are you going to be married . . . right away?"

"No," said Kathleen, "not for a long time."

Hannah was quite still. Her bright color

faded a little, and she looked away from the other girl. She dipped her scarlet-tipped fingers into the silver bowl and pulled out a gardenia.

"Who sent these?" she demanded. "Pat? Of course, that's like him, dozens of gardenias . . . Why not?"

"Why not what? Hannah, do stick to one thing at a time, my head's not normal yet."

"Why aren't you going to be married right away? I thought from something Pat said —"

"Pay no attention. I'm not going to be Mrs. Bell until Mother and Father get back. And, by the way, it's a secret, Hannah. No spilling. Promise? I don't want to tell them, because they'd come back at once and that isn't fair to them. They're to have their year abroad, and then when they get back we'll announce it and Pat and I will be married."

"I thought you didn't believe in long engagements. I've heard you say so a dozen times."

"I don't, but this is different. I can't do anything to upset them, to make them hurry back. Can't you see that?"

"Oh, I suppose so. It's so long since I've had anyone I had to consult," said Hannah. She pulled the gardenia to pieces and then looked at what she'd done in dismay. "I'm sorry," she said, "I didn't mean to."

"That's all right. Hannah, don't tell anyone, will you?"

"But I've told Paul," said Hannah, flushing. "I called him this morning."

Kathleen smiled. She thought, You didn't lose any time. But she could not be angry. She understood perfectly. She said equably:

"I don't mind. He won't say anything if you ask him not to."

"He's said plenty already," said Hannah with energy. "He wouldn't believe me at first. Said I was lying. We'd had a terrific bust-up last night, after he took me home. And was he wild when I told him you'd been hurt. He wanted to tear right up, said I had no business letting Pat bring you here. As if I could have stopped him had I known. Paul's such a fool!"

Kathleen said, "Well, call him again, say I'm fine, tell him that the engagement isn't to be announced."

Hannah said, "All right . . . but he'll probably barge in here himself. He said he was going to."

There was a knock and Emily came in with the tea tray and a message. The doctor had telephoned, the result of the X-rays was as he had expected. No injury. He would look in, however, tonight just to see how Miss Roberts was getting along.

When they were alone, "Molly," said Kathleen, "is marvelous. And so darned good to me."

"Molly?"

"Pat's mother."

"Oh. Is he the only child?"

"No, he has a sister, much younger, still at school. Her name's Carmela, and from her pictures she's very pretty."

"Well, you won't have many in-laws to cope with. Do you expect Pat will want you to come here and live when you're married?" asked Hannah curiously.

"We haven't got that far. He owns this apartment," said Kathleen, "and his mother and sister are very comfortable here. I don't imagine Carmela will stay single long. She's too attractive. I hadn't thought about the apartment, Hannah."

"Well," said Hannah firmly, "if you stay you'll have to do it all over. It's the damnedest place I ever saw."

"I hardly saw it, last night," said Kathleen. She looked around the room. It was over-elaborate, a great deal of satin and lace and draperies and painted furniture. But it was pleasant enough.

"Wait till you get a load of downstairs," said Hannah, shrugging. She set down her teacup. "I must run along. When will you

161

be home again?"

"Oh, probably tomorrow," said Kathleen. "I want to go to the office, if I can."

"Are you really going on working?"

"Of course," said Kathleen with spirit, "what else could I do? It will be months before my wandering parents return."

"It may be complicated," said Hannah, "working for the fiancé."

"I fail to see it, so I intend to; and, yes, by golly, if I'm worth it I intend to get that raise he promised me."

Emily appeared again. She said, "Mr. McClure to see Miss Roberts."

"I knew it," said Hannah, and whitened to her lips.

"Ask him to come up," said Kathleen. She smiled at Hannah. "You'll do the honors?" she asked.

Paul came in almost headlong. But he stopped when he saw Hannah. He said, "Gathering of the clan, eh?" He marched over to the bed and stood looking down. "Sweet Kate," he asked, "what hit you?"

"It felt like a pile driver," she admitted.

"Hannah doesn't give a very good report," he said, and sat down at the foot of the bed. "Come, tell all. Give."

She told, briefly. "So you see," she concluded, "I'm all right. No fracture, nothing.

Head's too hard, I guess. I'll be all right by tomorrow and back at work."

"But," said Paul with a glance at Hannah, "I understood from Mlle. Winchell here that work was all over: Girl Marries Boss."

"Not exactly and not yet," said Kathleen. She embarked on her explanation. "And so you see," she ended, "it's a secret. Please, Paul, don't tell anyone. If it gets around at all it's bound to reach the family."

"All right," he said. He rose and jerked a thumb at Hannah. "Come along, Bad News," he said briefly, "Kate looks tired. I left some flowers for you, Kate, downstairs. I can't compete with gardenias or lilies."

"I brought the lilies," said Hannah proudly.

"You're sweet," Kathleen told him. She did feel tired. She wished they'd both go.

"Get out of here," said Paul suddenly to Hannah. He picked her up, set her wildly protesting outside the door and then closed it. He returned to the bed, and looked down. He asked, gently, "You're happy, aren't you, Kate?"

"Terribly, Paul." Her eyes pleaded with him for understanding. "But a little bewildered. It must have been the bump on the head."

"I've often thought," he said, "that you were dropped when you were a baby. I won't

163

pretend I'm happy about this . . . why should I be? But if you are — Well, that matters, it will have to matter."

He leaned down, touched his lips to her forehead. Straightening up, he said, "Well, good-bye, Kate . . . be seein' you. Or won't you be allowed callers?"

The door closed before she could answer. She was staring at it, wondering what she would have answered, when it opened again and Paul put in his head. "By the way," he said, grinning, "I met your Pat's mother a little while back. Treasure her, Kate. She's unique."

Mrs. Bell came upstairs an hour later, to find Kathleen lying in the dark, watching the snow sift silently down past her unshaded windows.

"Hasn't Emily been in to turn on the lights?" she demanded.

"She came, but I liked it this way. Snowing hard, isn't it?"

"Hard enough. How do you feel?"

"Almost good as new."

"Fine. Pat's run the legs off me, telephoning. Who's that Hannah girl?"

Kathleen told her and Molly shook her head.

"I didn't think much of her. Flibbertigibbet."

"She's all right when you know her, Molly."

"I dare say. I liked that young fellow. He was in pretty much of a dither." Molly looked at her sharply. "In love with you too, isn't he?"

"He thinks so," said Kathleen, smiling, "but he'll get over it. I think that he and Hannah, one day —"

"Oh, so that's it." Molly dismissed them both from her mind. She sat there talking quietly about Pat, about Carmela — "She'll die with excitement when she hears about this" — until Pat came in.

Books, magazines, more flowers. He was vitality itself, bursting in, dropping things on the floor, seizing her in his arms. Didn't she look well, wouldn't she be all right by tomorrow, had she missed him, he'd been nearly crazy all day, the office was demoralized . . . they'd have to throw a party.

"Pat, sit down," said Kathleen, "and listen to me. No, Molly, please don't go."

He sat down, obediently enough, his bright blue glance first on one, then the other. "What's up?"

She told him, making her explanation once more. They would have to wait until her parents returned. And meantime no one was to know, except themselves and Hannah . . .

"and, of course," she added, "Paul McClure. Hannah's told him already."

Pat was scowling. He tried to beat her down by sheer weight of argument. It was silly. They could cable her parents, they could reach them on the telephone. She was old enough to know her own mind, she didn't have to wait for anyone's consent.

"It isn't that," she said wearily. "I don't intend to ask their 'consent,' they wouldn't expect it of me, Pat. But they must go on with their trip. They wouldn't. They'd come rushing back."

"The girl's right," said Molly, "and don't try and talk her out of it. That's the way I'd want it if I were in her mother's shoes. So hush up."

But he was still arguing after dinner and after the doctor had come and gone.

Toward ten that evening Kathleen looked at him, her eyes blue-shadowed. She said, "It has to be that way, Pat, or not at all."

"You don't give me any choice!"

"I haven't any myself, dear," she said, "can't you see that?"

"No." He could not brook delays, authority other than his own. He tramped around the room, his hands thrust deep in his pockets. She said, putting up her arms:

"Please, Pat — I'm dreadfully tired."

He took her quite gently in his arms, and kissed her. "O. K.," he said, "have it your own way. I still think it's nonsense."

"We've been so close, my people and I. I can't do anything to hurt them. You and I have all our lives before us, darling. We can wait . . . and . . . we'll be together . . . so much."

"That's just it," he muttered. "You really want to go on with the office?"

"Don't you want me to?" she asked.

"Of course, but . . . it's going to be hard," he told her.

"I know," she said, "I do understand. But I want to be with you, Pat, I want to go on working, I'd hate doing nothing. If you won't have me there, I'll have to find another job."

"No, you won't," he said with energy. "Your job's with me, as long as we live."

Later Molly came in to send Pat away and get Kathleen ready for the night.

"Did you bring him around?" she inquired.

"I did," said Kathleen, "but it wasn't easy."

"And it won't be," said Molly, "but you were right. Stand by your guns. This is one of the times when it's better to cross him." She bent and kissed her. "Good night, and sweet dreams."

Chapter X

Kathleen left the Bell apartment fully recovered except for the slight soreness when she explored her scalp with careful fingers. She had fallen in love again, this time with Molly Bell. She sang that little lady's praises to Hannah until her audience yawned in her face. "Spare me the prenuptial raptures, darling," Hannah implored; "wait until you're married. As a prospective mother-in-law she may be honey and roses, but remember that honey is made by bees and roses have thorns."

"Unworthy of you," laughed Kathleen. She caught her friend in an immense bear hug. "I'm so happy," she confessed, "I'm afraid it will creep into my letters abroad and arouse dark suspicions."

Hannah repeated this conversation to Paul upon the next occasion of their meeting. She was always enchanted to report to him how radiant Kathleen looked, how glowing. Paul swirled the ice around in his glass with a cold tinkle. He remarked, "She's right, they'll smell a — rat."

Hannah looked at him. "You have taken

a dislike to Pat, haven't you?"

"Is that woman's intuition?" he inquired. "My, isn't it marvelous. I've often wondered how it worked."

"Don't be that way," said Hannah. She looked away from him, across the smoky room of the little French café in which they were dining, and added soberly, "Of course, I know you're crazy about her, Paul."

"We won't go into that, if you don't mind, Hannah."

"Sorry. But what I mean is you've always been a fair sort of egg. You wouldn't go around hating people glumly just because —"

He said swiftly, "You mean that the fact that Bell and Kate are engaged wouldn't make any difference in my feelings for him if I had happened to like him in the first place?"

"How sweetly you put it," said Hannah. "Yes, that's the gist of it."

Paul shook his head. It seemed to Hannah that his thin face was leaner than ever. He's working too hard, she thought, and then with a pang, no, he isn't, it's Kate's fault.

"I'm not magnanimous," he said calmly, "I'd not feel overfriendly toward any guy who was headman with Kate. But in this case — Well, I just don't like the man, Hannah. I wouldn't even if Kate were out of the picture."

"He's attractive," said Hannah stubbornly, "very good-looking."

"Check," said Paul.

"He has charm," went on Hannah, "a sense of humor, a sort of arrogance which doesn't rub you the wrong way because it seems part of his personality."

"Double check . . . except the last part. It happens to rub *me* the wrong way."

"And," said Hannah, "from all one hears he's very generous."

"I suppose so," said Paul. He picked up his glass and set it down. He said gently, "But I don't like the so-and-so. Let it go at that. And suppose we don't talk about it any more."

"O. K.," said Hannah meekly. "How's the play going?"

Back at the office Kathleen was conscious that everyone knew or at least guessed about her and Pat. No one said anything openly but it seemed to her that Jim Haines was markedly hostile, and that the girls in the outer office a little too eager to catch and hold her attention. One or another of them came running to her on any pretext at all hours of the day. Even Sadie, whom she knew and liked best of all the staff, asked no questions.

Thanksgiving, a holiday which Kathleen had dreaded, had been very happy, after all. She had gone as a matter of course to the Bells'. Carmela had been there, the prettiest dark youngster, vivacious, devoted to her mother, terribly proud of Pat, and ready to meet Kathleen halfway. "I knew I'd love you," she cried, and cast herself on Kathleen's neck.

On this day Pat had given Kathleen her ring. They had argued about it before. "Not until the engagement is announced," she'd said firmly. "How could I have a ring and not wear it?" But he had bought it despite her veto. A square-cut diamond. Too big, she thought, gasping as it flashed back at her from the leather box, and too beautiful. But there it was and she loved it and couldn't wear it and was terrified to have it in the apartment. She hid it under lingerie, she parked it in slipper toes, and worried all day about it at the office. Finally she bought, at considerable expense, a little steel safe set in a bedside table and felt comparatively secure.

Hannah, who had made round eyes at the ring, said, logically, that any strong-muscled burglar could pick up the table and walk out with it, safe and all. "But how would he know it was a safe?" asked Kathleen.

Hannah reported all this to Paul. She said, "You should see the ring. She wears it at home, sometimes. Every time she puts her hand to her face I think she's eating ice. Honestly, Paul, it is to knock the eye out. About ten carats. Bertha, the Brewer's Bride. Oh, hell," she concluded, laughing, "I'm just envious. In my new black Eloise, with the high mink collar and the wallpaper fit and wearing just one immodest diamond, I would slay my tens of thousands."

She looked at him out of the corner of her eye but he was not listening. He said suddenly, "I'm having trouble with my second act. Unless you've a second act curtain, Hannah, you haven't a play."

Well, she thought grimly, it was evident that she hadn't a second act curtain. She couldn't understand herself at all. When Paul had been in love with her and she with him they had been careless with their love. They hadn't hoarded it. They'd been crazy and gay and spendthrift — and rarely serious.

It was only after the last of a succession of quarrels, arising from trivial causes but assuming gigantic proportions, that she had realized how much she loved him.

She'd tried hard to put him out of her mind. She thought she had when he had come back, on a basis of casual give-and-take friendship. But when she saw him desperately and suddenly in love again, and not with her, her old passion for him returned, redoubled. And he was different with Kathleen, she thought, knowing him as well as she did. Gay and casual enough on the surface but there was something frighteningly tenacious and dark underneath.

By her code of living, she should have turned her back on him for good when she saw what was happening. But she couldn't. Now Kathleen was to marry another man and Paul was carrying the torch and caring little who guessed it. And here she was, here was Hannah, trying, she told herself baldly, to get him on the rebound, shameless about it, indifferent to the reactions of any observer, not even caring if Paul knew.

Christmas came on a weekend that year and it was a green Christmas. So Pat put his mother, Carmela, and Kathleen in the car and drove them up to Placid where there was snow. Kathleen would have preferred an old-fashioned holiday, such as she best knew, in the Riverside Drive apartment, but Pat would have none of it. He wanted a gay time and lots of people. Besides, Carmela did too and there were sure to be dozens of young men at the club.

173

So up they went, leaving early on the morning of Christmas Eve, Pat driving his big car and Garman trailing behind in Mrs. Bell's car laden with packages.

After all, thought Kathleen, perhaps it was as well. She missed her family dreadfully. She could telephone them, ship to shore . . . and did, hearing their faraway voices with an almost intolerable delight. She could say, "Hello, darlings, a Merry Christmas to you."

She told them she was at Placid, at a house party, but her mother asked anxiously, "Have you a cold, Kathleen?" and she said, steadying her voice, "Not a sign of one. I'm just crying a little, that's all."

Yes, perhaps it was as well to be surrounded almost entirely by strangers . . . to admire a big impersonal Christmas tree and see holly wreaths she had not helped her mother to hang. And to forget that this was the first Christmas since she was born that a stocking had not hung for her on the mantelpiece.

Pat was lavish with his gifts: a sapphire bracelet, perfume, a fitted traveling bag . . . "for our honeymoon," he explained. Mrs. Bell gave her lingerie and a tiny miniature of Pat painted from a picture she had of him as a youngster of six, with curly black hair and bright blue eyes. Carmela gave her

174

stockings and a kiss.

She had things for them all: a cigarette case for Pat, handmade silver, very lovely, gloves and sachets and a pretty pin for Molly, and a compact for Carmela. She had brought with her the packages which had come to Hannah's for her: Hannah's gift of a suède bag from Eloise, with a jade clasp, remembrances from other friends and the bulky package from Paul.

She could not believe her eyes when she opened it and saw the leather-bound manuscript of *Nothing Is Lost*. On the title page he had written, "I still believe it, sweet Kate."

Pat said, "What's that?"

She showed it to him. "You must read it . . . It should read almost as well as it plays. But he shouldn't have given it to me."

Pat said, shrugging, "It's a conceited sort of gift, don't you think?"

"No," she said, staring at him, "I don't think that."

There was a little coolness between them. Molly felt it. She asked, coming into Kathleen's room on Christmas night, "What's the matter between you and the boy?"

"Nothing. Oh, just that Paul McClure gave me a play of his in manuscript and Pat didn't like it."

"The play?" asked Molly, twinkling.

"No, the gift." She put it into Molly's hands. "You didn't see it, did you? Well, read it. You'll like it."

Molly bore it away with her and returned it in the morning. She said gravely:

"That's a fine play, Kathleen. I don't pretend to know anything about such things but this made me cry and it made me laugh and it made me proud to be a plain ordinary human being. What's he done since?"

"Very little. Oh, he's been successful . . . but nothing like this again."

"You and Pat made up?"

"Of course. That didn't mean anything."

"He's jealous," said his mother warningly; "all the Bell men are jealous. Watch out for it, Kathleen."

They had a little skating, they had a sleigh ride and a long tramp through the woods powdered with snow. There was dancing and pretty girls and attractive boys down from college. Carmela broke three hearts and was perfectly satisfied. She'd had a keen Christmas, she said.

They returned to town and to work and, on New Year's Eve, Kathleen and Pat went out to celebrate and see the New Year in. He asked her where she wanted to go and she said she didn't care and then remembering something Hannah had said, added,

"Oh, why not the Jungle? It's new and very amusing, they say, and I've never been there."

He raised an eyebrow. "Neither have I." Then he laughed and his eyes narrowed. "After all, why not?" he murmured.

They dined, went to a play, and then on to the Jungle, a tangle of pseudo-coconut palms and grass shacks and banana trees, with a new clever master of ceremonies, and the hottest orchestra in town. Kathleen wore the new Eloise, her major extravagance, and felt repaid for it by the expression in Pat's eyes when he looked at her. It was a picture dress in coppery velvet with a full wide skirt, a tiny waist, and appliquéd in curious flowers, copper and mauve.

"You should have worn your ring," said Pat.

She wore no jewelry save two wide, old-fashioned gold bracelets with matching earrings which had belonged to her grandmother.

"Not here, darling," she said, "with a columnist behind every palm!"

There was a girl singing at the Jungle . . . a small blond girl with a beautiful figure. She wore a few leaves tastefully arranged here and there, a towering headdress, and nothing else. She danced a little, a sort of combina-

tion hula as no Hawaiian has ever understood the hula, and a few gestures wholly her
own. She sang, in a darkly colored, astonishingly deep voice, and people applauded her
wildly.

Pat applauded too and the blond girl saw
him and waved across the room.

"Who is she?" asked Kathleen, beginning
to feel a little sleepy and wondering how late
in the New Year it was.

"I used to know her," he said carelessly,
"her name's Sandra — at least that's what
she calls herself."

"Just Sandra?"

"Just Sandra. Kathleen, you're so lovely
tonight. This is our year," he told her, "just
beginning. How can you sit there and be so
unkind?"

"Unkind!"

But she knew what he meant. He had
argued with her at Placid; he had argued
with her in the car this evening, between
acts, over dinner, over the New Year's wine.
Why must they wait, why must she be so
stubborn, would nothing change her mind?

The girl called Sandra had finished her en-
core and vanished. Now she reappeared in a
slim black evening frock and came straight to
their table. She smiled at Pat, whose face had
darkened, and nodded carelessly at Kathleen.

"How about a glass of champagne," she said, "for old time's sake?"

The waiter brought a glass and a chair. Pat made the introductions. Sandra said, her elbows on the table, "Well, here's to crime." She set down the glass. She said, looking at Pat with big, mascaraed blue eyes, "I haven't seen you for months, sweetheart."

He answered, shrugging, that he hadn't been around much.

"Oh, but I've heard things," Sandra told him, "I read the papers, and I get around." She leaned back and surveyed Kathleen. "So this is the new girl friend," she murmured.

"Sandra!" said Pat sharply.

"Oh, no hard feelings," said Sandra. She drained her glass and rose. She stood there, leaning forward with fingertips just touching the tabletop, and spoke to Kathleen.

"Wish you joy of him," she said clearly. "If you ask me, he's pretty much of a heel. And I should know."

She turned and walked away, swinging her pretty hips.

Chapter XI

There was a brief, uncomfortable silence. Kathleen looked after the girl. She was very young. Her cheekline still retained that heartbreaking curve of youth. Eighteen? Nineteen? Kathleen, so little her senior, felt forty. The girl had stood close to her only a moment but she felt as if she had seen her a hundred times and knew her features by heart; the short tip-tilted nose, the big shallow blue eyes, the full mouth, the arched plucked eyebrows which lent her an expression of startled surprise. But the mouth was harder than a nineteen-year-old mouth had any right to be and the hair — so fair that it was almost white — had been skillfully touched up. Youth remained, however, piteous and touching, in the curve of the cheek, the tender nape of the neck from which the blond curls had been brushed upward. And in the lines of the figure, which would one day be a little plump if Sandra did not watch her calories and deny herself champagne.

Kathleen turned her sober regard to Pat. He was smiling, but a slow color crept up under his eyes. He said jauntily, "Skip it!"

Excellent advice. Kathleen found herself remembering with astonishment how short a time she had known him and how little she knew of him. For her knowledge extended only as far as what she herself had seen and heard, and what her heart told her. The rest of his life, his existence prior to their first encounter, was utterly unknown to her, a sealed book except for those few chapters which everyone might know. She shook her head as if to clear her eyes. She said quietly, hoping to heaven that she did not sound jealous or suspicious and knowing with a sickening certainty that she was both:

"Tell me about her."

"There's nothing to tell," said Pat, and beckoned a waiter to refill their glasses.

"But you know her?"

"Well, naturally."

"Well," she repeated slowly, "and naturally. I see, of course, you know her — well."

He said, irritated, "Don't pick me up like that, honey. Nothing to it. Pay no attention. I met her a year or more ago. She was in the chorus then, out of the Middle West, corn tassels in her hair. A cute little trick. I've forgotten where we met or how — cocktail party, I suppose, or night club or something. I took her out a couple of times . . . three-four maybe. After I met you I hadn't time,"

181

he said, smiling, "or inclination. So that's that. And she's sore. You know how these kids are, always on the make for a free meal, a pair of stockings, what have you? It isn't personal at all, except as far as her vanity is concerned."

Her eyes were the gray of a stormy sea. They regarded him steadily for a moment. He was leaning forward, earnest; anxious to hold her attention and her credulity. His heavy voice was pitched low and his blue eyes were anxious. He was as open as daylight, she thought, and as honest. She smiled suddenly and put her hand across the table and touched his. She said gently:

"Darling. I'm sorry."

His face lighted at once and he looked at her with pleasure and relief. He said, "It was that way — of course, it looked pretty fishy."

"No, it didn't, not really. Only —" she laughed — "Hannah would feel at home in such a situation but I suppose I haven't been around much. Awful confession, isn't it?"

He said, grinning: "You were jealous!"

"I was," she admitted, "terribly. Just for a moment. I imagined all sorts of things, and a house of cards tumbling down around my head. Forgive me."

He said, "I love your being jealous."

His eyes were intimate and caressing.

Kathleen flushed a little.

"I didn't like it," she said frankly. She looked across the room and saw Rosa Davenport and her son in the doorway, arguing with a captain. She called and waved to them and as they came over, "They're Eloise, Pat."

"Eloise?" repeated Pat blankly, looking at the approaching couple: Rosa superbly gowned, Sammy drifting along in her wake.

"We'll ask them to join us," said Kathleen. She was disappointed, but not sharply, that her evening with Pat was to be interrupted. Not so sharply as she might have been had not Sandra entered the picture. She felt ashamed of herself, let down. And, although she tried to assure herself that she had something of which to be ashamed, she was not wholly certain.

"It's absurd," said Sammy, in his high, rapid voice. "We had a table booked but we went on to Mitzi's after the theater and what with one thing and another we were held up."

Kathleen accomplished the introductions. She said, "Sit here, with us, there's room and to spare."

Rosa sat down. She said, sighing, "I'm half dead. Sam has the oddest ideas of celebrating a New Year. Odd to me, at least. My idea of a real festivity is to go to bed, with a book, a glass of milk, a carton of cigarettes, some very red apples, and a box of cream peppermints!"

Sammy waved his hands, which were, Pat saw to his horror, really beautiful. He cried: "But we have to relax!"

"Mitzi relaxed," said his mother with a chuckle. "She relaxed all over the place. There were a million people in her dressing room. We shooed them away. She and Galbraith were coming here with us. But, no, she had to go home first. To powder her nose, to change her frock, to telephone her mother in California. God knows what. And all the people who had been in the dressing room turned up, too. It was God-awful. When we left finally someone was pouring Galbraith into a cab and Mitzi was having hysterics because that damned Pekinese had eaten her second best rabbit's foot."

"Mitzi?" asked Pat, looking from one to the other.

"Mitzi Lambert," explained Sam carelessly. He turned to Kathleen. "I assure you," he said dramatically, "that if she puts on another pound I'll be forced to make her an entirely new wardrobe. Her present clothes were not designed for extra poundage. In the last act — you've seen it, haven't you? — in that white chiffon she looked like the neck of an ostrich which is eating oranges — whole!"

Rosa laughed.

"Well, if she does gain, it's good for business." She regarded Pat with interest. "I've heard a good deal about you," she began.

Sam said, "Don't bother, darling. He's a bachelor. No wife to dress."

Pat looked at Kathleen and laughed. He said, "You can never tell when my status will change."

Sam looked at her too. He knew who Pat Bell was, he made it his business to know who everyone was. Besides, Hannah had been talking. He said:

"If I do say it as shouldn't, you look next door to divine in that little number."

"I love it," said Kathleen, "even its silly name."

"Name?" said Pat.

He was gradually realizing who the Davenports were. Eloise, Inc. "Do they actually name clothes?" he inquired.

"You must see our spring showing," said Sam. "This," he touched Kathleen's shoulder — "this is called 'Mirage'."

"It doesn't make sense," said Pat.

"Why should it? By the way, after we left Mitzi's, we went around to the Bubble and Squeak."

"What in the world . . ." began Kathleen.

"The new place," answered Sam patiently. "Very smart. Give it another month and it will be on top. Cecily Jane is singing there. British music hall stuff. The whole place is very 'old England.' A crazy combination of the Kit Kat and Simpson's. Massive beef shoved around on a rolling table." He shuddered. "Magnificent ale. Prints on the walls, and paneling. But Cecily is rather naughty in a nice way, they've a good orchestra and a dancer — a blond young man with very intellectual feet. It's a must-dress, any evening. You see a good many people there. Hannah, for instance, tonight, ravishing in our cherry pie frock — and, of course, Paul McClure. They're probably still there. Why not join them?"

He had drunk a glass of Pat's champagne. No more. He was an abstemious young man.

Kathleen objected quickly, "But it's all hours!"

"Lord," said Sam, staring at her, "you don't intend to go home before breakfast, do you? Tell her it isn't done, Bell. Besides, as a favor to me? I'd like to see my Mirage get around."

Pat had his second wind. The episode with Sandra had passed off very well. Damn San-

186

dra anyway. She had threatened to make trouble for him, if she could. But how could she? She hadn't a thing, not a bill, not a check, not a voucher, not, of course, a letter. She couldn't prove a thing. He hadn't thought of her in months. He wished, regarding Kathleen, that she was a little more worldly-wise, in the sense that he understood the term. But she wasn't. And therefore Sandra without any proof might make trouble.

But that danger had passed. He felt vital and alive and ready for another four hours of merriment and clamor. He said, "How about it, Kathleen? Personally I'm all for it."

So they went on to the Bubble and Squeak and found it still almost full despite the hour. McClure and Hannah were there, but not alone. Hannah, in her striped white and cherry-colored frock, wore a paper cap rakishly on her dark head. She looked pretty enough to eat. Paul was having a good time too, he had a rattle and a miniature machine gun and he was making plenty of noise.

Pat fixed the captain with his eye. The captain didn't know him but he soon would.

"A lot of tables," said Pat.

"I beg your pardon?"

"You heard me. A lot of tables."

Hannah was standing up, calling to them. In a very few minutes there were tables

187

pushed together and Pat found himself host to McClure and Hannah and their friends. "I can't introduce them," said Hannah confidentially, "as they seem to have joined us incognito. One is a duke or a housebreaker, I'm not sure which. The dark one's an ex-bootlegger. Very respectable. Anyway, it's fun . . . and Happy New Year."

Champagne. Caviar in blocks of ice. Something hot under glass. More champagne.

Sam and Rosa drifted away first.

"I can't take it," sighed Rosa. She looked at Hannah and said, "You shouldn't."

"Speaks the employer," said Hannah merrily. "I'll have a hell of a head tomorrow. But Eloise, Inc. must go on. And I've a new idea, a brand-new idea: purples, violet, magenta, mauves, coronation stuff. Stubby, heavy jewelry. We'll all be ladies again. Purples and violets in sports things and leather and gold gadgets."

"Shut up," said Sam gently. "If you should have an idea, there may be people around who will overhear and beat you to it."

"Go home, Sammy," said Hannah, "and leave me alone." She was sketching on the back of a menu. She was a little drunk and enjoying it. She could forget when she was a little drunk how pleasant and friendly Paul had been all evening. She didn't want him to be pleasant and friendly, not to her. That wasn't his way when he was in love . . . not this kind of pleasant friendliness, smiling and amiable.

Sammy went, and Rosa, but Hannah and Paul stayed on, and the incognito others who were having, they assured Pat earnestly, the time of their lives. After a while the dark man whom Hannah had designated as an ex-bootlegger fixed Pat with a wavering, blood-shot stare. He asked, "Haven't I seen you before, somewhere?"

"Two other fellows," Pat responded inevitably. "Well, why not? I get around."

"Somewhere special." The wavering regard became meditative and glassy. "I know you, you're Pat — Pat Bell. Big sewer-and-ditch guy. I met you at a free-for-all at Sandra's a year or so ago. How is Sandra?"

"Fine," said Pat evenly, "she's dancing at the Jungle."

"Good lil Sandra," said the other man sentimentally, "sweet lil girl. Crazy about her myself. Didn't have a look-in with you around, you old so-and-so." He dug a sharp elbow into Pat's ribs and bubbled with laughter. "Lots more dough," he said sadly, "and what it takes."

Pat regarded him coolly. "I haven't seen

Sandra in some time until tonight."

"Tha's right," said the dark man, remembering, "I heard about it. Been away . . . South America. Crazy place, full of revolutions. Got into one myself and didn't know how to get out. Came back here last week and ran into dear old friend at the bar. What bar?" he inquired, staring at Pat. "Damned if I know. Dear old anyway pal of mine, closer than a brother. Haven't any brother. Can't think of the mug's name, doesn't matter. Anyway, I says to him, 'How's Sandra, pretty lil blond girl, wouldn't give me a tumble . . .' and he says, 'Oh, Sandra's all right, she was pretty sore when her sweetie gave her the air. Wanted to drink iodine. But we said, don't drink iodine, nasty taste, have a Martini instead.' "

Pat was white around the mouth and Kathleen looked sick. Paul, who had been listening intently, spoke. He said pleasantly, "Old man, I have a message for you."

The ex-bootlegger or whatever he was — it wasn't bootlegging, at any rate — looked up, distracted. "Poor lil Sandra," he murmured, "like to punch your nose for you. What's your name again, anyway?" he demanded, turning on Pat.

"Listen," said Paul clearly, "someone wants to see you outside."

Hannah was talking to the alleged duke. She had heard very little. Now she stopped and listened. The duke — who was a hardware salesman from Columbus — was listening too.

"Who me?" said the dark man. "Lady?"

"Pretty lady," said Paul soothingly, "little and dark." He made curved gestures with his hands.

"Like 'em pretty," said Sandra's friend, and staggered to his feet. Paul rose and took his arm and guided him with extreme skill, talking all the time, from the room.

"Well," said Hannah. She turned to her ducal companion. "Who in the world is he?" she asked.

That gentleman shook his head. "I haven't any idea. I never saw him before tonight. My date stood me up and I blew in here and I found him in" — he grinned — "the gentlemen's lounge, crying because his date had walked out on him. So we teamed up and after a while found ourselves with you."

Pat said shortly, "He didn't know what he was talking about. Drunker than a coot!"

Hannah looked from one to the other. She asked curiously, "Am I speaking out of turn if I ask whether this Sandra is a person or a figment of alcoholic imagination?"

"She's a person," said Kathleen evenly,

"and very pretty too. An old friend of Pat's. We met her just now in the Jungle."

Paul came back. He was smiling. Kathleen watched him make his easy way toward them. If he had been doing much drinking all evening, he didn't show it: he could carry his liquor as well as Pat. He was taller than most men and his lean, fair-skinned face was singularly distinguished.

"It's all right," he said, smiling, reseating himself. "I found out where he's staying. I even discovered his name. He had business cards: Togs for Tots. Hannah, your bootlegger dream is over. Anyway I dumped him in a cab and sent him off to his hotel. But what are Togs for Tots doing in South America?"

Kathleen said, low, "Thank you, Paul."

"A pleasure," he said cheerfully.

Pat was talking to the hardware salesman and Paul said quietly, "I haven't wished you a happy new year, Kate."

"Thank you," she said again. "It seems a long time since midnight." She looked white and tired and his heart ached over her and his fingers itched to — to —

Hell, what was the use? If he wrung Pat Bell's neck or slapped his handsome face, where would it get him?

He looked at Hannah.

"How about a little spot of home-going, Cherry Pie?" he inquired.

A little later they had said good-bye to the hardware duke and Pat had paid the check. Then he was driving them over to the East Side. Kathleen sat in front with him. She did not speak.

When they reached the apartment house he stood there a moment on the sidewalk in the gray light of early dawn. His eyes were anxious. He said, "You didn't really believe all that drunken — ?"

"I don't know what to believe, Pat," she said unhappily.

He said, "Listen —"

"It's late," she told him, "I'm so tired, Pat."

"I'll see you tomorrow," he said.

Tomorrow . . . was today. They were going off for the weekend with Carmela and Molly Bell. Driving down to Atlantic City.

"All right," she said listlessly.

When she entered the lobby Paul had gone and Hannah was waiting for her. "Paul sent his compliments," she said, "felt he needed the walk home." She yawned. "It's been a very large evening."

"Hasn't it?" said Kathleen.

She was in bed but not asleep when Hannah knocked at her door. "May I come in?"

"Of course."

Hannah came. She looked like a precocious child in her white wool robe, leather belted around her little waist. She curled up on the foot of the bed and pulled a comforter around her.

"I can't sleep, I've stayed up past sleeping," she said, and lit a cigarette. "What time are you leaving?"

"Oh, about two."

"Then you can sleep till one. Kate, what was it all about tonight?" She spoke gravely. She added, after a minute, "You know how I feel about you. If anything's wrong . . ."

Kathleen said after a minute, "I don't know whether it is or not. Probably I'm being a fool." She told Hannah briefly of their meeting with Sandra at the Jungle, and of the explanation Pat had made. She said, "I was jealous, of course — she's awfully pretty, really, Hannah . . . and the way she looked at him . . . but I tried to believe him and succeeded, I think. And then of all things that garrulous drunk turning up at the other place."

"I didn't hear everything," said Hannah; "begin at the beginning."

Kathleen told her as best she could. There was a little silence. Hannah said, "I wouldn't take Tots Toggery too seriously."

"But he knows her," said Kathleen, "he

knew Pat, he remembered him."

"What of it? Toggery Tots gets around. Probably has headquarters here in town and knows a million pretty blondes. Skip it."

"That's what Pat advised."

"Of course. Look here, Kate, you love Pat, don't you?"

"You know I do."

"Then what's all the shooting for? You're grown up, you're over twenty-one. You can't think seriously that Pat suffered no entanglements before he fell in love with you?"

"Of course not."

"Then what of it? Suppose he did know her, better than he admits? Suppose even that Totty was correct in his implications. Suppose this Sandra What's-her-name and Pat — What of that? It's over, it's done with. Honestly, Kate, you don't mean to lie there and tell me that it would make any difference? I mean, if you demand a Galahad these days — or any day, for that matter — you're going to be left on the mourner's bench," Hannah said, putting her cigarette in an ash tray.

"It isn't that," said Kathleen slowly. "I haven't thought much about the women Pat must have known before he met me. I haven't had time, I've been too happy. Too headlong, too suddenly in love perhaps.

Naturally, I realize he's had affairs. Dozens of them, most likely. But if you had seen her eyes, and the way she said —"

"Forget it," said Hannah briskly. "She'd lost out . . . a girl of that type will say anything. You needn't cheapen yourself by believing her."

Young, the line of cheek and neck, and body; the shallow eyes, the bad little hands with their vulgar nails, sunken deeply in the flesh, too long, too pointed, too scarlet. Young, common — vulnerable.

Kathleen said:

"Maybe you wouldn't understand. What I love most about Pat is his straightforwardness, his honesty. His simplicity. There's nothing complicated about him. He's just Pat. Lots of faults, lots of virtues, all honest. He's as plain to read as printing. He loves people and good times, he's — I don't know how to say this, Hannah; it sounds awful and yet it isn't. He's a snob, in the most honest sort of way. I mean, he's impressed with the things he hasn't, an old name, an inherited fortune. He likes society with a capital S, as a kid who adores dressing up in uniforms and watching parades. He's utterly open about it, and I love it in him. He doesn't pretend he doesn't want or like the things he hasn't. I have told myself a million times that if this is what he wants I'll help him get it. He deserves it. He works hard. He's good and generous and kind. And he hasn't grown up. This girl doesn't matter to me in the way you think. If he loved her, all right. He's out of love with her now and in love with me. But if he did love her I don't want him to deny it. That's being a traitor to yourself, it's mean and shabby. I want him to say, 'Yes, I was in love with her. It didn't last.' And I want to feel that when they split up, Hannah, that they did it cleanly and decently and honestly. Can't you understand?"

She waited for Hannah's reply. But there was none. Curled up in the comforter Hannah was breathing as quietly as a child. The cigarette still burned, a thin wasp of smoke in the ash tray beside her.

Kathleen reached over to take the ash tray and put it on the bedside table. She shook her friend gently.

"Wake up and go back to bed," she said.

Hannah woke and yawned.

"Where — how? Oh, golly," said Hannah in distress, "I ran out on you, didn't I? Did I miss much?"

"Not a thing," said Kathleen, laughing. "Go to bed, idiot."

Hannah unwound herself from the quilt and put her feet on the floor. She staggered across the room drowsily, her mules slapping. She said, "I drank too much. Paul wouldn't. It made me mad. Well, another time we'll have a heart-to-heart. I just wanted to set you straight."

"I've set myself straight," said Kathleen, relieved. She felt better for her confession. Just as much as if Hannah had listened. "Good night," she said, "I'll be all right."

Chapter XII

Pat turned up at two the next day and Kathleen was waiting, packed and ready to leave. He came upstairs to fetch her and when she let him in — for Hannah had gone to friends on Long Island and Amelia was off — she put her arms around his neck and kissed him, sweetly.

"That's for the New Year," she said.

He had come in some trepidation. Now his face cleared like that of a child who has dreaded a scolding and finds that he has been let off. He lifted her clear of the floor in a vast embrace. Setting her down he kissed her, not once but many times, holding her close. He said, "My God, but I love you, Kathleen."

"I'm glad."

He said, "Let's sit down and talk it over."

"What?"

"How much I —"

"Your mother's waiting," she reminded him.

They went downstairs and out to the car. Carmela was there, in her Christmas furs, and Molly Bell. Kathleen kissed them both, wished them a good year and got in front with Pat. The drive to Atlantic City was swift and uneventful. They had charming rooms with great windows opening on the wide blue water. The sun poured in, the waves beat on the sand. There was a big living room, filled with flowers, for them all to share. Pat had ordered a radio installed. "Mom hates to miss her programs," he said. He thought of everything.

It was a singularly happy weekend. Afterwards Kathleen was to look back on it as one of the happiest times she had ever spent. A school friend of Carmela's was at the same hotel with her family, including a good-looking brother. So they saw little of Carmela. And Mrs. Bell discovered an acquaintance from the old days, bundled up in rugs, riding in a rolling chair. So they rode together and Pat and Kathleen had a good deal of time to themselves.

They walked for miles. They bought each other silly souvenirs. They went to the Steel Pier and to the movies. They saw a hockey match. They rode in rolling chairs together holding hands under the rug. The weather was perfect, serene and sunny with a snap in the air and the blue water creaming in. They rode the ponies on the sand, at Pat's suggestion. He said, laughing, "I might as well begin here, as any place, and besides, if I fall off, it looks soft."

They did not speak of what had occurred on New Year's Eve except on the very first night when, riding back to the hotel in the chair, he said, "Look here, darling, about Sandra."

"Let's not talk about it now, if you don't mind, Pat. I — I do believe you," Kathleen told him.

But he said eagerly:

"There was nothing, I swear it."

"It wouldn't matter," she answered, "if there had been anything. As long as you didn't lie to me. I couldn't bear that, Pat."

He saw the pitfall too late. He had lied. If he hadn't, she would have forgiven him and understood. Now he had to go on lying — or half lying.

"A few drinks and a lot of parties. Maybe I did give her a whirl," he said, "but it didn't mean a thing."

"All right," said Kathleen, holding his hand. "Look at those silly gulls, asleep on the waves. Greedy and noisy, aren't they? I hate their beady little eyes. But in the light they are perfectly wonderful."

They had a little while alone together evenings when Carmela and Molly had said good night and they were left by themselves in the living room. She could lie in his arms then and feel their strength around her, and return his kisses.

"Why do you keep me waiting, darling?"

"Because I must."

He was always urging her, imploring. "Your people will understand."

"Probably, as they love me. But I can't let them down."

"Stay up a little longer, stay here with me."

"No, Pat. Good night, darling, good night."

Better that way, better that their engagement should be conducted, so to speak, at the office, in restaurants and theaters and night clubs . . . better that they shouldn't be too much alone together. Better for them both.

They drove home after dinner on Sunday night and on Monday she was back in the office and glad of it. Sadie said, when they lunched together, "I hear you were at Atlantic City."

"Now, where did you hear that?"

"It was in the paper, of course. Social item!"

Kathleen laughed. "I had an awfully good time. The air was marvelous . . . chairs and ponies and movies and lots of fun."

"It's an open secret, really," said Sadie

calmly, engaged with a leaf of lettuce.

"What is?"

"You and the chief."

"Sadie," asked Kathleen, "look at me. If it's a secret you'll keep it, won't you?"

"Sure. But people are talking. Haines is sore as a boil."

"Why should he be?" asked Kathleen indignantly.

"Oh, he hasn't minded the —" Sadie caught herself, flushing. "I mean," she went on, "he hasn't minded when the boss ran around a bit . . . this girl, that girl. You know how it is. But he knows this is serious."

"How does he know it?" asked Kathleen, smiling.

"He knows you, doesn't he?" asked Sadie in honest astonishment. "He sees you every day. We all do. It would have to be serious."

"I think you mean that for a compliment," said Kathleen, "thanks."

"You're welcome," said the dark girl. "Jim's a queer duck. You know why. He's wrapped up in the boss. Thinks the sun rises and sets in him."

"I felt he wasn't liking me much lately," said Kathleen seriously. "It's jealousy, then?"

"In a way. Look, if you marry Pat Bell —" said Sadie — "well, I suppose Jim thinks you'll wean him away from all his cronies."

"Why should I?" asked Kathleen, astonished.

"You're different," said Sadie, becoming inarticulate. "And the people you know. They'll be the people he'll know, see?"

"I see. Well, it can't make any difference," said Kathleen. "I am going to marry him, Sadie. But not yet, not until my parents return from Europe. And I don't want it announced before then. Understand?"

"Of course," said Sadie. "Everyone's pulling for you, Kathleen. They all like you."

Except Jim Haines, thought Kathleen.

She saw him the next day on her way out at noon. She stopped him, a hand on his arm and he swung around, a tall, overthin man with a pale, twitching face.

She asked, smiling:

"Got a lunch date?"

"No," he said, "but —"

"Take me then? Fifty-fifty. I want to ask you something."

It wasn't the first time. When she had first come to work she and Haines had lunched together quite often and she had taken her new problems of office routine to him and he had solved them for her.

"All right," he said ungraciously.

When they had been served, "Jim," she said, leaning forward, "you've been very nice to me, ever since I came here. You've helped me, so much."

She had never before called him by his Christian name. He looked at her suspiciously under heavy eyebrows. He answered, "It wasn't to my advantage not to help you, Miss Roberts."

"I understand. But you've seemed hostile toward me, recently." She looked at him with level eyes. "It is because of Mr. Bell, isn't it?"

He became very busy with his sandwich. He said, after a minute, "What makes you think so?"

"Let's not fence," said Kathleen. "I know the entire office has been speculating. I told Sadie the truth yesterday, and now I'll tell you. We're going to be married, but not until my mother and father come home. I can't have it made public before then. If they were to know I was engaged they would come home at once, and they mustn't."

"I see," said Haines. He looked a little gray and drawn. "Thanks for telling me."

"You're Pat's good friend," said Kathleen, smiling, "and so you should know. But I swore Pat to secrecy. It was my fault that he hasn't told you."

Haines's face was more friendly, and his small eyes, dark and sorrowful as a monkey's, lighted. "I wish you both all the luck."

"I know you do. I want you to feel that — I don't interfere . . . that I won't. I'd never interfere in Pat's friendships. They mean a lot to him. He'll have them all his life. They're worth everything, his old associations, and loyalty like yours."

He said, relieved, "Well, I didn't know. He deserves the best, of course, and you're that. But you're different from most of the — the girls he's known."

Perhaps Haines knew about Sandra. She kept her face very still. "Not different, really," she said. Then she managed to smile. "Just myself. I'll try to make him happy, Jim."

He looked at her a moment. He said, "Gee, it's too bad you have to wait. This big job coming off and all . . . you ought to get married and celebrate."

"Job? Oh, the subway. But that isn't settled yet, is it?"

"It's in the bag."

"But the bids . . ."

"Next week. We can't miss. What do you suppose he's had Dan McClaren round so much for?"

Dan McClaren. City politician. Of course, things were handled that way, she supposed, on jobs like these. Inevitable if distasteful.

She knew little about it. "Tell me about it, Jim," she urged him.

A new city subway. A big job, a long one. He added, "We'll underbid, all right. If we didn't, it wouldn't matter. They read off the figures aloud, see? They can read what they please."

"But, Jim!"

He looked at her and his face became a mask. He said smoothly, "It isn't quite like it sounds."

But it was like it sounded, perhaps. And he added hastily, "They won't have to, this time. We'll get the bid by a big margin."

"But how can we afford — ?"

He shrugged. "Lots of ways," he said.

There was only one way in which it would be easy, she thought. After all, she wasn't entirely stupid about the contracting business. Scamped materials . . . you had to make your profit, so you bid low and scamped on materials. Horrible, she thought, and possibly murderous. She drew a deep breath. No, Pat couldn't. It wasn't in him to do such a thing. He could use political pull, everyone did, there was nothing disgraceful in that. But he wouldn't endanger men's lives. Besides, there were inspectors . . . he couldn't get around them.

She said, after a moment, "Jim, I don't

207

know how to say this . . . you may be angry at me. Believe me when I say I'm not prying or curious. I just want to be of use if I can. If there is anything I could do for Mrs. Haines, to make things easier for her? Books, perhaps . . . does she read much? Or magazines?"

His face worked. He said huskily, "No, she doesn't read. I — Would you go see her someday, with me? She likes to see people and she hasn't many friends who remember. But I shouldn't ask you, it isn't very pleasant. Sometimes, she doesn't seem to want me, she cries because I come alone."

"I'll go with you next time," she said gently, terribly sorry for him.

She forgot the subway job entirely, immersed in this personal and human problem. And went on forgetting it until two things happened. She picked up her telephone to place a call one morning. It was an extension of one of Pat's wires. She listened only a second and then set the instrument down carefully, her lips tight. She had heard something. Not much, for Pat was cautious. But enough — almost enough.

And the next day the wrong letter came to her desk and she opened it.

She was dining with Pat that night, quietly, at a place they both liked. He was in high spirits. Tomorrow the bids would go in. He said, raising his glass, "Here's to profit. What do you want out of it — a mink coat, a diamond bracelet?"

"What do you want, Pat?" she asked him.

She had been quiet all evening but he had not seemed to notice. He answered, smiling:

"A long honeymoon with you, darling. Europe, Honolulu, anywhere you wish."

"Pat . . . ?"

"Yes, dear — wait a minute. Did I tell you how lovely you are this evening? But sober. I miss that funny little dimple at the corner of your mouth."

"Listen, Pat, this is serious." She stirred her coffee, lifted the cup to her lips, set it down untasted. "Serious and important. That city bid . . ."

He was quiet now, too quiet. His eyes narrowed, a little. He asked, "What about it?"

"Lots of things. Things I don't like. McClaren . . ."

He laughed easily, with genuine amusement.

"Poor old Dan . . . he's a nice guy when you get to know him. Eye for the ladies. Has he been hanging around your desk?" he asked.

"No, of course not."

"Why, of course? If he annoys you, tell

me, I'll handle him. But, if you love me, be nice to him. Not too nice, you understand."

"I understand perfectly," she replied. "But I don't mean McClaren personally. Just the whole setup. The bids. You underbid — naturally."

"I hope so," he said, with caution.

She struck her hand on the table with sudden force. A glass jumped, silver clattered. Someone dining near by looked around curiously. She said:

"You *know*." Haines's phrase came to her. "It's in the bag," she said, "and how could it be if you're honest? I don't know much about your business, Pat, I wasn't hired to know anything about it. But from what I have seen and heard, you'll have to cut your costs, shave them to the bone to make any profit. Cheap materials. Getting by when you can."

He was angry, she saw his eyes and shrank mentally. His eyes frightened her. But his voice was steady, it was even amused.

"Hey," he demanded, "who's been talking?"

"No one."

He frowned. He said presently, "You and Jim lunched together —"

"That's so. He's been rather — less friendly to me lately. I thought I knew why.

210

I didn't want to make any trouble between you, even unconsciously. He adores you, he is loyal. So I set him straight."

"What did he say to you?"

"Nothing that you'd mind his saying," she said instantly, "we talked mostly about his wife."

"He mentioned her?" asked Pat, incredulous.

"No, I did. I offered to go see her."

Pat smiled at her. "That's like you," he murmured, "you're a sweet kid, Kathleen —" he dropped his voice — "and mine."

"Not yet," Kathleen reminded him. She sat very straight and spoke swiftly. It had to be that way or not at all.

"I heard you talking," she told him, "to a man named Janisch. Over the telephone, by mistake. I had picked up mine and the wire was open. I hung up — but I heard something. He's an inspector, isn't he?"

Pat's jaw was set. He nodded briefly. "Go on," he said.

"I saw a letter, it was in my desk basket. Another mistake. To a man named Cameron."

"Well?"

"Just this. If you go through with this job the way you have planned it, Pat, I won't marry you. And that's final."

Chapter XIII

He looked at her with blank incredulity. Then he began to laugh and, to her utter amazement, his laughter was entirely genuine.

"But that's marvelous," he said, "that's —"

Then he saw her face. His laughter died and there was a brief silence. He asked finally:

"Did you mean that?"

"Yes, Pat." She was frightened, watching his brows draw together and the lines around his mouth become firm and frozen. She was terrified because he exercised such compulsion over her senses that she feared for her own stability. If they were alone, if he could take her in his arms . . . But they were not alone.

He said quite gently:

"But you're being silly, darling. You're — forgive me — meddling in things you don't understand at all."

"I understand enough," she said slowly. "I realize you didn't engage me as your secretary to understand. I was to fill a — decorative position. Personal secretary, social secretary. But anyone, Pat, with a modicum of intelligence can put two and two together and make —"

"Eight," he interrupted swiftly. "You're crazy, darling." He leaned back and his mouth relaxed. Laughter crept back into his eyes. He said, "Crazy and silly and I love you. But this is out of your province. Also, you are jumping at conclusions. I — we aren't out of order. We'll submit the lowest bid, I hope. We'll get the job and we'll complete it. It will be a good job, Kathleen, the best."

Looking at his open face, unable to look away from the frank clear eyes regarding her, she could almost believe him.

People came in whom she knew, sat at the next table, leaned over to speak to her, to ask how her parents were, her aunt . . .

She said presently, "We can't talk here, Pat."

"Of course not. Hannah home this evening?"

"I think not."

"Then suppose I come back with you?"

She hesitated for a moment. She had not encouraged his coming to the apartment when Hannah was not here. And she was, she knew with a tightening of her heart, afraid to have him come now, of all times. But because she was she lifted her chin a little and her eyes shone, with defiance. Not of him but of herself. She said, "All right, Pat."

"Good." He smiled at her, and beckoned the waiter. "Check, please," he said. He looked about the informal room, commented on the women's hats . . . "Screwiest I've seen for years, but I like them, they're funny and cute." He spoke of his mother . . . "She wants you to come to dinner soon . . ." and of a letter he had had from Carmela . . . "She's certainly nuts about you, Kathleen — and why not?"

He was entirely at his ease. It wasn't assumed, she thought unhappily. Either he believed in his ability to win her over or else he believed that he had nothing to fear. Or else, she thought further, he doesn't see, he can't see that what he is doing is all wrong.

Now she could remember a hundred little things. She could remember laughter in the office . . . knowing laughter. "He's put it over again, he's a wonder!" She thought of the jobs he secured for people — some of whom could be helpful to him — and of his relations, with certain politicians. "Kathleen, get me six seats for the Music Box, will you, for Dan McClaren . . . Kathleen, write so-and-so and get two more seats for the Army-Navy, Peterson wants to go." Oh, a lot of things like that. Small, seemingly unimportant favors for his friends. Then there was the checkbook in the safe, his special account. She did not see it or handle it. She drew his checks on his personal account, his mother's allowance, Carmela's, rent, school fees, servants, shops . . . and he signed them. She had as little to do with the accounts of the construction company as with that special account. She knew about it, however; she saw the statements come in each month and the checks. "Just leave it on my desk, I'll check it over," he'd said at the beginning of their association. She balanced the personal account but never the special. Once she had seen, without attaching any importance to it, the balance for one month. A large balance . . .

Why a special account? Why not just his own and the company's? For he was the company, no one else owned ten cents' worth of the Bell Construction Company.

They left the restaurant and drove to Hannah's. Inserting her key in the lock she hoped frantically that Hannah was home, after all. That she had misunderstood her, that she had returned, that she had acquired another headache. But the apartment was empty, Amelia had gone, Hannah was not there.

Rose petals from overblown blossoms

drifted silently to the polished surface of a table. She said, over her shoulder, "Go into the kitchen, Pat, mix yourself a drink, while I take off my wraps."

She came back, presently, in the little red wool frock with bands of Persian, to which Hannah had persuaded her. She had reddened her mouth and powdered her nose. She had observed, with detached interest, that her hands were shaking.

Pat was sitting on the big couch. His highball stood on a small table beside him. He had touched a match to the logs laid on the hearth and the fire had begun to burn brightly, humming to itself, informed with its own secret, radiant vitality.

"Come here," he ordered.

She came reluctantly to sit beside him, in the far corner of the couch.

"I said here!"

He reached out an arm and pulled her to him. "That's better," he said, "relax, lie back. Now then, infant, what's it all about?"

She asked, "Must we talk about it? I don't like your methods, Pat. Unless you change them, I won't marry you."

This time he did not laugh. He said soberly:

"I wish I thought you didn't mean it."

"But I do."

"You're a funny kid — and stubborn. You love me, don't you?"

"Yes," she said, "but that doesn't make any difference."

He regarded her, puzzled. His understanding of the relationship between the sexes was extremely simple. You met a girl and you desired her. You fell in love with her, as the saying went, so you had her, if possible. Sometimes you tired of her and then you had her no longer. He had always tired, until he met Kathleen Roberts.

He was in love with her, he wanted her. More than that, or rather beyond that, she stood for something besides mere desirable flesh and blood. For breeding, for background. He liked her quick mind, her quiet voice, the fine lines of her body, the contours of her face. She was what his father had called "class." Not cold, not as he understood it, sophisticated and sated, but warm, and a little unworldly, and wholly natural. Hannah — Hannah, now, she was the smart, shining, sophisticated type. He could crack with Hannah and have fun with her but he was uneasy with her, for all of that.

It had never occurred to him, once he had admitted Kathleen's attraction, that she would be open to any proposal except that of marriage. He prided himself on his knowledge of women. There were just two sharply defined kinds of women and a third, a borderline type. Kathleen was not borderline.

Also, in his understanding a woman either loved you or she didn't. She might play you for a sap, because you had money and were a spender, or she loved you for yourself. If she loved you for yourself, you could be rich or poor and it didn't matter. Nothing mattered to her except that you loved her and were faithful to her. Your business didn't matter. That was your concern. You could lie, steal, cheat and bargain, that wasn't her affair. But if you looked at another woman, if you two-timed her, she'd go after you hammer and tongs, tooth and nail, and raise hell generally because she loved you. You could do murder, you could do time, and if the relationship between you was clear she'd stand by you. You saw it every day, in the headlines. But let a guy make a misstep, interest himself in another woman, and the woman who loved him would turn him in. It was as simple as that, to him. He believed that women were concerned only with their personal, intimate feelings toward their men, their personal, intimate relationship.

That was as it should be. A man was head of his house and head of his business.

He said, "It's dog eat dog in this game."

"Need it be?"

"You don't understand, Kathleen," he told her, "it's over your head. Don't try. Can't you trust me?"

She said unhappily, "No, Pat, I can't."

"But —"

"Listen." She sat up straight, moved a little from the circle of his arms. "I'm in love with you. I can't help it. Chemistry perhaps. It doesn't signify how we explain it. I'm in love, that's all, I want to marry you, I want to be your wife and," she added, unfaltering, "I want your children. But your personal integrity is just as important to me as, say, your fidelity to me. If I marry you I must respect you. That sounds old-fashioned and rather like a bad play. But it happens to be true. That's the way I'm made, I can't help that either."

He said, "If I could make you understand —"

She said coolly:

"You do admit, then, that there is something crooked in this subway business, that if you underbid you will have to sacrifice something, someone, in order to make your profit."

There was a white line around his mouth. He said sullenly, "I don't admit it, it isn't so

. . . you're out of your head . . . someone's been talking to you." He took her shoulder in a grip that hurt and turned her around. "Who is it?"

He never trusted anyone in his own organization farther than he could see them. But he could have sworn that they were loyal enough.

"No one," she said steadily.

"I don't know what's got into you," he said. Then he stopped. He added, after a minute, "McClure?"

"Don't be absurd," said Kathleen, "what could Paul have to do with it?"

"I don't like him," said Pat, "and he doesn't like me. There's always talk about construction companies. Competition makes enemies. He could — Yes," he added, "that's it. McClure —" he laughed — "with his plays and cocktail parties! He isn't even half a man, Kathleen. Oh, I've heard him talk and heard people talk about him. Handsome, witty. The Noel Coward of America." He shrugged. "Someone said that about him the first time I met him here. He'd do anything to put me in wrong with you, he's in love with you, not with Hannah. Anyone can see that. I've always known it, it didn't matter to me, not after you told me that you loved me. New Year's Eve . . . why, it was written all over him. That play of his, the one he gave you at Christmas . . . sure, I read it . . . full of high ideals. Where will that get him? What's he done with them? Living on a couple or three hundred a month that his old man left him, eating other people's food, drinking other people's liquor, a party boy, with a lot of half-baked talky notions. They're all there, in his play."

She said, "It's a fine play, Pat, and an honest one. But he has had nothing to do with this. He knows nothing about your business."

"Oh, sure, I'll grant that. But he'd say plenty if he thought it would do me any harm."

"Leave Paul out of it," she said wearily; "this lies between you and me."

"What do you want me to do?" he asked abruptly.

"You can withdraw your bid."

"It's too late, even if I could consider it. I think you must be out of your mind, Kathleen. Do you realize the people dependent on me for their livings . . . the employment a job like this creates?"

She said, "I've been thinking of the school building."

He said angrily, "Was that our fault? It was inspected and passed. And no one was killed, except the watchman."

"That's one life," she said. "Is any job worth one life?"

"Accidents happen," he told her, "on every job."

"I know. But sometimes unnecessarily. If that very low bid is accepted, and if you make a profit —"

"I'm not in this for my health, Kathleen!"

"No," she said, "you're not. There's nothing healthy about it." She rose and looked down at him. "There isn't anything more to say, and I think you'd better go."

He came to his feet and took a step toward her, pulling her into his arms. "You think so, do you?" he murmured, and kissed her eyes and her mouth and bent his head to the little hollow in her throat.

"Let me go," she said, stifled, "please . . . I can't think clearly."

"I don't want you to," he said, in triumph. "Listen — you can't dismiss me like this. You love me, as I love you, you want me, as I want you. Forget it, Kathleen, what has it to do with us?"

"Everything," she said.

She was perfectly white. After the first blind moment she had schooled herself to an utter lack of response. She would not give him back his kisses. She stood there quietly, a statue of a woman. And presently he re-leased her.

He said, "This isn't the end, you know," and walked away. She stood where he had left her, watching him, in the little foyer, pick up his overcoat, shrug himself into it, jam his hat over his eyes. She saw him open the door and did not move.

The door closed.

Chapter XIV

The following day was Wednesday. Kathleen, ready for the office, was breakfasting when Hannah emerged from her bedroom. "Golly," said Hannah, "how do you do it?"

"Do what?"

"Get up so early. It would kill me."

Kathleen might have responded that, as she had not slept, she was glad to get up. She smiled. "I'm used to it by now," she said. "Nice party last night?"

"So-so. The usual drunks. The usual gentleman who wants to discuss the international situation with you, while emphasizing his good points by eying yours."

"Was Paul there?"

"No; he ran out on me, gone somewhere for a week or two, someone's camp in the woods. He'll freeze to death or get pneumonia. But he's on the last act and says there are too many distractions here. Sent you his best. How about you?"

"We had dinner at the Golden Louis," reported Kathleen, "and came home early."

Hannah sat down and looked at her. She said:

"Fight with the boy friend?"

"What makes you think that?"

"You look dreadful. And," added Hannah, "you've been crying."

"I'm a fool," said Kathleen. "Or am I?"

Hannah's drowsy face quickened. "That's for you to decide," she said, "I hope nothing's wrong."

She did hope it. O God, she thought, don't let there be anything wrong between her and Pat. Her supplication stemmed from a confusion of motives. She was sincerely fond of Kathleen, she desired her to be happy. Hannah had never felt that Pat was the man to fulfill this requirement. If Kathleen had also come to that conclusion, then there would be Paul to consider. Hannah thought wryly, I didn't know that there could be so much music in a second fiddle.

Kathleen pushed her plate away, drank the remainder of her black coffee. "I'll be late," she said, rising. She stopped beside Hannah, touched her shoulder, "Don't worry, I'll be all right. It's all over, Hannah."

Hannah followed her, exclamatory, questioning. But she answered merely, "I'd rather not talk about it now . . . please, Hannah." And on the way to the office she wished that she might never talk about it again. She thanked heaven that no knowledge of her engagement had reached her parents. It could be as if that had never been, on the surface. Hannah would keep her counsel, except for Paul. She herself would go see Molly Bell, she owed it to her. And she would tell Jim Haines and Sadie.

There had been nothing in any word or attitude of Pat's to reassure her. She thought, on the way to the office, if I could be blind and deaf to everything but emotions. If I could be like Hannah, who wouldn't care what Paul did or didn't do. Hannah would break with a man because of another woman, hurt vanity, a crazy quarrel, but never on a matter of principle. Lucky Hannah!

If you could stop loving people when you wanted to, when you felt them no longer worthy and yourself degraded, if you could say, Pat stands for one thing and I for another, therefore, I don't love Pat.

But she was never more aware of loving him than when she walked through the office, mechanically answering the greetings of those she encountered. She had a coward's hope that he would not be there. But he was, having come early, and the green vase on her desk was filled with lilies of the valley, shaken white bells, innocent and fragile, and perfumed with spring.

She went in as she always did and stood

beside his desk. Her heart pounded and the palms of her hands were wet. It had been such fun, every morning. Overacting the brisk secretary-boss business.

"Good morning, Mr. Bell."

"Good day, Miss Roberts. You are looking rather pretty this morning."

"Thank you. Here are your appointments for the day."

"How splendid. Let me see. Dinner with Kathleen. That's an appointment I must be sure to keep, Miss Roberts."

Like that, with variations and laughter. "Why can't I kiss you good morning, young woman? Don't you read the magazines or go to the movies? Every well-trained secretary kisses her boss at nine A.M. sharp."

Not today. This was another morning and it wasn't good. He was standing by the windows when she came in and swung around, his eyes eager and anxious. It nearly killed her, that look, the expression of a small boy dreading a scolding, a small boy who has been careful not to step on cracks all the way to the office in the bright belief that a miracle will occur and things will be as they have been.

"Kathleen!"

She said, "You didn't expect me? The lilies are lovely, Pat."

"I didn't know what to think . . . I'm glad you like them." He came closer, took her hands. "You haven't slept."

"No, Pat."

"I didn't," he told her, "it was hell. Well, we've both slept on it — or not slept on it, rather. You — you can't mean it, Kathleen."

"I haven't changed," she said.

"But you have, you can't stand there and tell me that you love me yet won't marry me because you don't approve of the way in which I conduct my business. Darling, it doesn't make sense."

"It does to me."

He said, still unbelieving, "You've got to listen to me." And while her heart cried out that, of course, she must listen, that it was not fair to him if she did not, that she must give him every chance, he made his mistake, he said the one irrevocable, revealing thing. *"You haven't any proof,"* he said.

Having said it, he laid all the proof she needed in her hands.

She was silent, looking at him with level, tragic eyes. He caught himself up then, blustered, stormed.

"Be quiet," she said, as she might have spoken to a child, "everyone will hear."

"I don't care!"

"You must." She stopped, considering her

words. She said, "I can't stay on here, Pat, it's an impossible situation. I'll find someone else for you, before I leave, someone suitable."

"But —" He looked at her, aghast. He asked simply, "Do you mean I'm not to see you any more?"

She said gently, "We can't be friends, can we?" Saying that, she realized that they had never been. Lovers, almost from the first, headlong lovers. Never friends, never growing from the gentler cooler relationship into the happy violence, the warmth of loving.

"But," he asked, "what am I to tell —"

Like a boy who has asked his friends to a party and then has to tell them the party will not be given. Her heart constricted for him. If she could look at him calmly, with detachment, with dislike, asking herself how in the world could I have loved him, but she could not. For she knew why, and why, God help her, she still loved him.

"So few know," she said, "we've told no one except your mother and Carmela. I'd rather talk to your mother myself, Pat. Then, of course, Hannah and Paul."

"He'll be delighted," said Pat bitterly.

She went on, "He won't be delighted, Pat, if I'm unhappy." She added, "Here in the office, I told Sadie and Jim Haines. I'll talk to them too. It will be easier for you."

She left his office and shut the door and went about her usual routine. At lunchtime she saw Sadie.

"Going my way?"

"Sure . . . why?"

"Let's dunk a bun together, shall we?"

At the marble-topped table Kathleen said soberly:

"Remember what I asked you to keep a secret, Sadie?"

"Who wouldn't?" said Sadie.

"It's still a secret, but in reverse." She tried to smile at the other girl's startled expression. "I mean, it's all off . . . and I'm quitting."

"I can't — I don't believe it. But why, Kathleen . . . or shouldn't I ask?"

"It doesn't matter why. It was a mistake, that's all. We found it out in time," she said, astonished that the clichés came so easily. "I want you to help me."

"Gee, Kathleen, anything I can do —"

"If you knew someone to take my place who can handle the work? It hasn't been much work, to be honest: engagements to enter, phone calls to answer, people to let in or keep out, a checkbook to balance. You must know someone, Sadie. If you do, I'll talk to her."

"I know at least eight," said Sadie; "I'll go

through them with a fine comb. Kathleen, I'm — sorry."

"Thanks," said Kathleen, "I know you mean that."

She looked with real affection at Sadie's dark, clever face. She wanted to say, Sadie, in your job you must know a lot about the Bell Construction Company. I'm not asking you to talk out of turn, but, tell me, do you approve of their methods?

She couldn't. She knew as surely as if she had seen it how Sadie's expression would change, tighten, close against her, a door shutting. She was no longer of them — if, indeed, she ever had been. She was an outsider.

Her opportunity to speak to Jim Haines came later in the day, just before she was leaving. She had not seen Pat since before luncheon. He had left the office then. She was shutting up her desk, thinking her own unhappy thoughts, when Haines came in. He asked, "Just going?"

"On the verge," she told him, smiling.

He said awkwardly, "I hate to ask you this, but Sunday . . . I'm going to see her Sunday, and I wondered —"

"Of course," she told him instantly, "what time?"

"Sure I'm not breaking up your day? I

mean —" he looked toward Pat's door — "you'd have a date Sunday, I thought, sure thing."

"No," she said, "no, I haven't a date." The office was quiet. Beyond the closed door they could hear the voices of the girls, getting ready to leave. She added, "I have to tell you something. Jim, it's all over."

"You and Pat?" he said, incredulous.

She nodded, turning her eyes away. He took a step close, seized her wrist. "Why you — you —" he began, in a still, hot fury.

"Jim!"

He dropped her hand. "I'm sorry," he muttered.

"That's all right," said Kathleen, nursing her hand.

"I understand. You're fond of him, and not of me. Anything that hurts him hurts you. It's perfectly comprehensible."

He said, "I don't suppose you'll want to go Sunday."

"Haven't I said I would?" she asked angrily. "Don't be stupid. That has nothing to do with my personal affairs, Jim!"

"O. K.," he said briefly, and turned away. "Three o'clock."

When she reached home that night she found Hannah arranging roses — masses of them, white and waxed, pale yellow like thick country cream, deep sunset pink, and dark, dark red, dewy, glowing, the shape and color of a remembered kiss.

"Oh," said Kathleen, "how lovely."

"They're yours," said Hannah, "every last one, drat 'em." She put her finger in her mouth. "My heart's blood."

"Pat?" asked Kathleen.

"I assumed it. Lavish gent." She shot an oblique look at her friend. "Maybe you're making a mistake."

Kathleen was reading the card. She tore it up, dropped it in the wastebasket. "I'd already made it," she said, "worse luck."

"It's none of my business, Toots," said Hannah briskly, standing back to look at the last vase, "but it's dangerous to quarrel. I used to think it was fun but I know better now. Even a little one's dangerous . . . like chucking a match in a forest. You think it will burn out. But it doesn't. There's a conflagration, and where's your forest?"

Kathleen picked one of the shorter stemmed roses from a crystal bowl and drew it through her fingers. She said, "It isn't a quarrel."

"Your mind's made up?"

"I'm afraid so."

"And the peace offering?"

Kathleen looked at the rose in her hand.

She said, "You can't buy confidence, not even with beauty."

"Don't talk like an eighteen-ninety novel," advised Hannah in exasperation. "Either you love the sap or you don't. If you love him you'll go to town for him, all the way. If you don't, the hell with him."

"I wish I found it that simple," said Kathleen.

Pat's card had said, "I'm coming to talk to you, tonight."

Kathleen went into her room. There was mail there for her, a letter from her mother. She sat on the edge of the bed and read it. They had left the cruise ship, they were staying in Italy. In the spring they would go to England. "So much war talk," her mother wrote in her thin, large hand, "it's terrifying. You hear it on every hand, and in, I may add, every tongue." She added that she was glad to get off the boat, for good, and that everything was all right. "Your father looks marvelous. He thinks he's even better than he is and I'm having a time holding him down. But we've met a thousand people we know, there is always someone coming to see us, asking us out. It's hard to save his strength. I'm so anxious to see Elsie and Butch again. I'd hoped they'd join us, but at present it doesn't look like it. Darling, your letters are such a joy. But you don't say how you are." Her father had added, in his beautiful copper-plate hand, "We wish you were with us, as the postcards say. How about changing your mind, quitting your job and coming over?"

That would be a solution: Italy and sunlight, and later, the hills and moors of England and the look of the far blue sea. Butch and his old pipe and twinkling blue eyes and the dogs at his heels, and her aunt, always the same, sturdy, dependable, incredibly frank.

You can't run away, she told herself, it would be the same anywhere. If I ran too far I'd begin to wonder, was it a mistake after all? I'd want to come back, I'd want to see him again, I'd want to be sure, and I wouldn't be sure.

She went out presently and Hannah asked, "How about a drink? I'm eating at home for a wonder."

"I'd like one," said Kathleen. When Amelia brought the shaker, she poured the two glasses and handed one to Hannah. "Let's drink," she suggested, "to something that wasn't to be."

"Oh, for heaven's sake!" said Hannah, in disgust. She drank, nevertheless. She asked, "What are you going to do now? Stay on?"

"Until I find someone to take my place."

"Emotionally or officially?"

"Either . . . seriously, in the office. And I'm going to get another job."

"Rosa will give you one," said Hannah, "her secretary's leaving the first of the month. Why not go see her? It will be different from the Bell Construction Company and Rosa's no glamour boss. She'll beat you down in salary too, but it's a job. If you like I'll speak to her tomorrow. I wouldn't be surprised if she took you on. She likes her hired help to have connections. Sammy would be delighted; he'd say, Oh, yes, my mother's secretary, niece of the Duke of Ainslee."

"Don't be idiotic."

"It isn't so silly as it sounds."

Kathleen said, "Pat's coming here tonight. I don't know where to get him to head him off. If I know him he won't have gone home where I could reach him. Do me a favor, Hannah."

"And go to the movies?"

"And *don't* go to the movies."

"All right," said Hannah, "but don't expect me to keep out of even a private fight. I love 'em."

Pat rang the bell at half past eight. Hannah opened the door for him. He spoke to her, smiling, in the foyer. "Buy you a lunch some-day if you'll remember an engagement, Han-nah," he said.

"No can do," said Hannah.

It would have been awkward except for Hannah, although it should have been awkward because of her. She talked of everything and nothing, a new perfume, scandalously alluring, a new frock . . . "divine and costs like the national debt" . . . and of a new play . . . "Here today and gone tomorrow. As the curtain fell on the second act, rigor mortis set in."

Kathleen said little, leaning back in a cor-ner of the couch. And Pat's retorts were hardly brilliant. Conversation languished and died, despite Hannah's valiant efforts. She viewed its corpse in silence. Then she said, shrugging:

"Maybe I'd better clear out."

"It's a good idea," said Pat, without a flicker.

"No," said Kathleen firmly.

Hannah looked from the man's dark face to Kathleen's marked pallor. She said re-signedly, "Well, why not battle for an audi-ence? I'll referee."

"That's a better idea," said Pat suddenly. "Look here, Hannah, you know your way around."

"None better," she admitted.

"Kathleen's gone crazy," he said. "She says she loves me . . . there's no need for me to tell you how I feel about her . . . but she's broken our engagement because she doesn't like what she believes to be my business methods."

Hannah's little jaw dropped. She looked at Kathleen and asked:

"So help me, Kate, is this true?"

"It's true," said Kathleen, without moving. If Pat decided to drag Hannah into it, it wasn't her fault. But resentment rose hot within her.

"You're nuts," said Hannah. "Why should you care . . . about anything? I mean . . ."

"I know what you mean," said Kathleen. "It doesn't happen to be the way I look at things."

"If I loved a man," said Hannah, who did, "and he got his living by blackmailing innocent girls, robbing women and orphans, I wouldn't approve, I might even ride the devil out of him about it, but I'd stick."

"Bravo!" cried Pat.

Kathleen looked at the other girl with wide, miserable eyes. "I'm sorry, Hannah. I know you think I'm a reincarnation of Elsie Dinsmore, but there it is. I can't help it."

"You go home," Hannah ordered Pat,

238

"and let me talk to her."

He went, without reluctance.

When she was alone with Kathleen she said, "You needn't, if you don't want to . . . it's not my business. Only, I'm curious. Do you mean to tell me that you think Pat's crooked?"

"I think he's dishonest," said Kathleen.

"Why doll it up? Crooked's as good a word. Do you know it?"

"No," said Kathleen, "I don't if by knowing you mean black-and-white, actual proof. But I know enough —"

"Most big business," said Hannah gently, "isn't conducted along the lines of the Golden Rule. You may even find that out at Eloise, Inc."

"I'm not marrying Eloise, Inc.," Kathleen reminded her, smiling faintly.

"And not marrying Pat?"

"That's right."

"Yet you still love him?"

Kathleen got to her feet and threw her cigarette into the fire. She stood there, looking at the dancing flames.

"I love him," she said quietly, "that is, most of me loves him. I love the way he walks and his voice, and his eyes and his hands, and —" She stopped and Hannah saw her tremble, as if she were chilled. "My body loves him, and I haven't an atom of respect for him, Hannah. I thought I had. I thought I loved him because he was different, because he was honest and decent and frank . . . even his faults seemed that. But my mind rejects that now, and him. There's no future in just loving, Hannah, and no percentage."

She turned from the fireplace, went into her room and shut the door. Hannah did not follow her, until much later when, tossing her novel aside, snapping out the lights, she stood at the door for a moment and heard Kathleen crying. She said, "Kate?" very softly and her fingers touched the knob. But the door was locked.

On Sunday Kathleen drove to the place where Jim Haines's wife lived her dim, distracted life behind bars. It was a pretty grim sort of place, very institutional. They did not talk much during the long drive. Once, when they were nearly there, she spoke to him, keeping her eyes ahead. "Jim . . . about Pat and me. I have to tell you this because I felt I owed it to you to tell you how things were between us then. They've changed, because of incompatibility, as they say in the divorce court. I made a bad mistake, Jim. You mustn't blame either of us if you can help it."

He answered, his eyes on the road, the little car running free and swift under his guidance:

"I *thought* he was crazy."

"You didn't like me," she said gently. "You didn't want him to like me."

"I knew it would end like this. Something new for you," he said, "something different. Then I suppose you got thinking about your people. Social register, aren't they? Pat's old man came over in the steerage."

"That's unkind," said Kathleen, "and it has nothing to do with what happened between us. Do you think I'd care if Pat came over in the steerage, do you think I wouldn't be proud of him if he'd fought his way up — honestly?"

The car jerked a little. Jim said, after a moment:

"Sure, I thought you'd mind. But the other day . . . when you said you were going to make him happy. I believed you then."

"I meant it," she said.

"What happened?"

"I can't talk about it, Jim," she said. "I can be loyal too."

She went with him into the big gray building carrying her package of bright picture magazines and her heart shrinking with fear. Fear of the unknown, of the abnormal. She was not prepared for the young woman who was brought to meet them in a little bare reception room under the escort of a quiet, middle-aged attendant. The attendant spoke to Jim. "She's been looking forward to seeing you. She's been quite lucid lately, Mr. Haines. The disturbed periods are farther apart and less violent."

His haggard face lighted with a radiance unendurable to see. He said, "Francesca!" and put out his arms and his wife ran into them and clung to him, sobbing. "I thought you weren't coming any more," she said.

Dark and slim and very lovely. She looked young, as if the years had passed her by. But her eyes were strange. Kathleen drew aside with the attendant. The woman said, "She's like this sometimes. Very gentle and easy to handle."

"I always come, honey," said Jim, smoothing the black, silken hair, cut short and close to the little head.

She drew herself away and looked at Kathleen. "Who's that?" she demanded. Her voice was high, like a child's.

"Miss Roberts," Jim answered, "she came to see you, to bring you some magazines."

"She's pretty," murmured Francesca. She looked at Kathleen with friendly eyes. Then they clouded. She drew back, against her husband, stammered, "She — she's your girl now, Jim?" pitifully. Kathleen's throat closed and her eyes filled.

"No," said Jim quickly, "of course not. You're my girl, all the girl I'll ever have. She's just a friend."

But Francesca was crying now, clutching at him, looking at Kathleen with hostility. The attendant moved close. And Jim said desperately, his eyes asking Kathleen's pardon, "She's Pat's girl, dear. *Pat's.*"

There was a sudden stunned silence.

"Pat's girl," repeated Francesca. "Pat's?" She spoke musingly, she spoke sanely. "Why, that's awfully funny!" She came closer to Kathleen, looking at her, her eyes very bright. Then she said, on a high sudden note, "But I was his girl too, of course I was!" She began to laugh. "That's it," she said, "only Jim didn't know. I was afraid to tell him. Pat said he wouldn't. I loved Jim."

Haines's voice burst from him, it did not sound human. He spoke his wife's name, twice.

"Jim," Kathleen cried, "she doesn't know what she's saying!"

"Make her keep quiet," said Francesca. "I don't like her. If she's Pat's girl, she'll be yours, like I was." She began to laugh.

Jim said slowly, calmly:

"At first he came to see her, with me. But she was so much worse when he came. So he stopped. She's never mentioned his name before."

His face changed. He was utterly livid. He shook off the restraining hand the attendant put on his arm, took his wife by the shoulders and shook her. Her face was mad and lax. She went on laughing. He demanded, "Tell me about Pat — tell me about Pat."

But now she was crying as well as laughing, struggling, blaspheming. Kathleen felt physically ill. The attendant said sharply, "That's enough, Francesca!" and took her away from her husband. She spoke to her in an undertone. Leading her away, she said, over her shoulder, "I'm sorry, Mr. Haines, but you've upset her dreadfully."

Jim groped for a chair and sat down. They could hear Francesca shrieking down the corridor. Kathleen put her hands to her ears. Jim said dully:

"All these years . . . *Pat!*"

Chapter XV

The dreadful sounds in the corridor died away. There were other sounds, normal, human: heels clicking by, a snatch of conversation, and then a face looking in for a moment, curiously.

Haines muttered, "I need a drink."

Kathleen touched his shoulder. She said quietly, "Let's get out of here and find one, Jim."

His car was parked with dozens of others in the severe semicircle before the institution. Walking toward it, she saw that he staggered. His face was something that she would not soon forget. She was so torn with pity for him and for the girl — she looked like a girl, one thought of her as very young — that she did not now consider what she had heard, in relation to herself.

She asked, "Want me to drive?"

"No, I'm all right," he told her dully.

She was frightened when he took the wheel, backed out, pulled away. It was suicide to let him drive, she thought, but she did not wish to irritate him by arguing. She sat still, trying to relax, her hands folded.

Snow and ice had remained from the last storm but the highways were clear. She saw, with relief, that he drove steadily, without effort.

He said, "I know a place, it isn't much."

"That's all right, let's go there."

He did not speak again until they had reached the sprawling roadhouse, plastered with signs, built like a monstrous log cabin. There were a number of cars outside. When they went in, it was dark, and smelled of heavy cooking, smoke, and liquor. He walked ahead of her like a man in a nightmare and found a table.

People sat in groups, talked, laughed, drank, and ate. The walls and ceiling were latticed, laced with artificial leaves and roses. There was a big fireplace and a great radio playing loudly. Someone at the next table said, "I wouldn't miss Charlie McCarthy for *anything!*"

The cloth was clean, the silver. A waiter sidled up. "Straight rye, double," said Jim. The waiter looked at Kathleen and she shook her head. "Coffee for me," she ordered, "a large cup and black, please."

"Hurry," Jim told the waiter, on a note of urgency.

He did not speak while they waited. He simply sat there staring ahead of him. No, not ahead; into the present, into the past. She tried to think. She tried to make excuses. Now it was coming home to her, what it meant to her, what it must mean. But Francesca Haines was not in her sane mind. You could discount everything she said, you had to discount it.

The waiter brought the drink and then the coffee. Jim drank, and set down the glass. He began to talk.

"I met her," he said, "at a block party. You've never been to one? Lots of lights . . . and people. It was summer, there was dancing. She was —" he halted and went on — "I'd seen her before, of course, we'd been to school together. But this was the first time I'd met her really. You know what I mean, maybe."

He stopped. "I know," said Kathleen softly. She did not want him to talk in that dead even voice while he stared at nothing. She did not want to hear what he had to say. She must. Let him talk, for his own sake.

"I didn't know Pat," he went on, "except by sight. I saw him for the first time at the wedding. I thought he was swell. His people and hers were related."

He beckoned the waiter. "Make it the same," he said.

The coffee was scalding hot. Kathleen set

the thick cup down again and waited until it cooled.

"I knew there had been someone," he said, "before I came along. She'd been in love with him, he'd treated her badly. She wouldn't talk about it. I didn't make her, I never asked her his name."

He was silent for a long time. The waiter brought the second drink.

He spoke again, wiping his mouth carelessly on the back of his hand.

"After — it happened the Old Man, Pat's father, sent for me and gave me the job. Later I learned that Pat had persuaded him to. He said I must have a chance."

He laughed and Kathleen shuddered.

"That's all," he said. For the first time he looked at her. He added, as if he realized for the first time who sat there beside him, "I couldn't stand you around, you knew that. I thought, if Pat marries this dame out of the top drawer, he's in for a beating. After you talked to me that day I told myself I was wrong, he's a lucky guy. But then you told me, as if it didn't mean much, that it was all off. I thought, I was taken in, after all. I thought, If she hurts him . . . but then I figured, if I was right the first time, she'd hurt him worse if she married him. Well, you were smart."

"Jim," said Kathleen, "never mind me. I don't matter. You aren't going to believe . . . ? She didn't know what she was saying, she isn't like other people."

"She's crazy," he said, "and you don't know anything about loving. She's crazy, and she's shut up away from me and I'll never have her again. She was — she liked to laugh. Like a kid. She liked keeping house, like a kid. She'd make something new to surprise me, a dress, a new dish. She had wanted to go on the stage, and she did for a little while. He helped her. But when we fell in love, she didn't care about the stage any more. She *did* love me, you heard her say so."

"Of course, she loved you, Jim."

"That was it," he said. "Oh, I know what the doctors said: her mother was like that after she was born. But she was gentle and quiet except when she was laughing or angry. Then there was a spark in her, she was beautiful then. She would have been all right, except — I can see it now — except because of the way she must have worried. For fear I'd find out. He used to come to the flat, after we were married. He'd take us out, now and again, to a show, supper. Not often. I'd say, 'He's a swell guy, isn't he?' and she'd say, 'Yes, sure, sure, he's swell.' "

He beckoned the waiter again. Kathleen

said, "Oh, no!" in despair, but he did not listen.

"That's it. She was sick, before the baby was born —" he choked a little on that — "dragging herself around, pretending she was all right. All the time she was thinking about Pat. About what had happened. What *must* have happened. When she was a kid, really. Seventeen perhaps, eighteen. She was almost twenty when we were married. She might have thought, I'll say something, he'll know. Maybe that was why she fought against taking the ether. She had the taint in her blood. She didn't know it, they'd never told her, they told her her mother was dead. She would have been all right," he said stubbornly, "if — if — *God!*" He slammed his fist down on the table and the empty glass jumped. "It needed just that," he said slowly, "to tip her over."

The waiter came with the third drink and Kathleen said, "Jim, don't drink it, please!"

"Why? I'm all right." He drank it, more slowly. "I don't even feel the stuff. I never do at first." He looked at her with his haunted eyes. "I start drinking, I don't feel it. I think about her and I start —"

She said, "Why? You aren't helping her or yourself."

"If there could be another woman," he

said, looking away, "it would be easier. Just for a while, to help, to make you forget. But I can't stand other women, they sicken me."

He was silent. He set down the empty glass. "I should kill him, I suppose," he said quietly. He looked at her and his eyes were the saddest things she had ever seen. They were full of tears.

She said rapidly:

"You're jumping at conclusions." That sounded familiar; yes, of course, Pat had said it to her. "You know — nothing. What if she was in love with him as a youngster? There might have been no more to it than that. When she loved you she forgot everything else. What happened afterwards would have happened anyway. Jim, try to think clearly. She had nothing, perhaps, with which to reproach herself. But today, when she remembered, it was distorted in her mind. Believe that. Go to the doctors, talk to them."

He asked stupidly, "You don't want me to kill him?"

"Oh, Jim!" She could have cried for his stupidity, his bewildered, strained mind. "What good will it do? You're all she has . . . all she has left in the world, all she must cling to. Can't you see that?"

He said, with sudden violence:

"Damn him!" He swore steadily for a

minute. She sat still, listening, longing to put her hands over her ears as she had a little while ago. "I've always done his dirty work," he said, "he's crooked as a corkscrew, he's no good. A lot of good-looking front. He looks at you with those honest blue eyes, and you think, no matter what he does he's right."

The tears crawled down his face. The hovering waiter looked distressed. Kathleen put her hand over the lax hand on the table. She ordered:

"Look at me."

He did so. He said, after a moment, "So you loved him too."

"Yes," she told him, "that's right. Perhaps I still do. I did, until a little while ago. Now what I feel I don't know. I don't want to know."

"All these years," he said as he had said in the reception room, "being grateful, thinking he was the swellest guy on earth." He moved his shoulders. "You won't get shut of him that easy. I could do it for us both."

He was silent again. Then he said, and laughed, "I can't move. Damned silly, isn't it?"

Kathleen beckoned the waiter. "Stay here with him," she said, low, but Jim Haines did not even try to listen. "Don't bring him anything more, stall him if he orders. I'm going to telephone."

She went out to a pay station and shut herself in. Close, evil-smelling. She called Hannah's number. Hannah would be home, there were people coming for cocktails.

"Hannah? This is Kate. Can you tell me where Paul is? It's important."

Hannah said, "Off with the old? No, I won't tell you."

"Hannah, listen to me. It isn't for myself. It's for someone else. I can't tell you about it . . . not now . . . but it's vital." She was pleading, she was almost crying. "I need his help — for someone. You said he'd gone off, in the woods somewhere. Was it to that place on Long Island he owns?"

"It's a shack," said Hannah, "in Suffolk County, on Peconic Bay. Woods all around. You turn off just beyond Mattituck. It's called Forest Point. Kate, what's happened?"

"I haven't time. Don't worry about me, I'll be late getting back."

Jim was still at the table. His head was on his arms, he seemed to sleep.

She paid the waiter and tipped him. She said, "Help me get him to the car."

They got him out there together, and people watched curiously, the tall, very thin, very drunken man out on his feet, Kathleen in her fur coat and little hat, her face firm with determination, the big waiter in his white apron.

"Three double ryes," commented the waiter. "Out like a light."

"He's had a shock," Kathleen said.

"I'll say he has!"

They hoisted him into the back seat, put a rug over him. Kathleen got in front. She thanked the man, who stood there looking after her as she pulled away. She thought, If only he'll stay out!

They were already on Long Island, but they had far to drive. Twice she lost her way. It grew dark early, there was a scattered snow flurry. It grew colder, the snow froze on the windshield.

It was late when they reached Mattituck. Jim had wakened, thrashed around in the back seat, risen to his feet, fumbled with the door. She slowed, stopped, spoke to him sharply. "Sit down, we're almost there."

"I've got to have a drink."

"You'll have one soon," she said.

The road to the cottage was rutted with ice, the car slued and slipped. If he wasn't there? She hadn't thought of that before. Her breath caught in her throat.

Slue and slip, bump, slue and slip. Trees,

pine trees, clustered together. Stars, now that it was not snowing, and a blackness beyond which might be water. Lights, the lights of the cottage.

She drew a deep gasping, sobbing breath and stopped the car. The windows were uncurtained, there was a porch. The house was small, one story. The trees had been cleared. Paul's car stood there, a rug over the radiator. She could see him moving about inside. There was a fireplace, bright with flame. She was cold, she realized, and began to shake with cold and fatigue.

He had come to the door. She cried, "Paul!" and his voice answered.

"Kate?" he said. "My God, what are you — ?"

"Don't talk now, help me get him inside."

Four rooms. A living room, the fireplace, a couch, some chairs. A kitchen table, a typewriter on it, manuscript paper scattered about. Beyond, a little bedroom, a bathroom. On the other side a kitchen.

Haines was out again. They got him inside, put him on the couch. The door shut them in together.

"Who is he?"

"Jim Haines."

"I thought it was Bell," said Paul. "He's very drunk."

He wore corduroys and a flannel shirt. His face was thinner than she remembered. It was brave. He said, "Give me that coat, you're shivering. Have you had anything to eat?"

"No." She sat down docilely, let him take her coat and hat. She pulled off her gloves and held her hands to the flame.

"You must try to understand," she said. And he nodded, looking from her to the ghastly face of the other man.

"I haven't any right to tell you this," she went on, "and I can't tell you all of it. This man, Haines, is in Pat's office. His wife is in an asylum." She told him why, briefly, and saw his face twitch. "He — drinks, periodic drinking, twice a year perhaps. Pat —" she faltered over the name and his heart quickened questioningly — "Pat knows, ahead. Lets him off, takes him back. He was rather hostile to me, at first; lately we've been better friends. I went with him today to see his wife. Something upset him." She looked up, her rain-gray eyes pleading. "Something she said. He wanted a drink, I thought it best to humor him. We went to a roadhouse, and — this happened. I called Hannah, to ask where you were."

"Why didn't you take him home?"

"I was afraid to — I needed help."

"Where does he live?"

"On the Island . . . not far from town."

"Kate, you're —" He couldn't say "crazy," not after what she had told him.

She said, "He's got an idea about Pat. He — he wants to kill him, Paul."

"That makes two of us," he said grimly.

"Please, Paul —" she made a gesture toward him — "please. This is serious. I can't tell you everything," she said, her mouth a firm, red line, "but you must help me. You must keep him here until he's sober. I'm afraid that, after this, he'll go off again."

"Then what?"

"There must be something we can do."

"Why didn't you go to Pat?" asked Paul.

She said quietly, "Our engagement has been broken."

There was a silence. Then he said, "I see." He looked at her. "I'll get you something to eat," he said. "There's some hamburger left over, and if I do say it, I make a mean pot of coffee and elegant fried potatoes."

She sat there, too tired to move. She watched Jim, sleeping deeply as if he were dead. Once his face alarmed her and she leaned over to take his pulse.

After a while she got up and dragged herself into the little bathroom, scattered with heavy masculine towels and shaving things.

When she came back Paul had pulled a table close to the fire.

He sat back, smoking, watching her eat. He asked, "What about you?"

"Me?"

"Getting back to town."

"It doesn't matter. I thought if only I could get him here . . ."

"He'll come to life," said Paul, trying to smile, "and want to murder me too."

"Don't say that, Paul, don't." She shivered, pushed her plate away.

"It's snowing again," he announced, going to the windows, "and rather harder this time."

She pulled her coat around her shoulders and went out with him. The stars were obscured, the snow swirled from every direction, the wind was rising, singing through the pines.

"You've a flat," said Paul, exploring with a flashlight in his hand.

"I thought so when I bumped over that last section of road," she told him.

He took her arm and hurried her into the house. "You can't drive back alone," he said, "flat or no flat. You could take my car, of course, but the storm's rising, there have been warnings on the radio."

She said, looking at Jim, "When he wakes

and finds himself in a strange place with you
—" She looked up. "I'll stay here and drive
back early tomorrow morning."

Jim woke presently and sat up, his head in
his hands. He raised it, looked around. He
muttered, "Where's Pat? Got to find . . ."
He focused his eyes on Kathleen. "Oh, it's
you. I feel like hell."

She sat down beside him and took his
hand.

"I brought you here," she said clearly, "to
— to a friend. This is Paul McClure. There's
a storm, Jim, so we're going to stay here
tonight."

"I want a drink," he said, not caring.

"He'd better have it," advised Paul; "sometimes it works." He came forward with a bottle and a glass, poured a short one. "Here
you are, feller," he said.

Jim drank it and leaned back against the
cushions. He said presently, "I feel — better."

"That's right," said Paul quietly, "you lean
back there, try and sleep again."

"Tell me about the play," said Kathleen
presently.

"It's all but finished. There's a night ahead
of us. Want to hear it?"

"I'd like to," she said.

"How about making yourself comfortable?

I've an extra pair of pajamas and a robe, some nice woolly socks and slippers a mile too big."

It was a strange night, with the storm beating outside and Jim there on the couch. Sometimes he slept, groaned, snored, spoke brokenly, wildly. Sometimes he was quiet, sleeping or awake.

Kathleen, in the warm robe and the pajamas, sat beside the fire in a big shabby chair and listened to the play. The snow thudded and hissed against the windows. The fire burned. Now and then Paul leaned forward to put another log in it.

When he had finished reading he said, "Well, that's that. Needs a lot of polishing."

"What have you named it?" she asked.

"*Remembering sorrow.*"

She said, "I can't talk about it. It's — fine. Better even than the other, your first."

He asked, as if in desperation, "Is it honest enough? Or do the words make it false? I've a wretched facility, Kate."

"It's honest," she said, and found her cheeks were wet.

"You're tired, I should be drawn and quartered." He picked her up in his arms and carried her into the bedroom. He put her down on the sheetless bed, drew blankets and quilt over her, opened the window on a crack. "Go to sleep," he said, "I'll stay with Haines."

She slept, almost at once. Once toward dawn she woke, frightened, wondering where she was. She heard voices next door, Paul's voice, and Jim's, talking steadily, as if they had been talking for hours. She closed her eyes and slept again.

Chapter XVI

Morning was clear, a pale-blue sky, brilliant sun, no wind, and a whiteness over all. Kathleen woke to the smell of coffee and called out, sitting up in bed.

Paul came to the door with a frying pan in his hand. He asked, "How'd you sleep?"

"Woke up just once, right before dawn."

"We came through once," he told her. "I got Jim into the bathroom. He was pretty sick. I was sure we'd wake you."

"Not me. Like a log. I'll be out of here in a moment." She added, low, "How is he?"

"O. K.," said Paul briefly, and closed the door.

She dressed, washed, and went out. Her handbag was in the living room and she opened it to look at herself in the mirror, powder her nose and redden her lips. The front door opened and Jim came in. He wore an old mackinaw of Paul's and his arms were full of kindling. "I think it's dry," he said, "it was under the shed."

He saw Kathleen and the kindling started to slip from his arms.

"Watch yourself," she said cheerfully,

"and good morning."

"I'm ashamed."

Paul came from the kitchen. "Come and get it," he told them. "There's only one egg. That's for Kate. Coffee though, bacon, and some bread and butter."

They sat in the kitchen and ate and drank. No one spoke except to comment on the weather. Then Paul pushed back his cup.

"Haines and I have been talking," he said, "and I've an idea."

Kathleen looked at Jim swiftly. He was ghastly in the sunshine, red-rimmed eyes, a beginning beard, his face white and drawn. But his regard was that of a sane, unhappy man.

He said, "I told him how — what you did for me. I've also said I can't go back to the office."

His eyes added, I haven't said why.

"It seems," said Paul cheerfully, "that he doesn't like our mutual friend any more. We didn't go into the reasons. They don't matter. So he'll send in his resignation."

Jim began to tremble. He said, "I can't see him again." He looked at Kathleen in stark appeal. "I'm — afraid."

"I'll tell him," said Kathleen quietly. "Will you leave it to me — how much or how little?"

263

He nodded and Paul said briskly:

"He tells me he's all right for money."

"What would I do with money," said Jim, "the way I've lived?"

"I know a place," said Paul, "he'll like it. It's in Virginia. We'll drive down there and get him settled. It's a good place, good doctors, good everything. Put him on his feet again. He doesn't want to go, much, but I've persuaded him. After he's O. K., I think I know of a job. In Pennsylvania . . . uncle of mine."

"Perhaps it would be best," said Jim. His regard swerved to Kathleen. "I could come back," he said, "and see her — often."

Paul said, stacking the dishes:

"It will work out. We'll stop by his house, pick up his things, go to the bank. I'm at a loose end. Play's done, I feel let down. Don't want to touch it for the final rewrite for a while. Thought you'd keep it for me, Kate, till then. Meantime, you take my car and get back to town. Stop at the garage at the crossroads, send a man out to fix that flat. When you're through with my car you can put it up." He gave her the name and address of the town garage where he kept it. "I'll come back by train and give you a ring."

What had they said to each other, in the graying dawn? How much had Jim told, how much had Paul guessed?

She started back to town, driving Paul's car, about nine o'clock that morning. Paul stayed outside, waiting, while she said good-bye to Jim.

She said, "I couldn't leave you there and I couldn't take you home and go away not knowing what had happened."

He said, "You don't know how grateful . . . perhaps I can show you."

"Jim, do you remember what you said last night?"

"Forget it," he said, "he isn't worth it. I'll get hold of myself, somehow. The bottom's dropped out. It would be easier to drink myself to death. I'll take the hard way. Let me say this . . . the hard way for you, for him too." He jerked his shoulder toward the door. "I didn't know there were men like him."

Paul came to the car with her, hatless, smiling. She warned, leaning out, "You'll take cold."

"Not me. Give my love to Hannah. Take care of yourself."

"I won't try to thank you. I just thought, shelter for the night, advice, all that. I was at the end of my rope, Paul. I thought of you."

"That's the good part of it," he said.

"We'll talk when I come back. I'm not doing anything. Haines will be all right. He hasn't known much about anything except hell for a long time. We'll see him through this."

She drove off, smiling, her heart warmed. But presently she must think of what she had to say to Pat.

She stopped at the garage to send the man back, she stopped along the road for a sandwich and coffee. When she reached the office she parked the car on a side street and went in swiftly, aware that eyes followed her and that there were whispers.

She shut her own door behind her, Pat's flew open and he was there, big, vital, almost beside himself. "Where in hell have you been?" he demanded. "When you didn't show up — Jim hasn't come either. What's this all about?"

She said, standing by her desk:

"He isn't coming, ever. He asked me to tell you that."

"Don't be mysterious," said Pat. He looked bad, talked loudly. He came, took her in his arms, and she suffered it. She had no love for him, she had nothing for him, yet her senses remembered and responded and she loathed herself.

She detached herself and stood back.

"All the way here," she said, "I've been

thinking what I should say — how much, how little. It has to be much. Yesterday I went with Jim to the place where his wife is kept. She was quite . . . reasonable at first, quite happy. A gentle, foolish little thing. Then she wanted to know who I was. Pat's girl, Jim said, after a while, to reassure her. And then she — she —"

"Well, what?" demanded Pat impatiently. "What's this to do with us? Where've you been, why isn't Jim here?"

"He knows," she said, "about you and Francesca. Or he guesses. I don't know how much is true. He believes that it was worrying about it, wondering if he'd find out, that sent her off her balance. He — he's been drunk, Pat, very drunk. He wanted to kill you."

"Of all the damn fool — !"

"You can't get out of this," she said quietly.

He turned away from her, and went to the window. "Well, what of it?" he said over his shoulder. "I was a hot-blooded kid and she . . . she was head over heels. It didn't last, it couldn't. I wasn't ready to marry, didn't want to. She fell in love with Jim, and married him. Afterwards when things went haywire I did what I could for him, I evened it up. It wasn't my fault, Kathleen." He turned and came toward her. "You've got to believe me."

"Even if I did," she said, "it wouldn't make any difference." She looked at him coolly. "You are utterly despicable," she said slowly.

"You'd punish me for that, for what happened long ago? She was in love with Jim, they were happy, I tell you, I didn't figure in it at all. When she went out of her mind — it was inherited insanity, it had nothing to do — You get hold of Jim, send him here."

"You don't really want to see him," she said, "you're relieved because you'll never see him. He's going away today. To a place where he can rest and be taken care of and perhaps be cured. When he gets back there'll be a good job, away from you, away from New York."

"Who fixed this up?" he demanded.

"I did."

"Well," he said shortly, "good riddance. To go off like that . . . after all I've put up with, all I've done."

"All you've done," she agreed.

She opened the desk drawer, took her personal belongings from it. She faced him again, and spoke quietly.

"I'm leaving," she said, "not waiting until I am replaced. Sadie knows of someone who will come in and —"

"You can't go!"

He was violent again, in anger, in dismay, seizing her, forcing her mouth to his, kissing her savagely and without pity. "You love me, you belong to me, you —"

"If it's love I feel for you," she said, when he released her, "it would have been better if I'd never been born."

The door closed behind her and he stood there staring at it. Presently he swore and went back to his office. The small boy again, saying, I'll show her, she'll be sorry.

He dialed a number. Presently someone answered and he asked, "Sandra? This is Pat. Look here, honey —"

Kathleen stopped in the chief engineer's office on her way downstairs. Sadie was there at her desk and Kathleen spoke to her swiftly.

"Something's happened," she said, "I can't stay on. Be a good egg, Sadie, and get hold of that girl you spoke of, or all eight of them and make appointments for them to see Mr. Bell." She held out her hand. "This isn't good-bye," she told her, "we'll meet again."

"I doubt it," said Sadie, "but — good luck, just the same. Look, the boss has been raving. Jim Haines turned up missing."

"Yes," said Kathleen, "I know."

She went out to Paul's car, drove uptown to his garage and left the car there with his instructions. She taxied back to the apartment, with the manuscript under her arms. When she walked in Hannah was waiting.

"Where in the world have you been?" said Hannah. "What's that?" She seized the manuscript, gave it a cursory glance. "Paul's! He never let me read it. Look here, Kate . . ."

Kathleen sat down. She was suddenly too tired to take off her outer things. She said, "Hannah, I've made so many explanations that I'm sick of them. Here goes again. Take it or leave it. I was with Jim Haines yesterday, Pat's right-hand man. We went to see his wife. She's in an institution for the criminally insane. Afterwards Jim got drunk. He has a grudge against Pat. He threatened to kill him. I called you at that point and then drove him down to Mattituck to Paul's. I had to take him where he'd be safe. The storm came up and I stayed."

"You stayed," repeated Hannah in a whisper.

"Yes, I stayed and don't look at me like that. I didn't go down there to spend the night with Paul McClure. I'm not in the mood," she said bitterly, "for romance in a cabin. I went because I felt Paul would help

270

Jim Haines. I stayed because it stormed, because Jim's car had a flat, because, in short, there seemed no point in my driving back through the storm although Paul's car was at my disposal. I drove back this morning, resigned my job, and incidentally Jim's. Paul is taking him south to a cure place. Afterwards he thinks he can get him a job. I drove Paul's car up, left it at his garage. And now is there anything else you want to know?" she asked, a little hysterically.

"Yes," said Hannah, "but I won't ask. I'm sorry, Kate." She went down on her knees beside the other girl. "I'll be honest. I'm terrified of you. It's over between you and Pat, and Paul's in love with you, don't you think I know it? Not with me, never with me again, even if he was once, which I doubt. But I was trying to be content. Half loaf, second fiddle. I thought, Anything's better than nothing when you're so much in love."

"Love," said Kathleen. "I don't want to hear about it, I don't want to think about it. I'm sorry, Hannah, there's nothing left in me somehow. I don't care about you and Paul. I don't care about anything. I want to work and I want to — I don't know what I want to do!"

Hannah said, "I spoke to Rosa Davenport.

You get the job. Will you go around there tomorrow?"

"All right," said Kathleen. She got to her feet. "I'm going to take a bath," she said, "and soak. Then I'm going to bed. Will you ask Amelia if I could have something to eat on a tray? Not much."

"I'll come in and sit with you," Hannah said.

"I'm sorry," said Kathleen, "not now. I've been such a fool and everything's so ugly and hideous." She shuddered. "Let's not talk," she said, "I want to sleep."

Hannah asked, "Would Paul mind if I read his play? Or would you let me read it and not tell him?"

"Oh, don't be humble," Kathleen cried at her, "don't be besotted and bewitched and small. Where does it get you? Why should he mind? It's a great play — honest and unafraid."

"Like Paul," said Hannah.

"How do you know?" asked Kathleen and went into her room and slammed her door.

How did you know anything? Pat. She had dismissed him because she didn't like his business methods. Standing there, righteous and self-contained and sorry for herself. "I won't marry you because you cheat," she had told him in effect. Bad enough. But

272

nothing to the other! She thought of Francesca and her smooth black hair, which was disheveled as she tore at it. "Pat's girl." Of Jim Haines, living his unhappy life, loving one woman, getting drunk because he could not forget his tragedy, loving one man and loyal to him.

Paul, fine like his play, honest and unafraid. It was nothing to her. She was grateful to him, he had helped her, he would help Jim. But she was grateful to him as if he were a stranger. He was in love with her, or thought he was. He had told her so at every opportunity. So what? So he had been helpful and dependable, not because he gave a damn for Jim Haines and the hideous thing that had happened to him, but because he was in love with her, with the woman who brought Haines to him. Selfless motives couldn't exist, in the man-woman relationship.

Jim Haines had to thank biology for what had happened to Francesca, before he met her and afterwards. He had to thank it for saving him from madness now, and Pat had it to thank for saving him.

Nice going.

She pushed aside the tray Amelia had brought her, turned her face to the pillows and wept. Presently she rose and put the tray on a table, bathed her eyes and face and turned out the light. Perhaps she could sleep as heavily as last night, not remembering Francesca's face, not remembering Jim's, not remembering Pat's as she had seen it last. And above all, not remembering that when he had taken her in his arms she had wanted to stay, to believe him, to debase herself and forget.

That was not love. And because it was not, she was bitterly ashamed.

In the living room, Hannah was smoking one cigarette from the butt of the other. She was reading Paul's play.

When she had finished, she thought, That's over my head, I don't feel like that, I don't think like that.

Paul did. How could she hope to mean anything to him if she could not meet him on his own ground?

She rose and mixed herself a drink. There was no sound from Kathleen's room. She thought, Poor kid, and tried to piece the thing together in her mind. There were great gaps. She couldn't assemble the pattern. She tried not to think of Kathleen down there by the frozen water, among the pines, in the little cottage, with Paul . . . a fire going perhaps, and the drunken man oblivious of them, sprawled out somewhere, anywhere.

It's no good, she thought, it's one of those things. She doesn't love him now, she's never loved him. It was Pat all along. Could it be Pat again, after she's forgotten this, whatever it is? He's persuasive enough.

She asked herself, Would you help him if you could? And she knew that she would.

You haven't any loyalty, she told herself, throwing a cigarette on the hearth. Except to Paul, and he doesn't want it. The best thing you can do, Hannah, is to get over him — again.

The telephone rang and she answered, looking at the little gold clock. It was very late.

"Kate?"

"It's Hannah, Paul."

"May I speak to her?"

"She's asleep," Hannah said, "she's pretty tired."

"I know. Tell her we're all right, and on our way. Stopping the rest of the night in Baltimore. He'll be in Virginia tomorrow, I'll phone her again."

"All right," said Hannah. She added, "I read the play, Kate brought it home with her. It's a knockout, Paul."

"Glad you think so," he said. "Give her my best, be sure and say that Jim's all right."

"I'll tell her," she said again. "Good night,

Paul." She hung up and turned from the telephone. He didn't care whether she liked the play or not, she thought. Damn it, he knew she hadn't liked it, he knew that it frightened her, that it spoke to her with the alien lips of a stranger.

Chapter XVII

Kathleen never forgot her interview with Molly Bell. She went up to the Riverside Drive apartment one early morning and sat with Molly in the overcrowded living room, crammed with heavy, expensive furniture, the latest thing in radios, and a grand piano, which no one played. All the way there she had rehearsed what she must say, but Molly helped her through the preliminaries.

"What's wrong between you and Pat? Oh, don't look so astonished, girl! He's been like a bear with a sore head. Snaps mine off when I ask him about it. Stays out nights. Not with you, I know that. You never left lipstick on his coat lapel, you don't use the kind of perfume — Well, no matter. And you aren't at the office."

"I'm not going back, Molly."

"So that's it. You've quarreled. Well, that's all right," said Molly, watching the younger woman with bright blue eyes, "it takes a knockdown fight to make a good marriage."

Kathleen shook her head. She looked badly, she had lost weight, pallor was apparent under a dusting of rouge, and her eyes were shadowed . . . the delicate skin around them looked bruised.

"I'm afraid not," she said.

"You've broken with the boy, then?"

Kathleen looked straight into Molly's eyes. They were so like Pat's in shape and color that her heart was sick within her.

"Yes, dear," she said, "I —"

But that was all. Suddenly she was in tears. She put her hands over her face and wept. Molly let her cry. After a while Kathleen fumbled for her handkerchief and Molly put a clean, primly folded square into her hand. "There, take that," she said.

Kathleen drew a gasping breath, mopped her eyes, blew her nose. She apologized, with a diluted smile.

"I'm so sorry . . . so ashamed."

Mrs. Bell nodded. "Good cry's what you need. This is your own affair, Kathleen. The boy's my son, but that's not the point. Only think carefully — if it's a silly thing, something that looks big and isn't? Is it jealous you are?"

Kathleen shook her head. She said, "You've been so good to me, I — You'll hate me now."

"Why should I?"

"Isn't it routine?"

"No, I'm a person," said Molly vigorously, "and I was one before I ever married Frank and had his children. I like you. You're a good, sensible girl. If this isn't just a lovers' tiff —"

"It goes deeper than that," Kathleen told her. "Call it incompatibility. Pat and I don't see things alike. That wouldn't matter if the things were unimportant, like" — she tried to smile again — "roast beef on Sundays, or opera as against musical comedy."

"I see," said Molly. "Well, I tried to warn you." She looked old suddenly and unhappy. "I told you he was a good boy. A good son. So he is, I don't lack for anything, Kathleen. There are things I don't like, he was always headstrong and perhaps I gave in to him. Still," she added musingly, "I doubt I could have changed him. I thought, Kathleen will. But maybe I was wrong. It's your life, I'll not interfere. You thought you were in love with him, you found out in time that you weren't. God be thanked it was in time because if it was after the two of you were married —" She broke off. "You don't care to tell me about it?"

"I'd give my right hand to tell you," said Kathleen somberly. But she could not. She had thought, It would be impossible to tell Pat's mother that his way of doing business

279

was not that of an honest man. How much more impossible to tell her about Francesca Haines!

"I can't," she said; "it involves other people. Believe me when I tell you that if I could . . ." She halted miserably. Then she looked at the other woman, her gray eyes dark as a rainy day. She said slowly, "Even after I broke with him, Molly, I went on loving him."

The older woman whitened. "Then it *was* something important."

"To me, yes."

"I see. And now, how do you feel?"

"Empty," said Kathleen.

She opened her handbag and took out two little boxes, the bracelet, the ring. She put them on a table. "I'll leave them here," she said, "for him."

She rose and Molly rose with her. She was taller than Molly but she felt small because of the other woman's tolerance. It was not what she had expected, she had expected the fighting Irish, the tigress in defense of her cub. She said simply, "It just wasn't to be, that's all."

"I could beg you," said Molly thoughtfully, "to give him another chance. It will go hard with him now, Kathleen."

Kathleen shook her head.

"I know," she said, "but I can't, Molly, I can't."

"Perhaps," said Molly, "you'll come see me sometimes? Drink a cup of tea? Two friends, that's all. We won't speak of Pat."

"I'll come," Kathleen promised, choked.

"You're not going away, then?"

"No, I'm going to work the beginning of next week, as secretary to the woman who runs Eloise, Inc."

"That's good. It's hard to be idle and unhappy."

"Would you write Carmela and tell her? I don't know what to say," admitted Kathleen, "she adores Pat, she'll think me pretty low."

"She's young," said Pat's mother, and reaching up, kissed Kathleen's cool cheek. "I can't hold it against you," she added, "but I'm sorry for Pat and for myself. You were a daughter I wanted for my own."

"I won't forget that," said Kathleen, "nor you."

She did not forget her, during the weeks which followed as winter melted into early spring, as early spring blew itself out in gusty winds under a wild blue sky. April came and the bright rain and pale-gold sunlight. And then it was May and her parents had been writing her from England for several weeks. Glorious there, everything much as usual.

Why didn't she give up her job and join them? And why had she changed jobs anyway?

Guarded in her replies, she wrote as she had written when she told them of the change, that this offered more opportunity, as in Bell's office she was merely a decorative adjunct. She liked Rosa Davenport, a slave driver if ever there was one, and she had become an adept in framing the courteous, friendly letters which stopped just short of dunning. "The people with the most money never pay their bills!" she informed her mother. "It's too amazing. And you should see me, the perfect secretary, dressed by Eloise. Because I must, it would be bad business not to. If all secretaries could afford this simple black number, with the touch of white here and there and the sublime cut, what a fashion show offices would turn out to be. But it's fun."

It was, in a way. She grew fond of Sammy, admiring his genius, tolerant of his high rages, his hysterics. And Rosa, she discovered, was a remarkable woman, driving herself and her employees but generous to a fault, always doing something for someone. She insisted on good work and no malingering, but she interested herself in their problems and love affairs, their finances, their health and families.

Kathleen's work was backstage with Rosa. She went through the workrooms with her every day, took notes as Rosa dictated. She wrote her business and most of her personal letters. She was sent on errands of mercy, to homes, to hospitals. She got the brother of one of the seamstresses a job, she arranged a vacation for the little errand girl. Now and then, when Rosa had special appointments with the great and near-great, she received the customers and talked to them until Rosa was ready to make her grand entrance. When Sammy designed the evening and Hannah the sports clothes for a new play, Rosa and Kathleen, with her notebook, went to rehearsals.

"The blue won't be right here," said Rosa, "it's the wrong color. Pink, I think, dusty pink, very young, very naïve. Sammy's off, there. The girl's a youngster at her first party. That ice blue is all right for an older woman, not for a girl just falling in love."

Kathleen helped Rosa arrange her parties . . . not only for the spring showing, which took place just after she came to Eloise, but the more private affairs for special customers, the party for the wholesale people for whom Sammy had designed an inexpensive line, and for the out-of-town buyers, representatives of a few exclusive shops from Chicago to the Coast which bought one of a kind, the Eloise recent ready-to-wear line. She met people in and out of the trade, she was busy and not unhappy.

She was seeing Paul. When first she saw him again after that stormy, crazy night on Long Island, he came to the apartment to report on Jim Haines, safely harbored in Virginia . . . "if he'll stay there. Write him now and again, Kate, will you? Of course, you will. There's good stuff in him. He's worth saving."

In May, heavier by several pounds, clear-eyed and with a look of fortitude and peace about him, Jim Haines returned to New York. He came to see Kathleen and Hannah, curious but unquestioning, went out and left them alone. He told her of his experiences in the Virginia place.

"Hell," he reported, "a good deal of the time. Oh, not the treatments, not the — thirst. But the other kind of hell, not physical. Thinking, remembering. Twice I tried to get away, back to town, to break his neck." He looked at his hands, they were brown now and strong from outdoor work. "That's over now. I'd like you to know that. He's safe enough, from me."

"I'm glad, Jim," she said.

"I know. I'm off to Pennsylvania tomorrow, to take that job. I'll keep it too, no — layoffs. I owe it to you and to Paul McClure. Did you know he drove down to see me, three times?"

"Yes, I knew."

"Sent me books, wrote me, kept in touch. That's a regular guy," said Haines.

She hesitated. "Have you been to see Francesca?" she asked finally.

"Yes. She didn't know me at first. It's been so long. She's better again. Quiet, like a child. After I left her I went to the place where we were that day. Same waiter, the big one, remember? I sat for a long time, near the bar. I could smell the stuff. I wanted a drink, I needed it, seeing her had — I can't tell you what it did to me. I ordered coffee, black. I drank a quart, I guess. Then I got up and went out. I had that licked too. I'll never need a drink so badly again."

He rose awkwardly, "I won't keep you," he said, "I just wanted to tell you how things were. I'll drop you a line from Easton. I —" He looked at her with shame and appeal. "How is he?" he asked.

Her heart constricted. It was not right or fair that a man should have the power to enslave those who had loved him, beyond hatred, beyond justice. She said, after a minute,

"I don't know, Jim. I haven't seen him, of course. I did see Sadie last week, she had very little to say; the situation was a little embarrassing, I suppose. I see Mrs. Bell every once in a while but we don't talk about Pat."

"He's been in the papers," said Jim.

"I saw them."

She remembered the first time she had seen Pat's name in the columns; "Pat Bell, Big Ditch Boss, is being seen around town again with Sandra, one of the prettier reasons to visit the Jungle."

Haines said after a minute:

"The subway job went through, all right." He stopped. "My last check came to the old address and was forwarded. And a letter. I didn't answer, and I sent back the check." He looked away from her. "I couldn't send back all the others," he said. "I thought, There's a lot in the bank, he always gave me more than I needed, more than I was worth. I thought, If I send that back — But I didn't. I had a trust fund made, for Francesca; if anything should happen to me, there's money to take care of the little for her, the things she'll need."

At the door she took his hand and held it firmly. She said, "Let me hear from you, Jim, and — keep your chin up."

She couldn't wish him good luck. His luck

was out long ago. It wasn't luck he needed.

Paul's play had been rewritten for the last time. It would be produced in the autumn. He came to see her and Hannah, took them both out, found an extra man. Sometimes she saw him alone. On the first occasion he said abruptly, "You know how I feel about you. I'm not going to talk about it. I want you to remember it when you want to remember it. Otherwise, forget it."

He had made no mention of the subject since then. There were other things to talk about, what was happening in, and to, the world, gossip of the theatrical center, the play, always the play, her new job, the latest word from her people. She was grateful to him, for his easy speech and for his omissions. It was possible that he still loved her, but the thought left her entirely cold. Love was the last thing she wanted from anyone now. Friendship, yes, a certain amount of give and take, a casual companionship. But never love, again.

Hannah had acquired a new beau. A very pleasant one, this time, a banker. He was about forty, and a widower. A quiet man with a sense of humor and the most beautiful, unobtrusive manners. "Joel makes me feel like the wrong side of the tracks in a nice way," said Hannah. "I find myself living up to him."

"You like him, don't you?"

"Well," said Hannah, "he's different. He thinks I'm young and foolish and believes that he was created to look after me. Very scare-making! I'll be dressing in white muslin with a blue sash, first thing I know. When I get off one of my specially elegant wise-cracks, he looks at me as if I were a bright child who has said something clever but doesn't understand what. It's disconcerting. He even wants me to meet the children."

"Children!" repeated Kathleen, laughing. "Oh, Hannah!"

"It's absurd," said Hannah gloomily. "I've met all kinds of people in my time — one duke, half a dozen tycoons, Elsa Maxwell, Noel Coward, and a princess or two — but when I think of the children of the late Mrs. Ransom, I could shriek. Two, you know, a boy eight, and a girl ten. They have govern-esses and such. Joel says they're nice kids. That's as may be, but I don't know how to talk to children under twenty."

"Who was their mother?"

"Childhood friend, one of those prear-ranged things. Nice, from what he says. Invalid ever since the little boy was born. She's been dead for several years."

"Hannah, you sound serious."

"I'm not," said Hannah, enraged. "Can I

help it if he has the symptoms? It isn't catching."

No, it wasn't catching. She liked Joel Ransom. She didn't have to be witty and brilliant or hard and on her guard with him. Such a quiet, decent man. "A stuffed shirt," she had said of him the first time she met him. All right. But stuffed, she found, with a very superior stuffing.

One nail didn't always drive out the other, not even a golden nail like Joel Ransom. There was still Paul and the way her heart behaved when she saw him. But ever since the night when she had read and laid aside his incomprehensible play she had tried to ignore her heart — ignorant organ, it lacked logic and common sense. Had Paul said a serious word to her, ever? No, not even when he believed himself in love with her. Their relationship was purely surface, she amused him, he liked being with her, he could be as much himself with her as he cared to be . . . but she had never been herself with him. Always trying to keep up, always trying to hold his attention, sharpening her tongue and her wits. With Ransom, she need not . . . she could be tired, she could be bored, she could be discouraged.

Perhaps, she thought, the first time Ransom proposed to her, and she refused him, perhaps a carpet-slipper marriage was better than a marriage represented by a pair of high-heeled toeless sandals. Carpet slippers weren't exciting, but they didn't pinch, they didn't hurt, you had no sensation of walking on daggers.

One bright day toward the middle of May, Hannah was in Rosa Davenport's office. So was Sammy. They were quarreling happily over something that seemed very important at the time, and Kathleen sitting at her desk in the little cubicle assigned to her was listening, smiling. Sammy waved his beautiful hands and burst into French and Hannah said bitterly, "Stow that, Sammy, it isn't going to get you anywhere." Rosa, sitting very erect in her utilitarian chair, was refereeing. All this excitement over a bolt of material. "It isn't your province," Sammy was telling Hannah, when one of the girls in the reception room came in and spoke to Rosa. "She says, she has an appointment," she concluded.

"Sandra?" repeated Rosa. "Sandra what-else?"

"That's all. 'Tell her Sandra's here,' she said," the girl answered, shrugging.

"Never heard of her," said Rosa. She looked at Kathleen. "Did you make an appointment for me?"

"No," said Kathleen, "I didn't. But I can

tell you who she is. She's singing at the Jungle. Or was, until it closed last week."

"Sounds unlikely," said Rosa. "Well, see her, do, there's a good girl, and find out what it's all about."

Kathleen got up and left the room. Hannah, looking after her, whistled.

"What's that for?" demanded Rosa crossly.

"Nothing. Only," said Hannah, "Sandra is Pat Bell's current heart interest, if you're to believe the papers."

Kathleen walked into the quiet lovely room. Sandra was standing there, smoking, her heels beating an impatient tattoo. It was a warm day but she wore, over her black dress, a bolero of silver fox. She tossed her cigarette into an ash tray and turned.

Kathleen smiled. She said, "We've met before, I think. I'm Miss Roberts, Mrs. Davenport's secretary."

Sandra held out her hand, the bad little hand with the dreadful nails. There was a bracelet on her wrist which Kathleen recognized. She said, "Of course, I met you with Pat." Her shallow blue eyes were filled with malice, and pleasure. "I heard you were here."

Kathleen said, "I'm afraid you were mistaken, as Mrs. Davenport remembers no appointment. She is very busy at present. But

I'll have someone show you the clothes, if you wish."

"Pat," said Sandra carelessly, "says this is the best place in town. All right." She sat down on a couch. She asked, "Would you show them to me?"

"I'm sorry," said Kathleen, a little white, "Mrs. Davenport needs me. But I'll see that you're well taken care of, Miss — Sandra." She beckoned one of the unobtrusive young women. Mentioned her name. Sandra's eyes widened. She thought, A princess . . . wait till Pat hears this!

Kathleen went back to her office. "Well?" asked Rosa.

"She wants clothes," said Kathleen, "she knew she had no appointment. Olga's doing the honors."

"Who's paying for them?" demanded Rosa.

Kathleen said carefully, "I think you needn't worry on that score."

Hannah, who had slipped into the other room, now came back, her dark eyes bright with laughter. She asked, "Did you get a load of that unseasonable little coat?"

"What coat?" asked Rosa curiously.

Hannah and Kathleen spoke almost simultaneously. Kathleen said, "Silver fox," but Hannah, laughing, corrected her. "No," she said, *Minx!*"

Chapter XVIII

Sandra had come and gone like summer lightning. She ordered three linen suits and matching hats, innumerable summer evening frocks and several prints for daytime. She ordered Hannah's traveling suit and top coat and the latest Hannah extravaganzas in shorts, sweaters, one-piece tennis dresses, and three bathing suits.

She was fussy at the fittings — when she came. Half the time she made but broke appointments. The fitter assigned to her, clever and temperamental, threatened to leave a dozen times before the clothes were completed and delivered to the lady's hotel. Once Kathleen had had to intervene when Sandra, storming through the rooms in a negligible costume of lace and silk, demanded to see Rosa, who was not there. Sammy rushed out, and in horror, rushed back. "Do something!" he begged. "This is a dressmaker's establishment not a burlesque. The creature is doing a strip tease!"

"The fitter's insolent," complained Sandra when Kathleen had herded her safely back into the dressing room.

The fitter, with tears of rage in her eyes and pins in her mouth, could only shake her head silently. Kathleen soothed, comforted, pleaded. "Well," said Sandra, relenting, "I do like the clothes."

The fitting went on and Kathleen went out. She had schooled herself not to think of Pat every time she was forced to think of Sandra. Now she did think of him, wondering how he stood these childish rages, the speech that was vulgar without the force and honesty for which vulgarity may be excused.

Hannah, who had been in the office at the time, shook her head. She said, "You're feeling sorry for Pat."

"Well, why not?" retorted Kathleen.

"Don't. He'd eat up that kind of thing. It's a complement of his nature," explained Hannah. "They can scream at each other, swear, throw things, and then go out arm in arm to dine and dance. Don't be sorry for him, Kate. He has a dramatic sense too, you know."

Kathleen sat down at her desk.

"You don't expect people here not to talk," she said. "Agatha will stick pins in her if she can. It will get out: Sandra Stages Scene at Eloise, Inc."

"We can stand it, and she'll love it. You forget, she's opening at the Elsmore Roof next week. We can't forget it, seeing we're dressing her. I think I'll go. I dare you to, Kate."

Kathleen looked at her. "Why should I?" she asked quietly.

"You've been in mourning long enough. Always going to 'quiet' places so that you won't run into Pat. Coward, aren't you?"

Kathleen flushed. "Make up your party," she said with spirit.

Joel and Hannah, Paul and Kathleen. Paul said, when he met her at the apartment, "Sure you want to attend this shindig?" and she answered, her head high, "Of course, I'm sure."

It was Joel's party. A good table, near the dance floor, after the theater. They came in a little late, just before Sandra made her entrance. Pat was already at his table with half a dozen men and women. Kathleen saw him as she followed the head waiter. She was entirely feminine and, therefore, glad that she had worn the new frock, that Hannah had persuaded her she was one of the few women who could wear her hair up and not look like her own grandmother. "We have to," said Hannah. "Next season's clothes are built around this crazy hair-do, and *all* the hats. Eloise's employees have to be six months in advance of the fashions, Kate. Be a sport and let Henri do your hair."

She had been a sport, she was being a sport.

They sat down and ordered and Pat, looking up from his highball, saw them. He rose and came over, standing there, big and smiling, in the way she remembered. "Hello, Kathleen," he said, "you're looking marvelous." He spoke to Hannah and to Paul, was presented to Joel.

"Mind if I sit down a minute?" he asked.

Sandra came on, to prolonged applause. She wore one of the most effective of the Eloise frocks. She looked like a child in it. Someone had been clever with her hair, toning it down. It was pale daffodil yellow now and the dress was white, and disarmingly young. She clasped her hands in front of her and turned her big blue eyes on her audience. She sang, in her husky, unimportant voice, the song which one of the cleverest men of his day had written for her. A naughty song, but not too naughty. The contrast of the words, the yellow head, the white frock was enchanting. The audience applauded, demanded more.

"Clever, isn't she?" Pat asked Kathleen.

"Very," said Kathleen, smiling.

If he had expected something, a flash of the gray eyes, a tightening of the serene red mouth, he was disappointed. But he stayed where he was, enjoying the situation, confident that Sandra, at least, was not enjoying it. He didn't know about Kathleen. She made no sign. He said, "You've been sweet — going to see Mom . . . she appreciated it."

"I appreciate the opportunity," said Kathleen. "I'm very fond of her, Pat."

Sandra was singing again. Pat ignored the outraged glances from near-by tables and went on talking. He asked, "Don't jump down my throat, but have you heard from Jim?"

"Yes," she said. "He's working in Pennsylvania. He's doing very well."

Their eyes met, and clashed like rapiers. Hannah whispered:

"Will you two kindly shut up?"

At the conclusion of Sandra's second song Pat returned to his table. Sandra, stepping down from the stage, followed him there. She sat there for perhaps ten minutes, drinking a glass of champagne and talking exclusively to Pat. She was very angry. Kathleen could see her color rise under the make-up, could see how her hands twitched, could hear her voice, sharp and definite, but no words.

Paul said lazily:

"Looks as if young Mr. Bell had made a bad break."

Kathleen said, "Paul, I'm tired, do you suppose Hannah and Joel would mind?"

"Stick it out," advised Paul in an undertone, "where's your pride?"

She whitened and looked at him without gratitude. "All right," she said, "I'll stick it out."

They left after Sandra's last number was sung in a slim black dress with a corselet of sequins. Outside, waiting for the men to collect their hats, Kathleen felt a touch on her arm. It was Pat, drawing her aside, to say urgently:

"Kathleen, look, will you let me come see you?"

She shook her head. It was strange and cruel, she thought, even now, feeling as she did, seeing him, feeling his most casual touch; her pulses pounded and she felt sick and lightheaded with excitement. She said, "Better not, Pat, there really isn't any reason."

"But I want to talk to you. I promise I won't say anything to offend you — I've got to talk to you, Kathleen, you never gave me a chance to explain."

"I'm sorry, Pat," she said, "it's no use."

The gardenias came next day, in a heart-

298

shaped box. They reminded her of those he had sent her after the automobile accident, when she was ill at his mother's apartment. She put them back in the box and gave them to Amelia.

"Why?" asked Hannah, discovering them, from the fragrance which emanated from the icebox when she opened the door.

"I don't want them," said Kathleen.

"Amelia can spare me three," said Hannah cheerfully. "I'm dining with Joel again. Kate, you're still in pretty much of a dither about Pat, aren't you?"

Kathleen moved restlessly, lit a cigarette, put it out almost immediately. She said, "I can't make you understand, Hannah."

"Try; I'm not so dumb."

"How did you feel when you saw Paul again, after you had quarreled?"

"That's not fair," Hannah told her, in a stifled tone. "That was different. That was a quarrel, and my fault mostly. And I'd learned to realize that what he had felt for me wasn't what I wanted."

Kathleen said slowly:

"When I told Pat I wouldn't marry him I was still in love with him. As much as ever. I couldn't respect him, but I loved him. Something else happened — afterwards." She looked at Hannah gravely. "I can't tell you what that was."

"It had something to do with Jim Haines," deduced Hannah. "I can see through a stone wall as far as most women."

Kathleen nodded. "After that," she said, "I — couldn't love him. I mean, it was out of all reason. I should have stopped instantly, I should have felt nothing. I should have despised him, I did despise him, yet . . . Oh, Hannah," she said miserably, "when I saw him last night it was like dying, and it was like coming to life."

"You poor devil," said Hannah.

"I know. It's a physical thing, it makes me sick to think about it." She tried to smile. "I'll get over it," she promised.

"It isn't easy," said Hannah. "I know."

The bell rang. "Joel!" she cried. "Take care of him for me, I'll get the gardenias and my bonnet. I'll be mysterious about the gardenias, don't give me away, Kate, there's a good girl."

After Hannah and Joel had gone, Kathleen had her dinner on a tray. There was a new book she wanted to read, there were letters she must write. She put on the hostess gown Hannah had given her on her recent birthday: pleated chiffon, simple, a pale clear green like the young leaves on the springtime trees. She was writing at the desk in the living room when Pat rang the bell. Amelia had left and she opened the door.

She said, "I told you not to come."

"I know. Just for a moment, Kathleen, I had to see you again."

"Very well," she said despairingly, "come in."

He looked, she knew, for the gardenias. They were not there. He asked, "Did the flowers come?"

"Yes," she said. "Pat, say what you have to say, and go — quickly."

"Last night," he told her, "Sandra gave me hell. She saw me at your table."

"She came to Eloise because of me," said Kathleen, smiling faintly, "which was good business for the firm — I hope."

Pat looked at her sharply. "You've changed."

"How?"

"You're different. A little hard. More like Hannah," he answered.

"That's good," Kathleen told him indifferently. Strange to be sitting here with him, only an arm's length away. Strange to be talking about things that didn't matter, and trying not to remember.

"Kathleen, do you remember — ?"

"I remember everything," she interrupted clearly. "It doesn't make any difference."

"We had such good times," he said slowly, "we loved each other so much. I haven't got over it, Kathleen."

"And Sandra?" she asked involuntarily.

"That doesn't matter." He shrugged slightly. "Someone to take out, someone to amuse you, to amuse. She's like a crazy kid. No brains — just all body. Jealous as a cat. Claws like a cat. At first, well, I thought you'd hear about her, thought it would matter to you."

"It didn't," said Kathleen, "but you're not being very fair to her, are you? You aren't fair to anyone, really."

"I was to you."

"No," she said, "never to me." She looked at him and laughed. "I fell in love with you," she said, "because you were different from the men I knew. Honest and open — rough diamond, if you like, nature's nobleman." She laughed again on a higher note. "Sometime or other in an impressionable childhood I must have read a book, and made up my mind that nature's nobleman was always the hero and the smooth sophisticate the villain. It was the wrong book, Pat."

He said, "That has all the earmarks of a dirty crack. I suppose you're thinking of McClure."

"No, I'm not thinking of anyone but myself. I'm thinking of my abysmal ignorance — or was it innocence? — and my naïveté."

He moved closer to her. He stated very firmly:

"But you're still in love with me."

She moved away definitely.

"No," she said, "I'm not in love with you, thank God."

"You can't be with me alone like this and deny it." He put out his arm, pulled her against him. "You can't let me hold you like this and deny it! There is something between us, something important. You can't deny that either. It's real and it's lasting. Don't be a fool, Kathleen."

She said, "I don't care what's between us, I don't want any part of it."

The doorbell rang sharply. He said, "Sit still, I'll attend to that."

She sat as he had left her, not moving, her heart beating thickly. She was faint, dizzy. A messenger boy, a special delivery letter — she didn't care. It was rescue whatever, whoever it was. She thought, If you could only teach women this, that because they want to be in a man's arms, because his kiss gives them pleasure, because, in short, they want him, it isn't always love. Not always. If they could learn this without having to experience it for themselves . . .

"Oh, it's you, McClure," said Pat flatly, when he had opened the door.

"In person." Paul came in, and looked across the room. He said, "I'll go if you want me to, Kate."

"Of course, she wants you to," said Pat lightly, "don't you, darling?"

"No," said Kathleen, "I don't." She smiled at Paul. "Come over here," she said, "and sit down."

"I can sit down too," said Pat.

It was an absurd situation. Paul laughed, offered Pat his cigarette case. He said, "You remember the story of the boy who was sitting on the front porch with his best girl when another lad came along. They both sat, as we are sitting. It was two in the morning before the second one went home. 'Well,' said the first in triumph, 'he set and I set, but I outset him.' "

Pat said, "I've a lot of patience." He leaned forward, smiling. "Look here, McClure, you're a wise guy but tactless. I saw Kathleen last night for the first time since our — our disagreement. I came here to talk it over with her. Be a good egg and run along, will you?"

"Did you ask him to come?" Paul demanded, turning to Kathleen.

"No."

304

"Do you want him to stay?" asked Paul.

"No," said Kathleen again, "I don't."

"Well," said Paul, "you heard the lady. Get going."

Pat's face darkened, a vein swelled on his forehead. He asked, "By what right —"

"Oh, don't be melodramatic," said Paul, "no right at all. But you heard her."

"She doesn't mean it," said Pat, not moving. "You're here, so she's bluffing."

"I don't think so." Paul put his cigarette in the ash tray and rose. He walked over and stood by Pat. He was as tall as he, but much less heavy. He asked gently, "Are you going or must I throw you out?"

"Paul, please!" cried Kathleen. She had been a fascinated spectator. The whole scene had played itself out before her eyes as before an audience. She had not felt that she had any part in it, not even when she was answering Paul's question. Now she was part of it again, she was frightened. "Please," she repeated.

"I won't hurt him," said Pat infuriatingly.

Kathleen got to her feet. She said, "This is ludicrous, it's — indecent." She turned on Paul, with sudden anger. "I can handle my own affairs," she said. She looked at Pat. She said, "You'll go now — I think."

"O. K.," said Pat, "I'll go, but I'll come

back. He can't always 'outset' me."

He went to the door without haste. Once there he spoke again. "Good night, Kathleen, it's been fun seein' you."

The door shut. Paul was white. "Had rather the best of it, didn't he?" he said. "Remember how he said, 'I won't hurt him.' If I'd hit him then —"

"Paul, don't be silly!"

"He would have knocked me out," said Paul calmly. "I'm no hero and no athlete. But he wanted hitting, badly. No sense, I think, in my staying. Sorry I barged in, Kate. Always doing something like that."

She said, "Paul, please be sensible. I didn't know he was coming, of course. Now that he's gone —" she drew a deep breath — "it doesn't matter that he did come, I'm over it," she told him, flushing. "What's left . . . well, I know it by its right name, it can't worry me any more."

"Good," said Paul. His eyes were bright but his face did not change. "Feel like celebrating?"

"I think perhaps I do."

He went out into the kitchen, mixed two drinks and brought them back. He toasted gravely.

"To your freedom," he said, "and, I may add, your happiness."

"Thank you," she said, smiling. She drank a little, and put the glass down. Paul, finishing his, looked at her thoughtfully.

"You look tired," he commented. He looked over at the open desk. "And you were writing a letter when interrupted. I'll clear out now." He came around behind her, dropped his hand on her shoulder. "Good night," he said, "and good luck."

"I don't need it now," she told him.

She went to the door with him and held out her hand. "Thanks for coming, Paul."

"I was not," he said ruefully, "a very heroic figure. Well, perhaps I was cut out for the author of the piece and never the hero. Good night, my dear."

Poor Paul. "I won't hurt him," Pat had said. No, never a hero, she thought, returning to her letter writing.

But her mind was not on it. She was free, having seen clearly for what it was the emotion Pat aroused in her. Or was it the shadow of an emotion — an emotional hang-over, perhaps, after long intoxication?

She would not see him again, she thought. But if she did, not even her traitor pulse could frighten her.

But the next afternoon she heard of him. The late newspaper editions were on the street when she came out of Eloise's. She bought one, walking toward the subway, and the headlines leaped out at her, struck her across her eyes, left her sick with horror. The subway job, Pat's job . . . a wall collapsing, and then fire. And men dead and dying.

Chapter XIX

Blindly Kathleen went down the subway steps. The uptown local station was not yet crowded. She sat down on a bench and opened her paper with shaking hands. She read the headlines, and the facts which followed them. She read of panic and the screams of trapped men. She felt so ill that she was afraid to move. A fat woman with a string bag full of badly wrapped parcels sat down beside her, put the bag on the floor and stretched her legs. Her feet were fat too, they bulged over the strapped shoes. She said cheerfully, "Good to sit down, ain't it?" and Kathleen said, "Yes," mechanically, her mind filled with horror. The woman looked frankly over Kathleen's shoulder. She commented, "Terrible thing. Hadn't ought to happen. Makes you feel funny inside to think about it. My boy's a steelworker. There ain't hardly a day when I don't find myself praying for him out loud, no matter what I'm doing — scrubbing floors or baking a cake, or out walking. He's working again now and that's a help to us all, with six younger to feed, but when I think of him, up there in the air —"

Kathleen said faintly, "It must be dreadful —" Her voice trailed off. The fat woman turned and looked at her closely. "Say," she exclaimed, "you look bad. Feel sick?"

"A little," said Kathleen. "I'll be all right. I'll just sit here quietly."

The woman put her hand on Kathleen's knee. The hand was fat, like the rotund, tied-in-the-middle body and feet. It was also rather dirty. There was a broad gold wedding ring on it. She said with a sympathetic chuckle, "Young married, ain't you? I know how it is."

The train roared far down the track and the woman rose. She asked, "Sure you don't want me to stay?" and Kathleen shook her head and smiled. "I'm fine," she said, "thanks just the same."

She watched the woman hurrying away, awkward, grotesque, the string bag bumping against her side, the waddling gait, the hat on one ear, the round face badly in need of powder, the shabby black handbag clutched under her arm, and thought humbly of the tremendous kindness of the human heart.

The train roared out again, crowds were beginning to pelt down the stairway. Kathleen rose and went on back up to the outer air. She left the newspaper where it was.

She taxied home, recovered but still shaken. When Hannah came in, flinging her hat aside, commenting profanely on the unseasonable warmth of the weather, she had herself under control. They were going out that night. Sammy was giving a staff party. And Hannah, lounging in the doorway of Kathleen's bedroom while Amelia set the table for dinner, said, "I suppose you saw the papers."

"I saw them," said Kathleen.

"Tough," said Hannah. "There's bound to be an investigation, everyone says so. I wonder if you'll be called?"

Kathleen cried, white:

"Oh, I hope not. I don't see why."

"You might be," said Hannah thoughtfully. And Kathleen had a vision of herself on the witness stand. "Your position in the company?" they'd ask her and she'd say, "Mr. Bell's personal secretary." Then they'd ask, "You knew a good deal about the methods of the company?" "No," she would tell them, "I knew nothing." And if they pressed her, if they inquired, "Just what were your relations with Mr. Bell?"

If it came, it would come. She would have to face it.

Sometimes it was harder to be right than to be wrong. She could take the paper to

311

Pat, she could point to the headlines, she could say, "*That* was why."

But there would be no triumph in it.

There was more to follow: the hideously personal interviews, with the widows of the dead men, the pictures of children clinging to their mothers' skirts or with their small heads bowed in pictorial prayer. There were more pictures taken at funerals, and there were photographs of Pat and a garbled description of his Riverside Drive apartment "the epitome of luxury," a biographical account of his life to date, and of his father's . . . an interview with his mother. "Molly never said that," exclaimed Kathleen, outraged. And an item concerning his "beautiful sister at a fashionable finishing school."

A week passed before she could find courage to go see Molly. When she did, there was considerable delay before she reached her. A strange man at the door, no one she had ever seen before, put her through a catechism. Who was she, why had she come? Then Molly, running along the hall, crying angrily, "Let her in. Don't keep her standing there, what's the matter with you?"

She looked badly, her round face drawn. She drew Kathleen into the living room, holding her hand tight. She said apologetically, "Ever since that fool girl reporter got past the door, Pat's hired this man to keep people out."

Kathleen said, "I wanted to come sooner. I lost my nerve."

"I understand. Thanks for coming at all." Molly sighed. "I can't believe the things they hint. They daren't come right out and say them. I can't believe them, Kathleen. Do you?"

The brave blue eyes, red-rimmed, looked straight into hers. Kathleen tried to say, "Of course not." She did say it with, she thought, conviction. But Molly shook her head.

"You're just saying it to help me. You do believe. You have — reason to." Her eyes widened and filled with difficult tears. "I'm afraid for Pat. He won't sleep, he won't eat. He tramps around the house, nights."

"I'm so sorry for him," said Kathleen, with utter sincerity, "for all of you."

Pat's mother spoke slowly. She said, "There'll be an investigation. There's bound to be, with all this political shake-up and an election coming on. It may be delayed. But you'll see. By autumn anyway."

There wasn't much Kathleen could do or say. She stayed long enough to drink the tea Molly provided, and then left her. She hated to go, the older woman looked small and forlorn, like an elderly child. Kathleen kissed

313

her and held her close. She said, "If there's anything I can do —"

The nine days' wonder died. She heard nothing of Pat except now and then a mention of the impending investigation. Her parents wrote her, they had seen the newspapers, thank heaven, she was out of it. "I could kick myself," wrote her father. "Do you think there's any likelihood of your being called in this? I'll get back pronto if you say so. When's it going to be?"

She cabled him, "Investigation date not scheduled, please do not interrupt trip, everything all right."

They would be home anyway in October and if, by that time — But she told herself repeatedly, I don't know anything, I wasn't a part of the business. I only guessed. But if they guess that I guessed?

She remembered the letter, the special bank account, the telephone call. If they asked her what she remembered?

Paul asked one night:

"You're worrying about the Bell investigation, aren't you? I heard it will take place in late September."

"Of course, I'm worrying," she told him sharply.

"You think you'll be called?"

"Won't all his office people be subpoenaed?" she inquired. "I should think it very likely. I'm getting frantic letters from Jim Haines."

It was Jim's chance to get even. He wrote: "When I first read about it I was glad. Here was my chance to cut his throat, and go scot free. I know enough to hang him. The prosecution wouldn't need any other witness. Bribery of inspectors, bribery of the higher-ups — and all the way down the line. I was so damned glad when I read that first headline I could have yelled. But I've been thinking about it. They'll call me, for sure, and I don't want to be called. I can't do it, to him. I can't because I hate him. It's too easy. It's a laugh, isn't it, wanting to obstruct justice because I hate the guy who should be punished? But how could I clear myself with myself? I couldn't be sure on the witness stand that my evidence wasn't for revenge, a cheap sort of thing. Cleaner, perhaps, if you'd let me stay drunk, kill him and take the rap. If I hadn't found out about Francesca, Kathleen, I'd have gone on the stand and lied my soul away to save him. What must I do now?"

She couldn't tell him; this was his responsibility, not hers. She couldn't say, "Do this, do that."

Paul asked:

"If you went on the stand — would you protect him?"

She looked at him with haunted eyes.

"I don't know," she answered slowly. "I can't bear to see him defeated, I can't endure to have Molly, but —"

"But you could quit him because you knew he was crooked?"

"I never told you so!"

"My dear, I'm not so stupid as that. Besides, Hannah talks too much. She offered me a hypothetical case . . . very hypothetical. You'd break your engagement for that, for the sake of your principles, and yet you wouldn't go on the stand and swear —" He shook his head. "Women beat me," he said humbly, "but if you weren't inconsistent as hell you wouldn't be a woman. Most women."

She said dully, "I don't know what I'll do, Paul. The occasion may never arise. In Jim's case it's different. He'd be an important witness."

"He has it in for Pat," said Paul, "he told me so that night."

She asked, "Did he tell you why?"

"No. But a man doesn't want to kill another man without a fairly valid reason. Money or a woman. It wasn't money, I take it." He looked at her sharply. "Hence, I sus-

316

pect it was a woman. I thought at first it might be because of you. Then I realized that was pretty silly. I knew about his wife, in the asylum. You told me that night. He told me later. I put two and two together."

"Please, Paul."

"O.K., I'm not asking for confidences, I didn't from him. What I'm trying to get at is, has he a personal grudge? He can wipe the slate clean at the trial. If he wants to."

She said, "He doesn't want to — because it *is* a personal grudge."

"Haines," said Paul after a moment, "is regular. Maybe his ethics are cockeyed, I don't know. But not many of us stop to consider our own motives."

The long summer dragged on, hot and breathless. Kathleen remained in town most of the time. Occasionally she went visiting, weekends. During the weeks there were out-door dining places in town or roof gardens or dinner somewhere an hour's run out. There was always some place to go, people with whom to go. And Hannah suggested:

"Let's take a vacation in September, after the fall showing. I'll wait for you, we'll take it together. Rosa will give you a week, anyway, even if you don't rate it yet. And Joel suggested that we take his house on the Island. The kids will be back at school then.

317

It will be after Paul's opening. It all works out. We can go down there and loaf in the sun. Joel has horses, we can ride if we like. He'll come down for the weekend, and longer if he can get away. He's got an elderly cousin there, housekeeper-manager. She'll do for the conventions. How about it?"

"I'd love it," said Kathleen.

Paul's play opened just before the middle of September, on a Monday. On the following Friday, Hannah and Kathleen were to leave for the Ransom house. They would see Paul there as he had announced his intention of going down to his shack, after the play opened, to rest and perhaps block out the new play about which he had been thinking for some time. But rehearsals had kept him busy, and the inevitable rewriting. They were opening cold in New York and he was, he said, scared out of his pants.

"Keep 'em on," advised Hannah, "when they yell 'author, author!' "

There was a good audience, carriage trade, the women displaying the usual ermine and mink despite the fact that it was a warm night. The critics were there, the Hollywood scouts, and three cinema stars who happened to be in town. Park Avenue came and Fifth and the usual group of writers, artists, actors who were "resting," night club people, Broadway.

"Holy cat!" said Hannah, startled. She had been observing with the smug smile of the prophet the preponderance of mauve and magenta, the "up" coiffures of the women. She had been taking notes, in a tiny book with a gold pencil.

"What's the matter?" asked Kathleen.

Joel was with them, Sammy and Rosa Davenport, and two or three others. Paul was in the back of the house, in hiding.

"Look over there, third row, center."

Other people were looking at Pat and Sandra. Sandra was nakeder than the occasion called for, her yellow hair on top of her little head and a jeweled bird glittering in a riot of curls. "Well," remarked Hannah, "it appears that after all there are birds in last year's nest."

Pat did not look as if very shortly he would face an investigation which might mean the business ruin of his life. He looked serene, even complacent. He looked confident.

"What's the gal doing these days?" inquired Hannah, "other than luring our feathered friends to her topknot?"

"I don't know," said Kathleen, "I read she'd left the roof."

"Probably raised it!"

The lights dimmed, people came in, falling over other people, the usual social rudeness was in full swing. The curtain rose.

From the first the play could hold them, the rustling stopped, the coughing. When the curtain fell on the first act there was a tremendous round of applause. "Oh," cried Kathleen, her eyes shining, "he's done it."

"Sure," said Hannah, "I knew he would."

But she still didn't know what it was all about. The play affronted her, it made her feel small and mean. She didn't like the sensation. Joel Ransom touched her hand. He said, "It's very good, isn't it?" and she nodded. He added, "This means as much to you, I suppose, as to him."

His eyes were clear and unhappy. Hannah felt a rush of affection for him. Stable and good and decent. He didn't make her feel mean and small and futile, he made her feel important. She slid her hand into his, smiling and wordless.

"Let's find Paul," suggested Kathleen.

Hannah made up her mind. Her heart was wrenched in her breast and her eyelids stung. But she said, "You find him, Kate. Joel and I are going to stay here, I can't face crawling out and crawling back again."

Rosa and Sammy had gone out to smoke. Kathleen made her way out, looking for Paul, but he was nowhere to be seen. Pat Bell, standing with Sandra and a group in the lobby, left them and came to her and drew her near the velvet railing.

"I expected to see you here, that's why I came," he said.

"Oh, hello, Pat," she said quietly. "It's a very fine play, isn't it?"

He shrugged. "Search me, I'm not high brow. You're looking — marvelous." He added, "Thanks, for going to see Mom, she needed it."

"That's all right, I wanted to go," she said embarrassed.

"Go on," he said, "say it, say 'I told you so.' "

She looked at him, her eyes luminous. She asked, "Why should I?"

"You wouldn't," he said, "of course, I might have known. Look, I'll do my best to keep you out of this mess, Kathleen, you know that."

Sandra detached herself from the group. She came up and slid her arm through his. She ordered, "Come along, sugar, we've got to get back to our seats." She viewed Kathleen smiling. She asked, "How's the shop, Miss Roberts?"

"Fine," said Kathleen; "you haven't been in to see us lately."

"No, I like a change," said Sandra carelessly, "you can understand that. You ran out on Pat, didn't you?"

"Sandra!" said Pat warningly.

"Perhaps you had your reasons," said Sandra; "rats do, when they leave a ship."

She pulled him away and they were lost in the crowd hurrying back to their seats. Kathleen followed slowly. That was that, she thought dully.

At the end of the second act she remained in her seat. And in the beginning of the third there was a slight commotion in the audience which distracted them and the players. Someone was leaving, deliberately. Kathleen turning angrily, saw a slim woman hurrying up the aisle alone. The audience settled back again, the third act played itself out to its dramatic conclusion. The curtain fell and there was cheering. How long had it been since a theater had rung to cheers? People were standing up, clapping, calling for the star, for her leading man, for the young girl new to Broadway, who had made her name tonight. For Paul . . .

He came out presently, looking haggard and unusually ill at ease. His curtain speech was short. Kathleen, standing, clapping with the rest, her heart singing for him, looked along the third row center — Pat was still there, standing with his hands in his pockets. Sandra was not visible.

It had been Sandra, then, who had left. They had quarreled in the interlude between the second and third acts and she had gone.

Kathleen's party surged out to the lobby, waiting for Paul. They found and took him, unprotesting, back to Hannah's apartment. Joel and Hannah, Kathleen, Paul, the two Davenports, and the rest.

"To your further success, my lad," said Hannah, toasting him.

He said:

"It wasn't success I was after. Not as you understand it, Hannah." He looked at Kathleen. He said humbly, "If I've made them stop and think, just for a minute, that's all I want."

She said, smiling:

"Don't worry, because it will be a success too. It won't hurt you, Paul — this time."

"The Hollywood scouts were around," he said.

"So what?" she demanded.

"So I stay here," he told her, "and go to work again."

Chapter XX

The Ransom house was a big affair, sprawled out on the sand. It had been built during Joel Ransom's boyhood and bulged with bow windows and great glassed-in rooms toward the sea. There was a captain's walk reached by an inner stairway. The bedrooms were spacious, many-windowed, and smelled of lavender and salt. The living room was sixty feet long, and no matter how much care you took, sand sifted in. It was in the rooms, in your clothes and hair and food, but you didn't mind.

Joel had another place, in Connecticut, where he could indulge his passion for roses and prize delphinium. But his children liked this house best and occupied it all summer, living on the sand in scant bathing suits, growing brown and hard. And Kathleen, arriving with Hannah and Joel that Friday, could understand their preference. You were so completely exposed to the great clean sea and the sunlight pouring in through the windows. You slept to the sound of wind and waves.

It had turned too cold for bathing but they

bathed nevertheless, emerging half frozen but laughing, running back to the game room enveloped in toweling robes while Joel mixed them a drink. The elderly cousin, Mrs. Keates, was pleasant, unobtrusive, and evidently delighted with them. She said she missed the children, back in town with their governess in the Park Avenue apartment. Mrs. Keates would stay on here until Ransom closed the house and then she would take over the Connecticut place, keeping it open as he was likely to come up weekends through the winter. There were three servants here: a good couple, and their son who did the heavy cleaning and made himself generally useful. They would return with her to Connecticut.

Kathleen found herself in a sense very much alone. She liked it. Joel and Hannah were there, of course, but she felt shut out of the charmed circle which Joel drew around the other girl. She was glad, and hopeful, for her. She walked with them, swam with them, played three-handed bridge . . . and thought her own thoughts. She felt rested, cleansed by sea and air and sun. She thought through her problem about Pat. She would go on the stand if she was called. She would answer questions truthfully but no more. She would not volunteer information. But before she did anything, she would make a clean breast of the situation to her father, ask, and follow, his advice.

She found that she missed Paul Mc-Clure.

He drove over on Sunday in a downpour of rain to spend the day with them. In the afternoon, after a heavy dinner, they left Hannah and Joel playing Canfield for pennies and went out to talk on the dark wet sand. Kathleen wore Joel's old windbreaker, a pair of slacks and a raincoat. She had an ancient hat pulled down over her eyes. She lifted her face to the rain and laughed, watching the angry sea, gray and sullen, come creaming in. Gulls cried unhappily along the beach and there was driftwood.

"I like it," she said.

Paul, trampling beside her, his hands in his pockets, said, "Looks as if Hannah and Joel —"

"I hope so," said Kathleen.

"He's all right," said Paul. "The sort of man who ought to have money. I like what he does with it and himself."

"So do I."

They were silent, walking in the rain. Paul said finally:

"Play begins to shape up."

"And *Remembering Sorrow* is sold out three months in advance," she said. "I'm so proud of you."

"For the three months in advance?"

"No. I would have been as proud had you failed."

"That's what I wanted to hear," he said contentedly.

Presently he asked:

"How about Pat?"

"What do you mean?"

"I mean —" he hesitated — "how do you stand?"

She said:

"Free. We drank to that, didn't we? But I wasn't quite free, even then. I am now. After seeing him the night of the opening. Whatever was left — and I wasn't exactly proud of *that*, Paul — was gone."

"And the investigation?"

"If I have to," she said, "I'll testify." She turned her face shining with rain toward him. Her voice was high because of the wind. "I won't do anything to hurt him," she said, "if I can help it."

"You and Jim? Damn the guy anyway," said Paul, "he's got something."

"Plenty," said Kathleen, "if only — Oh, never mind. Hadn't we better get back? Mrs. Keates promised me tea and I'd rather have tea than anything I know."

"Kate —" he caught her hand — "oh, don't look so alarmed, it's just to say I'm still here, waiting. Always."

She drew her hand away. She said, "I know that, Paul." She thought, But you can't fall in and out and into love again. You have to wait and think. She said, "I like you better than anyone I have ever known."

"Suits me," he said, "for a start."

He left after supper and she missed him, watching Hannah and Joel. And Hannah came in to see her that night after she was in bed.

"I'm going to marry Joel," she said, without preliminary.

"I'm glad, Hannah."

"Me too." The dark narrow eyes were soft. She said, "The kids like me. I'm terrified of them but they're sweet. And I love Joel, Kate. Maybe I'm not in love with him but I love him. I know the difference now. I think that maybe this way is better."

Kathleen asked, "But — Paul?"

"Never mind that," said Hannah. "Perhaps it was just stubbornness. Perhaps it was something left over. I don't know. He's in love with you and he won't be with me, ever again, no matter what you do. I'm over wishing he'd change his heart about you and you'd change your mind about Pat. It's up to you now. I'm out of it . . . and happy. I'd like you to believe that."

"Hannah, I do, and I'm so happy for you."

"Well, excuse these girlish tears," said Hannah a moment after, "but that's how things are. Good night, Kate."

In the morning Joel was to return to town. But he had caught a cold, he was running a slight temperature, and Hannah bullied him into remaining. She did his telephoning for him with a brisk little air, quite possessive, which touched and amused Kathleen. She ran errands, carried up soup, sat by his bed and read aloud. And Kathleen spent the day in the library or walking alone in the rain. For it kept on raining.

Joel was better the next day. But it still rained. Why drive back to town in an open car? Did he wish to catch pneumonia? Hannah demanded. Stay till it cleared, the world would not go to smash without him. So he stayed, a quiet, attractive man whose eyes followed Hannah wherever she went.

On Wednesday it rained harder than ever, the wind rose, and the sea came in. "It looks," said Joel, frowning, "like a bad storm . . . the end of that Florida hurricane maybe. I don't much like it."

"Old-fashioned equinoctial," said Hannah. She slipped her arm through his. "I like it," she said, "it's exciting."

Before noon a car came racing up the soaked driveway and stopped. Hannah was at the windows and turned a startled face. "Set another place," she said, "it's Pat."

He faced Kathleen, dripping, in the library. They were alone, Joel and Hannah having discreetly removed themselves.

"Get your things off," she said sharply, "and what in the world —"

"Rosa Davenport told me where you were," he said. "We're in a hell of a mess, Kathleen."

"We?" she repeated. "The investigation?"

"Oh, that. You may be called, I don't know, I'll try and fix it — no, it's Sandra."

"Sandra!"

"I married her," he said sullenly, "in April."

"Married!"

"I was drunk," he said. "When I came to — Well, I persuaded her to keep it quiet for a while. I said my mother would be antagonistic, it might take a time to win her over."

She said scornfully, "As if you cared! She fell for that?"

"No, but — Well, she had the ring and it was O.K. with her. I promised I'd get her a Hollywood test. We've been leading a cat-

and-dog life for some time. She got sick of it, wanted to give it to the papers. And I talked too much at the wrong time. She said not long ago, 'It's a good thing I'm your wife and won't have to testify when this investigation comes up.' " He looked at her, haggard. "But the other night at the opening —"

"Well?"

"She's quit," he said, "to divorce me. She'll name you."

"As what?" demanded Kathleen coolly.

"I don't know. Corespondent, she says. She knows I've been to see you at Hannah's. Or she'll sue you. Alienation of affections. Anything."

"But how — ?"

"I can't afford this now with the investigation coming on. I tell you, it will ruin me," he said.

He hadn't a thought for her, she perceived without astonishment, or what Sandra's play-acting would do to her. She asked, "Why did you come here?"

"You've got to come back with me and talk to her. Maybe you can make her see sense."

"That's out of the question," said Kathleen. "I've nothing to fear from her, Pat. Let her sue, so far as I'm concerned."

"Oh, you!" he said. "But how about me?"

They were still arguing when Hannah rapped at the door. "Luncheon," she said, "and make it snappy, Joel and I are starved."

Pat said, catching Kathleen's arm as she moved toward the door, "You won't go back?"

"Of course not, Pat, don't be absurd."

"I'll stay here till you do," he said grimly.

It was a curious luncheon. Hannah talked most of the time. Joel, watching Kathleen's white face, was worried for her. He did not like the little he had seen of Mr. Bell. The storm rose steadily and the servants began to show signs of disorganization . . . and the sea came closer.

By early afternoon there was no longer any question of Pat's returning to town.

There were not many neighbors on this particular stretch of beach, most of the houses had been closed for the season. But a woman fought her way up against the almost unendurable wind, carrying a child of two or three years. She was a caretaker left in a summer cottage until the first of the month. Her husband had gone into the village and had not returned. The water was rising steadily, she told Joel, clutching the wailing child, the porch had been swept off, she was afraid to stay.

He was talking to her, trying to quiet her,

and Mrs. Keates, perfectly calm except for a heightened color, was making tea on an oilstove as the electricity had long since failed, when Paul's battered car drove in. Kathleen ran out to meet him and shrieked when she saw the car's condition, "Paul, you crazy fool!"

He grinned. He was covered with mud and the car looked as if it had been through a tornado. "I started hours ago," he said when he got inside, "but there are trees down all the way. The woods around my place is in shambles. How the house stood I don't know. I kept thinking of you here . . . and the sea. What's Bell doing here?" he asked, seeing Pat standing by a window talking to Hannah.

"He came down on — It doesn't matter, it isn't important."

Joel said, "We'd better get the girls out of here."

"I doubt if you can," said Paul. "One bridge is down, and look at the water, but we can make a try for it. I just made it, coming in."

It was incredible, it was unbelievably terrifying. The waves raced by level with the windows; wreckage raced with them, doors, window frames, boats, pieces of timber. The gale screamed like a woman in labor. The noise was horrible. The loose shingles struck the roof sharp as machine guns.

The windows broke in, all those toward the sea. Glass shattered with an explosive sound. Joel cut his hand, and Hannah tried to bandage it. The child cried steadily and in the garage an automobile horn howled without ceasing because of a short circuit and lent the last eerie touch. No light, just darkness. A dead telephone, a silent radio, and the sounds of the elements mocking at man's ingenuity.

Pat burst into sudden profanity. He was white and sweat was on his forehead despite the cold damp, the rising chill. What dry wood was in the house burned in the living room fireplace, but the furnace was not in operation, in a cellar full of water.

"You can do as you please," he shouted, "I'm getting out."

There was a terrific crash as the doors facing the sea blew in off their frames and the water came with them, tons of boiling gray water swirling around their knees.

Pat had gone, racing out the door which faced away from the sea. Joel spoke to the woman with the child and to the servants. He took it for granted, it seemed, that Hannah and Kathleen would show no sign of panic. He said, "we'll try and make the bridge over the inlet."

The road was water now, rising and rising. They struggled out, and found themselves up to the waist in the cold steady swirl and in a terrific current. Joel had the child in his arms, and Mrs. Keates stumbled along with Paul's arm about her. The servants followed silently.

It was a long walk, with nothing stable upon which to walk. Part of the time you swam and helped those who couldn't swim. Hannah screamed at Kathleen suddenly.

"Pat!" she called. "There!"

They saw him, just ahead, doggedly swimming, alone, a black speck among other black specks. They saw the piece of timber that struck him.

Paul yelled, "Take care of her, Kate," and left Mrs. Keates and struck out for the figure ahead.

Kathleen watched, fighting to keep her balance. She cried, once, "No!" and then, "No, Paul!" But he did not, or would not, hear.

When they reached him he was supporting Pat's big unconscious body. He said briefly, "In the head, I think; it looks bad."

The woman whose child Joel was carrying began to cry again.

"It's too deep to stand here," shouted

Paul, and Kathleen struggling out of her sodden clothes and shoes, stripping herself to her underwear, swam toward him, trying to avoid the wreckage. "I'll help," she called above the hellish noise of wind and water.

The boat came then, a rowboat with two men in it. One called, nearing, "The bridge is out, you'll have to come with us."

"Take him," said Paul, "he's hurt. You go too, Kate."

She shook her head.

"The woman and her baby," she said, "and Hannah."

They were all together now. The man in the boat said, "we'll take all we can; rest will have to wait till we get back or send. All hell's broke loose."

They got Pat in the boat on the third try. Twice the boat overturned. Finally he was in, and the woman with the baby. Joel said, "Hannah?" but she just looked at him. She said, "You go, idiot, you're sick." But he laughed at her. Then Mrs. Keates was helped in.

The boat rowed off. That left four of them in the storm, clinging together. The water rushed past with a triumphant fury, the rain beat down, the wind screamed savagely. A door floated past and Paul flung himself at it. It would be a makeshift raft, he thought, and he and Joel steadied it and the two girls climbed on, half naked, shivering.

The men half waded, half swam alongside, holding the raft.

"Don't look, darling," said Paul urgently.

A body floating by, the body of a child, battered beyond recognition.

The raft went on, held back from its rush by the two men. They might reach the place where the bridge had been.

They reached it; the water was not so deep here, and there were other people waiting. Pitiful and distracted and brave, clutching a child, a dog, a cat, a jewel case . . . waiting for rescue.

The boats came at last and took them back to a land beaten but firm under their feet. Trees down across the road, high-tension wires, crazy wreckage, as if a madman had gone through.

They found shelter in a house in the village . . . dry clothes, whisky. Hannah sat beside Joel and held his hands between her own. "If you've caught more cold," she scolded. "Paul, can't you get a doctor?"

"The doctors are busy with people who've been hurt," said Joel, and put his hand on her black hair, "I'm all right."

"You're telling me!" said Hannah, sobbing.

Mrs. Keates was upstairs in bed. She had sustained a bad shock, she was an old woman. The woman with the child was waiting for word of her husband. Kathleen and Paul sat together in front of an oilstove. Kathleen had on a sweater much too large for her and a tweed skirt pinned at the waistband. Her hair was soaked, and there was a bruise on her cheek.

She said, "We must find out about Pat."

Paul rose and looked down at her. "I'm going now."

"Paul . . ."

He turned back.

"Yes?"

"You — saved him."

He shrugged. "The guy was knocked out," he said, "he couldn't save himself."

You couldn't search for motives here, you found only the decent human impulse and instinct. No grandstand play at saving the man your girl loved, for you knew she no longer loved him.

The tears ran slowly down her face. The storm was abating. Tomorrow would bring word of death and horror, tragedy and courage.

"Paul," she said again, "don't leave me — for long."

He came close to her. Joel and Hannah

were there, absorbed in each other. They did not hear him speak, he would not have cared if they had heard.

"Kate, get this straight. This is — drama. It's not everyday living. Don't let yourself be convinced that just because I held Pat's head abovewater —"

"It wasn't that, although that showed me the way," she said.

"I'll hope," he told her, his eyes very bright, "but I won't hold you to it. After this storm, serenity. You'll know then. I can't let you make a fool of yourself because you're over-wrought, because you're safe, because —"

She said, "All right, just go on hoping."

He bent and kissed her once, hard, on the mouth and turned away. She sat there, very still, her hands folded in her lap, heedless of Joel and Hannah, of the servants hurried in a corner, of the strange woman and child, of the other people crowding the little house. She thought, It was like that hen . . . like lightning. Different from — from the other. No less exciting but with a sense of security, of homing, underlying the excitement. What had Molly Bell said? "A rehearsal. Rehearsal for love." This was the play itself.

It was an hour before Paul came back. When he slammed the door and entered and they looked at him, they knew. Joel swore and Hannah stifled a little cry. Kathleen's eyes were wide.

She asked, "He's dead?"

"Yes," said Paul. He stood beside her but did not touch her. "That knock on the head. I — I couldn't get through to his mother, Kate. No wires. We'll get a car, I'll drive you up, it may take a long time but we'll manage."

"Poor Molly," said Kathleen brokenly.

She could weep for Pat, who had not escaped, and for Molly, who could not escape. Paul would understand why she wept. His arm was about her, holding her quietly. After a moment she stopped crying. She said, looking at him, and loving with all her heart:

"All right, Paul — let's go."